Praise for Paradise Prey:

"*Paradise Prey* is an intense Florida thriller with international stakes and Tess Titan is just the woman you want covering your back when the bullets start flying. A terrific first novel."
—Glenn Meganck, aka J.R. Ripley

"The opening line's a killer! A real page turner that has you rooting for Tess as she unravels a complex mystery while keeping her humor intact, and her murderous impulses in check."
—J.L. Miles author of *Roseflower Creek*

"Brooks has put Tess Titan's home, Paradise Pointe, on the mystery novel map! Her keen eye captures the quirks and characters of the Panhandle Gulf Coast, where the fantasy Florida meets the real world."
—David Vest, *Panama City News Herald*

"Florida's Panhandle comes to life with Jackie Brook's first novel. Tess Titan, her somewhat reluctant sleuth, tells it like it is. Knock her down, she gets right back up! We can't wait for more!"
—Elizabeth Fravel, Owner, Books by the Sea, Panama City, Florida.

To: Paula
Read and enjoy!
My best - JB

Paradise Prey

A Tess Titan Mystery

10-22-04
Jackie Brooks

By

Jackie Brooks

PublishAmerica
Baltimore

First printing

ISBN: 1-4137-3136-8
PUBLISHED BY PUBLISHAMERICA, LLLP
www.publishamerica.com
Baltimore

Printed in the United States of America

This book is for all the people who believed in me.

Acknowledgments

The author wishes to acknowledge the invaluable assistance of the following people: Rosalie Shaffer, National Marine Fisheries Service Laboratory; Kris Metzger, Harbor Branch Oceanographic Institution; Sandra Jordan, Dean, College of Humanities and Fine Arts, Murray State University; Dr. E. Hunt Scheuerman, ME; Sgt. John Corley, Bay County Sheriff's Office Criminal Investigation Division; Major Kent Thompson, Florida Fish and Wildlife Commission; Dr. Bruce Goldberger, University of Florida Toxicology Lab; Ken Rudisill, Horticulture Cooperative Service; Jim Kimbrough; Gloria Dale Skinner; Bob Mayer; Elizabeth Fravel; Michael Lister; Carol Tang; Chris Brickel; Alexander Jaszenko; Nancy Gillis; Kelle Witt; Liz and Jane; Captain Andy and Celia Redmond; and all the ladies of the PMs Society: Carole, Ruth, Marty, Adele, and Melissa. With special thanks to my husband and children for giving me the time to write; to my father and mother for their enduring support and optimism; and to PublishAmerica for making this book a reality.

Prologue

September 20, 1991

It was a shame to die on such an ugly day.

Eva had hoped for a pleasant afternoon ferry ride across the Channel, but as usual, the British weather wasn't cooperating. The rough sea forced the passengers into the enclosed deck. She chose to stand aft, spray from the waves soaking her overcoat.

There was no sky, only gray clouds heavy with bad weather. Fog closed in around the boat, shutting out any semblance of life beyond the vessel. The ferry fought to make headway against the tide. The craft appeared dead in its own wake.

Standing alone, as she had for most of her life, Eva experienced a feeling of peace. There hadn't been much time during her life to enjoy such blessings.

For as long as she could remember, she had raced to keep one step ahead of her nemesis. As grueling as the work had been, she never wavered from her goal. Her work was her obsession.

When it came to antiquities, her passion and conscience were at one. She would not stand by and watch international art treasures stolen or bartered to fund the resurgence of a crime family. She had the key to keep it all from happening, but today the key had to be passed on to safer waters.

No one on the ferry recognized her. That was God's last little joke—to have her live a public, titled life as a Contessa, then leave this earth as a servant to a secret that only she possessed the answer to.

The hairs on the back of her neck rose. She sensed her rivals were dangerously close. She'd felt their presence over the years, and was grateful when the detective she'd hired confirmed her suspicions.

At first, she couldn't understand why the renowned crime family was interested in her activities. But as the secret unraveled, her understanding was complete.

This imposing adversary had never approached her, never impeded her search. But today was different. They had caught on to her betrayal, and that seemed to upset the precarious balance of their relationship.

Eva was glad she'd taken the precaution of leaving her diary with a lawyer. She smiled at how surprised her American friend, Nell, would be receiving a package "from the grave" so to speak. She hoped Nell would live long enough to receive the package with its precious contents and complete the puzzle she'd spent her life solving.

She had wanted desperately to share her work with Nell, but that was impossible. If she had ever breathed a word of her work to anyone, it would not only have endangered them, but cost her the edge she'd kept against her enemy.

Proof had always been her goal. Without it, no one would have believed the truth. Until now, the story recited to her as a teenager was thought to be conjecture. A story about priceless antiquities stolen and hidden during WWII that would make any person as rich as a king was merely a tale to give hope to a new generation after the war.

But the proof Eva held now was irrefutable, and the Family was painfully aware of it. She knew they had no intention of letting her reveal the secret about the existence of the antiquities, no intention of letting her breathe life into an old tale. Eva had outlived her usefulness in their eyes. She had become a liability, and was expendable.

She had stayed one step ahead of them all the way to the end. She smiled knowing they thought they were dealing the final hand, claiming victory before the last card was played. They weren't counting on her cunning. They never considered she might cheat.

Eva shivered and pulled a scarf from her pocket. By the time she'd tied it tightly around her head, her apparitions had appeared—men with a purpose.

They spoke loudly to one another over the wind as they walked towards her. "Damn shame," said the young man on the left. "My papa liked the old broad."

Eva didn't scream or struggle, but locked eyes with each of them, as they lifted her over the rails and dropped her into the unforgiving sea.

Darkness came quickly. The edges of her pale lips curled into a tight smile. She knew she'd succeeded. She'd beaten them at their own game. Now they'd have to play by her rules.

Chapter One

I sat still as a rattlesnake ready to strike. Spine straight against the wood rail, my hands were raised as high as a tank top would allow without showing my middle age lack of will power. Small beads of sweat formed on my forehead about to roll into my eyes.

With my chin tilted upward, I sought the stare of my assailant. His body stood silhouetted against the intense rays of the Florida mid-afternoon sun, his face lost in shadow. Squinting against the glare, I tried to identify the stranger, a coup that might provide hope of a last minute reprieve.

As the compact figure moved towards me, my attention was drawn to his black and white Keds with the words "Blaster Master" scrawled in thick black ink on the white rims. I knew there would be no mercy.

The sea was calm, the sky crystal blue like a magazine advertisement. The modern-day replica pirate ship proved a perfect stage for the ensuing battle.

The ship sailed slowly under motor up the Bay Channel, carefully avoiding the shallow waters and sandbars of the State Park nearby.

Behind Mr. Blaster, the crew fought. One member gained control of the big gun and prepared to fire off a round. It was time to act. I watched as the charge was placed in the barrel; within seconds the hammer connected with the cap producing an explosion loud enough to scare the b'Jesus out of any unsuspecting soul.

Lucky for me, Mr. Blaster's soul was unsuspecting. He fell to the deck. His weapon slid across the planks and stopped neatly at my feet. I kicked the gun aside, and reached over my shoulder for my piece. My fingers wrapped easily around the trigger; there was warmth in its familiarity.

Jumping to my feet, I stood over the Blaster. He didn't look so invincible now.

"No mercy," I said.

He covered his head with his arms, and curled into a tight ball.

I aimed low. Squeezing off every drop of ammo, I sprayed him from toe to head. My trigger finger and heart stopped beating at the same moment. Was he finished? Had I finally ended this nightmare?

An unfamiliar twinge shook in my lower belly. It took over every bone in my body until I couldn't stand it any longer. I looked toward the sky, raising my arms above my head like a God pronouncing victory, and broke into a deep diabolical laugh.

"No fair!" screamed Timmy Jenkins from under my feet. "Mrs. Titan brought a Super Soaker 2001 with her!" He jumped up and dashed to the other side of the ship, seeking alliance with his young friends.

"Don't mess with the 'Master' Mom." I blew pretend smoke from the barrel of my water gun.

Applause came from the upper deck.

"Great job, Tess," yelled Nancy Peterson giving me a thumbs up as I turned and bowed. The ladies all laughed and went back to chatting.

I made my way to the bench, and hung my head over the rails to catch the faintest whisper of a breeze. A seagull was flying effortlessly right outside my grasp. Knowing it had my attention; the bird cawed obnoxiously to be fed. I guess he thought I was a tourist and wouldn't know that tossing a few scraps of bread out to him would bring on a squadron attack of wayfaring gulls. I was in no mood to be used for a free meal ticket or a repository for white poop splashes.

Sitting back on the bench, I tried to imagine myself on top of a cold, snowy mountain. The wind was blowing, and my toes were cold. I thought it might be working for a minute until I realized my make-up was caking, my clothes were sticking to me, and sweat was rolling down that little vee place between my boobs. "Disheveled" would have been a compliment at this point.

"Nice moves, Master Mom," said my neighbor and friend, Geena Richards, as she sat down beside me and handed me an exotic frozen concoction disguised in an insulated coffee mug.

Geena looked like she'd just stepped out of a page from *Family Circle* magazine. Her chestnut bobbed hair and make-up were flawless. The gauzy clothes flowed effortlessly around her size eight body, and the only perspiration I could spy was a dab of moisture above her upper lip.

"Don't let anyone know we've got these drinks," Geena whispered to me behind her hand. "They'd probably make us walk the plank...*after* they confiscated the goods."

"Tell anyone? You've got to be kidding. From the looks of it, we'll be lucky if there's enough to keep the two of us refreshed." I reached for the cooler and scooted it under my feet.

Geena blew some strands of hair away from her mouth. "I like this Pirate Ship idea for birthday parties, but they always seem to be held on the hottest days of the year."

I stretched my arms out behind me, resting them on the rails. "Yep. This September feels just as hot as August. It seems to be staying warmer, longer, each year. Pretty soon, we won't have winter at all."

"Just be grateful we live in the northern part of the Panhandle." Geena took a flier from her purse and made a fan fit for a queen. "You want one?"

"Does a Barracuda have teeth?"

She smiled and made me an extra large one. I waved it in front of me like a Royal might and pretending an English accent, added "The weather doesn't bother me as much as the food. Fast food just doesn't meet my epicurean standards."

Geena scooted the cooler back out and lifted the lid, "Well, Lady Tess, I packed a few delicacies for us. I figure we can slip away to the head and indulge while the kids are doing the Hokey Pokey."

I gave Geena a high-five. "I knew it would pay off to be friends with a bed and breakfast owner. You get the preparedness badge for the day. By the way, I call the sink to sit on!"

"You cheat, you know the toilet doesn't have a seat."

"That's okay, if it makes you feel any better, the sink drips and there's no paper towels left to wipe it up after fifty kids have filled their squirt guns."

"Hmmm, you walking around with a wet butt, and parsley stuck between your teeth. Yeah, that's a fair enough trade. Deal, Kemosabi." We tapped our mugs together in a toast.

"Treasure Ho!" yelled a shipmate hanging from a sturdy line.

"I love this part of the trip," Geena said. "The kids get such a kick raising that treasure chest out of the water."

"Yeah, you should have seen the hoops the Captain had to jump through to hang his treasure rope on the buoy out here. You would have thought he was trying to get permission to feed the dolphins."

The first mate started giving directions in his best pirate voice. "Arghh, me hardies, this treasure looks mighty heavy. We'll need all you swabbies heave hoin' to bring it on board today. Grab on to the rope, pull with all your might!"

I glanced up and down the line and spotted my Katie near the middle. Her lean, strong build was in sharp contrast to her fine shoulder-length hair and soft, contagious smile. Her best friend, Lindsey, was behind her.

"When did they get so big, Geena? It seems like only yesterday they were swimming in kiddy pools, and chasing butterflies around the backyard. When did they get to be beautiful, precocious nine-year-olds wanting to wear fingernail polish and go to skating parties?"

Geena smiled. "They tend to do that. I think it happens somewhere between folding laundry, and feeding the dog."

"Heave! Ho!" yelled the mate to his swabbies.

"I guess there won't be many more of these trips. It won't be much longer before they outgrow this." I watched the kids pull with all their strength on the thick anchor line. "Kevin stopped coming a few years back. He prefers checking out cars and girls now...in that order."

Geena and I joined a number of the other moms at the front of the rope.

"It's never been this heavy!" one of the kids said between grunts.

"It must be something really neat," said another.

Geena and I smiled at one another, knowing the moms had put extra weight in the chest to fool the kids.

At fifteen feet, the chest came into view. The sighting renewed excitement in the young crew. I could see fish circling the chest. This wasn't unusual since fish are instinctively curious creatures, but I was worried that some of the sealed candy bags had opened up inside the chest.

"Pull, pull," screamed the kids. "We've almost got it."

Time seemed to stop. The edges of the chest were blurred beneath the water's surface. It looked like you could reach out and touch it, but I knew better. The clarity of the water made the depth deceiving. The chest was probably still sitting a good eight feet down. I could see the fish more clearly now, darting back and forth as if they were feeding.

The harder the crew tugged, the more resistant the line became. The sea didn't want to give up its bounty today, but the children were determined to claim their riches. Finally, the chest broke the surface.

"I can see it, I can see it!" yelled one of the kids.

I could see it too. There was added cargo. Human cargo.

******

A partially decomposed male body was draped upside-down over the top of the treasure chest, looking like a well-dressed department store mannequin after an exhausting Labor Day sale. One leg was entangled in the rope. His feet were bare.

I put two fingers in my mouth and gave a loud shrieking whistle to get the attention of one of the crewmembers. I gave him the "cut" sign across my throat.

He got the picture and yelled to the kids, "Let go of the line, mateys. Looks like old Long John got to our treasure first and left behind his calling card."

The kids looked around at each other, whispering about the change in the usual routine. They dropped the lines, and started wandering around the deck wondering what to do next.

Instinctively, I grabbed for my cell phone, pushed the automatic dial, and waited interminable seconds before hearing the familiar voice of my ex-partner in the Florida Marine Patrol.

"Daniels here. Who the hell is this? And why are you calling me on this line?"

I could hear the roar of the 200-horse power engine in the background. He was on the water. I knew he couldn't be far.

"Nice public relations, Bubbles. You may want to work on your delivery a little."

"Titan? Is that you? What the hell do you want?" He barked back above the engine. "If you're calling, it must be trouble...always is."

"I'd love to two-step the day away with you, Jack, but I got a corpse tangled up in the Pirate Ship's treasure chest line. It's not a pretty sight. If you don't get here soon, I think the parents may start asking for refunds."

"Christ. You find the damndest things. Where are you?"

"At buoy number six, where they tie up the booty. You're gonna want a search and rescue team."

"Right, I'm in the pass, I'll be there in three minutes. Don't let anyone touch anything. Try to keep everyone calm. Oh hell, you know what to do, Titan. Just do it."

I could hear the engine of the patrol boat rev higher. He was probably opening her up to 50 mph for quick response.

I closed my phone, knowing all too well what had to be done.

Eyes glazed, Geena slumped at the rail. I shook her shoulder.

"Geena, I need your help. Are you up to it?"

She nodded. "You can always count on me, Tess. What do you need?"

"Take the kids below and play the Hokey Pokey and Limbo. I need you to keep them busy for the next forty-five minutes."

"No problem, I can handle that." She started a Conga line to the lower deck.

True to his promise, Jack pulled alongside the ship in a twenty-one-foot, center console, patrol vessel with seconds to spare. He wore his summer Marine Patrol uniform; khaki shorts, a matching shirt, badge, and web gear. The gear held handcuffs, pepper spray, baton, and a 9mm semi-automatic pistol.

Jack was pushing forty, but scaled the ladder like a twenty-year-old.

"Okay, Titan, where's the floater?" he asked, muscles flexing as he pulled himself over the rail. Blond hair stood out on his tan arms. His sun-bleached light hair was thick and windblown.

I pointed out over the water. "Under the buoy. The chest is attached to the line. He's the guy doing water aerobics upside down. Can't miss him."

"Cute, very cute. Search and rescue will be here in five minutes. Anything else I need to know?" Jack leaned over the rail to survey the wake on the side of the ship.

I rested my arms on the rail and looked across the emerald waters at Shell Island, a favorite site for both locals and tourists. "Yeah. It looks suspicious."

He positioned himself closer to me and lowered his voice. "Suspicious like a jumper, or a pusher?"

"Pusher'd be my guess. He's way out of his element here—trench coat, Armani suit, and Rolex. Not your typical local."

Jack turned toward me and grinned. "Jesus, Titan. He dangled for a few seconds and you saw all that?"

Jack had always known how to make me feel good. "Luckily, he barely cleared the water before the crew had the kids drop the line back. I think most of the partygoers thought it was a gruesome blow-up mannequin. Just part of the show." I raised my sunglasses and faced him. "The Captain is scrambling now for enough chocolate doubloons to give the kids. They were counting on the ones from the chest."

"Kids and chocolate. I wouldn't want to be in his shoes," he said.

We laughed at that, and watched a mother dolphin and her calf chase a school of fish. A few pelicans circled to take advantage of the free lunch.

It was quiet. The silence felt safe.

Jack pressed the heels of his hands to his temples, massaging an ache I imagined would be with him 'til sunset.

"You should come back, Titan. You know that. We could use you." The words flowed easily from his lips. He had a way of saying what was on his mind regardless of the effect.

I was both frightened and relieved by his invitation. "Thanks, Bubbles. But I think breathing all that testosterone again might be lethal." I tried to sound convincing, but doubted even my own sarcasm.

I'd left the Patrol nine years ago when Katie was born. My husband, Michael, agreed we could manage our first child, Kevin, while we both kept working. But he refused to let me continue when Katie was born.

At least that's the story we told. Only Jack knew the truth.

It had been a privilege serving in the Florida Marine Patrol for almost ten years. It was a demanding job that was considered prestigious among law enforcement agencies. Being the only woman on a twenty-man team in Gulf County added to my notoriety.

I had maintained my water-related certifications and six-month qualifications on my 9mm Glock. I don't know why I did it, I just did. I kept the gun in a lock box at the bank. It somehow seemed more appropriate having it lie on top of the life insurance policy. Besides, I didn't have the heart to sell it. It had been a gift from my father.

Musical sounds floated across the deck. The kids were singing "Happy Birthday" in a variety of keys and tempos. The laughter was intoxicating and genuine. Jack cracked his knuckles and looked like a fish out of water.

Pointing at a fast approaching outboard with three men in short diving suits, I nudged him on the shoulder. "You've been saved, my man. Here comes search and rescue."

I could see the relief in his eyes. He spit on his palms, and rubbed them together.

"Time to get to work," he slipped over the side back to his boat. Taking a few steps down the ladder, he lifted his head up towards me, "We'll need your statement. You can leave it at the substation if it's easier for you."

"I'll stop by in the morning."

"Oh, I almost forgot. Tell the kid happy birthday for me, Tess."

"Yeah. Tell the guys happy fishing for me," I said, under my breath.

The guys worked for another half-hour before they gave me the okay sign. I let the Captain know he could set sail for home. The kids returned to the upper deck, armed with tambourines. They were a-twisting and a-turning to Chubby Checker, and trying to do the electric slide. Geena and I stole away to the lower deck with the cooler and locked ourselves in the little damsel's room. It was our turn to unwind. We knew the girls were being picked up at the dock by another mother and taken to the movies.

"You got anything stronger than piña coladas in there?" I asked, hopping up on the wet counter.

"I think I've got the cure for what's ailin' ya, mate!" She plopped her backside on the open toilet seat, obviously in a state of denial. "I did a little acquisitioning while you directed traffic upstairs." She pulled six minis of tequila out of the cooler, and a bag of sliced limes.

"Girlfriend, you are it. You have my everlasting gratitude." I bit into a lime and took a long drink from the first bottle.

Geena waited until my face was plastered with satisfaction. "Forget that gratitude crap, I plan to collect in a more labor-intensive tender."

I leaned back against the mirror, and took another bite of lime. "Oh boy, I can tell I'm gonna hate this. What's this moment of liquid sanity costing me?"

"Well, as you are well aware, love bug season is almost here. I think

18

one neighbor providing another neighbor the kindness of a clean windshield and bumper for —what shall we say—two weeks? She said dangling the second bottle in front of me.

"One week," I replied, dangling the lime bag at her.

"Ten days."

"Eight."

"Deal," we both said. I grabbed the bottle. She grabbed the limes. It wasn't "Cheeseburgers in Paradise," it was better.

The tequila hits slid down real easy, while the image of the dead corpse etched itself deeper into my memory. *What was he doing out on the bay dressed to the hilt? Why didn't he have any shoes on? If he was pushed, couldn't he swim? Was he drugged first?* The questions started coming faster. I tightened my fist around the shot glass and drank more quickly. I'd never found a more tried and true recipe for lightening the ol' memory load. If you drank fast enough eventually you outpaced the memories. I'd learned this lesson the hard way, from too much experience.

The picture started to fade after the third shot. But the questions hung around for a while longer. *Who was this guy? And why did he die in Paradise?*

Chapter Two

September 13, 2001

My senses were being attacked on all sides. The sun shone through my window like a high-powered searchlight. I grabbed my sunglasses from the nightstand, and covered my head with a feather pillow. The pillow felt like a concrete slab slamming into my head. Tequila headaches are hell.

There was a clattering noise coming from downstairs, and my mouth tasted like a lizard had crawled up in it and died. The only part of me not thoroughly disgusted with being alive was my right big toe.

Gradually, the tantalizing aroma of Earl Grey and brioche lured me from my Sealy Posturpedic tomb.

I stumbled into a pair of elasticized shorts and left on the over-sized tee shirt I'd slept in. Geena was as close to family as it got. She'd seen me at my best, my worst, and everything in between.

"Good morning, sleepyhead. Nice shades. Hope the rattling around didn't wake you up." Geena slipped the brioche from the cookie sheet onto a serving tray, and poured me a cup of tea from her favorite pot. She was neatly dressed in a sleeveless cotton shift with matching sandals. I was checking out the color of her toenail polish when she added, "The kids are already up and gone. They had some Danish on the run, and caught the bus to school." She placed a cosy over the pot.

I took a seat at the kitchen table and tried prying my fingertips away from the pressure points on my temples. "Okay, slowly and very, very quietly tell me what's wrong, Geena?"

"Wrong? What do you mean? Can't a friend share a breakfast with another friend without being given the third degree?" She cut the brioche and brought it over to the table.

As hard as I could, I pressed my index finger on the pressure point in the middle of my forehead for as long as I could stand it. Some of the pain began to fade.

"That's a lovely sentiment, Geena, but let's cut the Betty Crocker routine. We've known each other too long." My eyes scanned the kitchen for the artificial sweetener. "We both know you love to cook— in your kitchen. You hate my kitchen. You only cook here when something is really bothering you. So spit it out. What is it? Is it about yesterday?" I got up and dragged myself around the kitchen looking for the sweetener bowl.

Geena set a plate of brioche in my spot.

"It didn't seem real until I saw the paper this morning." She laid the paper by my plate, and poured herself some tea.

I plodded back to the table and looked at the headlines. The surprise cargo had made the front page of the local section. Rather ironic considering the man was as unlocal as you could get. I estimated he was farther from home than a pod of manatees during the winter season.

Geena jumped up from the table and stomped over to the medicine cabinet. "I'd sue the paper if I was that guy. Look at that horrible shot the photographer got of him being rolled into that body bag. Isn't anything sacred? That's certainly one day in my life I'd like to forget, and I don't appreciate having it thrown in my face on page one of the paper...a paper that I pay an annual subscription to, I might add." She grabbed the aspirin bottle and knocked four of the tablets out into her hand, but not before checking the expiration date on the bottle.

I looked at the picture, and scanned the article. The photographer had gotten a clean shot of the body being transported by the EMS team to the morgue. The Medical Examiner would be having an early morning of it. My eye also picked up a headline about Mrs. Lubbock's pair of chinchillas being stolen. She was so distressed by her loss that she'd been admitted to the hospital with heart palpitations. I focused back on the body.

I knew everyone at the paper was just doing his or her job, but that was the wrong answer. I had been a viable part of the human race long enough to know that.

"You're right, Geena. It's not the way I'd like to be remembered in celluloid...a last picture like that." I gave up on finding the sweetener and added a teaspoon of the real stuff to my tea.

"I just don't like the way things are stacking up around here." She dropped two of the aspirin in front of me, and kept the other two for herself. "First it was transients with their petty theft. Then came the Spring Breakers with their drugs and underage sex. Now we have a body swinging from a treasure chest. Am I the only one seeing a trend here?"

Dragging the sugar bowl over to her side, she measured exactly two teaspoons into her cup, scraping the excess back into the bowl with a butter knife. "This used to be a safe haven. A place where we could let our guard down and leave our doors open. It was that peacefulness that attracted me to this town in the first place."

I watched as she stirred her tea. She used a quick, deliberate motion, forcing the brew to the lip of the cup, but never over the edge.

"Why, Geena, you almost sound sincere."

"Oh shut up and eat your brioche." She threw a balled-up napkin at me. "May I remind you that it's that same air of peacefulness that attracts the paying customers? I mean, what happens when Paradise isn't paradise anymore? Doesn't it bother you to know that these hoodlums and psychos are slowly stealing away our lives, as we know it? It's just too close to home, too close for comfort." She placed a piece of brioche on a plate for herself.

My eyes scanned the kitchen floor until Geena finally asked, "What are you looking for?"

"Your soapbox. If you think you're finished with it, be sure to shove it back under the table. I sure as hell don't want to accidentally trip over that thing," I said, almost choking on a nut from the bread.

"Serves you right. You can be so closed-minded sometimes. How would you have felt if that had been Katie at the front of the line looking over the rail when that chest came out of the water?"

Her words cut to the bone. "You always know just what to say, Geena."

"I'm sorry. That was uncalled for. I just think we've got a problem here, and nobody seems to want to recognize it. Maybe you could write something for the paper that would wake people up." She stuck her index finger to the table, over and over, picking up crumbs.

"I hate to be the one to tell you this after all these years, but I don't write wake-me-up, make-me-sweat-it-out-in-the-morning-before-I-go-to-work news. Remember me? I write that nice little column that's supposed to make you feel good about yourself and where we live." I took a gulp of tea. It wasn't sweet enough.

"You're right. I'm grabbing at straws. I just thought since this was your area of expertise that you might consider getting involved."

Getting involved is exactly what I didn't want to do. "WAS is the key word here, Geena. That was a long time ago. I wouldn't even feel comfortable asking questions about the case. I'm way out of the loop." I bit into the soft, warm brioche, and almost believed what I was saying.

"Don't try and fool me, Tess Titan." Geena got up and scrubbed the cookie sheet in the sink. "I saw you out there on the ship. You didn't even blink when that body popped up. You probably knew his name, weight, and zip code before the sunlight even struck the pant cuffs on that fancy suit."

She turned towards me. "When we all realized what we were looking at, the adrenaline paralyzed us with fear. You...it gave an edge. You knew just what to do." She dried the pan and put it away in the broiler drawer.

It was quiet as Geena loaded the dishwasher, and I finished eating my breakfast. The food improved my physical disposition, while the conversation had disturbed my mental one.

Fact was, it had taken me years to get rid of that edge—to ease the paranoia and judgmental attitude, and to blur the picture of the day I'd screwed up. I'd wanted—no needed—to find my soul. To forgive myself. To laugh and smile. To live life without the incessant reminders of the trash that lives among us.

I wanted to be a normal, ambivalent citizen unaware of and shielded from the atrocities of life. I couldn't have people depending on me to protect them when I couldn't even protect myself.

I thought I'd succeeded. I was the picture of normalcy, as I perceived it. A stay-at-home mom with a part-time job, two kids, husband, and a mortgage. I'd been the Girl Scout Leader, PTA Spring Festival Chair, and Home Owners Association President. I dug holes and planted trees for Arbor Day, went trick-or-treating for UNICEF, and saved the whales. All of this, only to be undone by one untimely moment. One act of fate that I had no control over had somehow shaken loose my façade, and now everything felt wrong.

I took my plate and cup over and placed them in the dishwasher. "Thanks for the gourmet breakfast, Geena. I owe you one." I started back upstairs, but on second thought came back down and peeked around the corner.

Geena wiped a layer of dust from the mixing bowl on the counter. "Do me a favor, don't cook me anything, okay?"

I watched as she cleaned up the counter a bit, then retrieved the artificial sweetener from its hiding place behind the toaster oven and returned it to the table.

I raced back up to the first landing. "Cook? No problem. That's a four letter word in this house!" I climbed the last three stairs, and realized I was out of breath. Sucking wind, I yelled back "I'll talk to you later. I've got to get to the photo shop and the fish market before all the good stuff is gone."

I had this gnawing feeling I should just order pizza tonight...without the anchovies.

******

I pulled onto the docks by the fishing pier, admiring the new boardwalk the Improvement Board had laid to attract tourists. The "Old Town" area was really coming back to life. A few antique shops had opened up, along with a music store, coffee bar, and a kayak rental place. The residents had rallied to get the Post Office to stay put, adding quaintness to the town that couldn't be bought.

The police substation was across the street on the corner. It helped to keep the riff raff to a minimum. I stood in the parking lot for a minute unable to decide whether to go give my statement about the Pirate Ship fiasco first or get my seafood for tonight's dinner.

Duty won over dinner. The substation wasn't in bad shape considering it was housed in a fifty-year-old building that used to be a bank. It smelled kind of musty inside, like an old bookstore. I found the nearest available officer and gave a quick, but complete statement of my involvement in the activities that day. I was done within forty-five minutes and felt some weight taken off my shoulders. I couldn't tell if I felt better because I thought I'd done the right thing by going there first or if it was because I could check it off my mental list of "things to do today." Considering it might be the latter filled me with new guilt. It was a no-win situation.

My eyes wandered across the street to the newly renovated park. It was quite impressive. The community saw an opportunity to add a tourist attraction to the old town and moved the only known four-headed palm tree into the park. Tourists came to snap photos and marvel at the curiosity, while locals just figured it was a freak of nature, an outcome of the tree growing too close to the water treatment plant.

I slung my satchel over my shoulder, grabbed my wallet, and walked over to get a carry basket at the docks.

I headed toward the back of Tony's boat. I had a regular line-up of fishermen I did business with: Tony was always first on my list.

"Hi ya, Tony. Any Amberjack today?" I tried not to breathe in the fishy smells.

"Sure have, Tess. I saved some for you. Had to beat off your neighbor, Mr. Breecher. He suspected I was holding them for you, which seemed to get him all riled up!" Tony laughed, while he packed the fish on some ice and double bagged them.

"Thanks, Tony. I've been craving some seafood stew, and it just wouldn't be the same without some of your Amberjack." I handed him a few extra bucks for a tip.

Moving quickly around the docks, I picked up some shrimp, scallops, and mussels. Seafood stew for dinner was startin' to sound real good. It was one of those quick-n-easy, one-pot meals that I prided myself in making.

The morning was well gone, and only a few cars were left in the parking lot. Most of the boats had closed up for the day. I loaded purchases in my arms, and fought to get the basket back in the stack. I almost had the basket in place, when a man appeared from one of the walkways between the boats.

He stared straight at me, then yelled something in Italian.

"Did you want a carry basket?" I offered him my basket and apologies at the same time. "I'm terribly sorry...I had no idea. Did I stack them incorrectly?" He walked right for me. I started backing away using the basket as a shield.

He pushed the basket aside and sprayed me in the face with pepper spray. I grabbed for my eyes, and felt the satchel being ripped from my shoulder. My throat started to close up. I staggered backwards. Tripping over a water hose, I fell off the pier into the bay.

I lay on my back trying to float and catch my breath at the same time. I could feel the carcasses of recently cleaned fish rubbing up against me. I tried not to imagine the number of boats that had illegally emptied their bilges in the canal that morning.

Someone had just purposely ruined my seafood stew dinner.

******

"Tess. Tess Titan!" called the voice from beyond, pulling me back from my market nightmare.

Tony had rescued me from my watery grave, and insisted on riding in the ambulance with me to the hospital. They had given me a tranquilizer to keep me from sitting up in the ambulance. The loss of my stew dinner had been a bitter pill to swallow, but it was the cold steel table freezing my butt that brought me back to reality.

I opened my eyes, only to be blinded by a stream of light being directed into my pupil.

"You're really getting slack, Dick. Couldn't you find any better way to torture me today? Or are all of your really special torture tools out to be cleaned?"

"Very nice, Tess. I can see that your romp with Charlie the Tuna didn't affect your social graces any," parlayed Dr. Dick Dashel.

I forced a smile, trying to keep my lips pursed, so the gauze holding my tooth in place wouldn't dribble out of my mouth. I knew he hated it when I called him Dick, but he hadn't earned any reprieve from me.

Dick was a pain in the ass—my ass to be exact. We had been rivals ever since childhood, when he proudly announced to me, at the ripe age of four, that his "package" was complete and that mine was just "completely missing." I had been devastated for weeks. His proclivity for poor taste in jokes hadn't changed much over the years, only proving to me, "once a Dick, always a Dick."

It was just my luck that he was working in the emergency room this morning. I couldn't help but wonder what strings his father had pulled to get him on the day shift, a benefit normally entitled to only the most senior physicians.

"Your x-rays came back fine. You didn't break anything, but

26

certainly not from lack of trying," he preached, while scrubbing his hands in the sink.

"You need to take it easy for a few days. You have a good-sized knot on the side of your head that may cause you some discomfort over the next twenty-four hours. Your ankle is going to be a bit touchy; you twisted it pretty good in that hose. And your jaw is going to be sore for a few weeks. You're lucky you didn't lose all your teeth with the way you hit that piling when you fell. You'd be wise to keep the gauze on that tooth for the next forty-eight hours to help strengthen the root system."

He dried his hands with a paper towel and headed towards the door, "No eating steak, apples, or...chewing gum!" he said, purposely as he opened the door to leave.

I knew he'd added that last part just to infuriate me. He knew that I was an incurable gum-chewer, unable to go for more than a few hours without a stick to sustain me.

My godmother, Nellie Sharp, an angel put on earth to save me from myself, was sitting unobtrusively in the corner in a worn armchair provided for visitors.

She was a lovely woman both in body and in spirit. Her 5'1" frame couldn't begin to equal her feisty stature. I had grown fond of her eccentricities, and relied on her love of life to save me from my lack of one.

Her hair was still auburn, though silver highlights were taking over her long locks. Occasionally, she would put a festive colored streak down one side or the other...orange, green, red, whatever the occasion might call for. Most of the time, she bundled it precariously with tortoise-colored sticks on the back of her head, adding a butterfly hair clip or two to complete the effect. She had always been a rebel at heart.

Nell was "of that age," whatever that meant. She didn't celebrate birthdays. "Birthdays are for people intent on getting older," she always said. "I feel younger each year." She'd been in her fifties for as long as I could remember, but then so had my mother.

As far as I knew, mother and Nell had known each other their entire lives, though they'd come from different sides of the tracks and went to different schools. I often wondered how two such very different people came to be friends.

They were like pickles and ice cream, or pizza and anchovies, you just didn't think they'd go together. But I never pressed the point. Nell had been a godsend to me my entire life. She was kind and considerate. She never missed events, however small, for the children or me. She was always there when I needed her, and knew when to be there even when I didn't have a clue. She was everything my mother wasn't, so I was sure she wasn't going to miss this opportunity to mend one of my burnt bridges.

Nell jumped up from the chair, catching the doctor's attention before he could leave. She grabbed his two hands in hers in a very grand motion. "I can't thank you enough, Dr. Dashel, for taking care of Tessa. It comforts me to know that we have someone we can depend on, someone who knows our little town and its people. Your father must be thrilled that you've returned home to practice."

I thought I'd gag. But Nell kept a perfectly straight face.

Overwhelmed by her warm gesture, Dick shook her hands and gave her a hug. "Why, yes of course, you're very welcome...I have to be running, you know, emergencies and all." He grinned like a Cheshire cat as the door closed behind him.

Too bad it didn't hit him on the way out! I got down from the table, and took a look at myself in the stainless steel mirror hanging over the sink. I couldn't help but smile. I had cotton balls hanging out of my nose, and a wad of wet, bad tasting gauze shoved between my swollen lip and gum line holding my tooth in place. The walnut-sized knot protruding from the side of my head was particularly sensitive to my touch. *So don't touch it, idiot!*

As I shuffled over to the locker to retrieve my clothes, I was smartly reminded of my sprained ankle sporting one of those attractive, flesh-tone bandages. I also noticed that I was way overdue for a pedicure.

"Tessa, Tessa, Tessa," smiled Nell, "I hope you look better than the other guy!" she teased, "though you'd be wise to take better care of your feet and your teeth. They're the only ones you get, you know."

I started to answer, only to realize the antiseptic had seeped into a little pool under my tongue, making me wonder if I should swallow or spit.

I spit. Cotton balls went flying everywhere. We laughed so hard, we had to wipe tears from our eyes.

"Nell, thanks for coming to the hospital." I limped over to the lockers to get my clothes while wiping drool from my mouth. "I didn't want to call Mother. I think today is the dress rehearsal for the Women's Club Fall Fashion Show. I know how much she's counting on that event to run smoothly. She's got quite an itinerary of affairs over the next week." I rolled my eyes and rested my hand on the locker.

"Oh pish posh. That's what godmothers are for, and don't go fretting about your mother. She'll be a shoe-in for the President of the Women's Club this year, with or without that fashion show. Now, let me help you with your things, then you can tell me what needs to be done to keep the Titan household up and running today!"

"Thanks, Nellie, you're a jewel." I finished dressing and grabbed my wallet. Instinctively, I reached back into the locker for my satchel, only to remember it had been stolen.

"Of all the bad luck," I said, staring into the empty locker.

"What's the matter, dear?"

"I picked up my copies of your photos right before I went to the market. I put them in my satchel, the one the mugger seemed so intent on relieving me of before I fell in the bay. So much for that Pulitzer."

My eyes lit up a second later. "Felix forgot to make the second set. He put one of those yellow stickies on the envelope saying the second set would be ready tomorrow." I closed the locker door with a sense of satisfaction." Maybe good did prevail over evil today."

Nell put her backpack purse on over her shoulders and offered me her arm.

"Well, there you go, dear. All is not lost."

"Only my stew dinner," I said as she opened the door for me.

"I think that was just as well too, dear," she scrunched up her face and stuck out her tongue.

Chapter Three

I was a little edgy. It'd taken an extra half-hour for us to run our errands and get home. I didn't want to miss the school bus.

"What do you think that little riotous crowd was all about in front of the veterinary clinic?" I asked Nell, as I pulled into the driveway.

"I'm not positive, dear, but it may have something to do with that exotic animal group that's meeting here this week." Nell picked up the prescription bags filled with painkillers and handed them to me. I learned long ago to never pass up the opportunity to maintain a stash of legal mind-altering drugs. You never know when you'll need those little buggers.

I slammed the car door with my good foot and looked at my watch. "I know the community was hoping for some added income from these meetings and conferences, but if this is any sign of what we can expect, it may not be worth the trouble."

I noticed my neighbor, Mr. Breecher, and his female "friend" getting ready to leave. He helped her into his car and shut the door for her.

Nell saw me staring. "I think it's nice he's finally found someone he's got something in common with."

"You're right. They can both join the 'tight-ass' club."

"Tessa! She might be a perfectly reasonable person. You know better than to judge a book by its cover."

I nodded sheepishly, not agreeing with a word of it. "Speaking of books, the bus will be dropping the kids off any minute. Would you mind running up to the corner to meet them, and bracing them for the appearance of their dear ol' mom?"

"I can do better than that, Tessa. How about I pick them up and take them to the afternoon movie over at the Village Green? That will give you a few hours to recuperate, put on a little make-up, and prepare to play the ever-resilient, brave mother role." She was already waving over her shoulder as she power walked toward the street corner.

I plopped down on the padded kitchen chair, and made a quick phone call to the market and our local constable to find that my satchel hadn't been recovered. The calls only served to confirm my growing suspicion. Why would the attacker take my satchel and not my wallet? The wallet was in my hand, and fell on the pier when I went into the water. It was an easy target, if that's what he was after.

I dialed Geena to commiserate.

"Geena, put the tea and scones on the table and get over here right away. You'll never let me live this one down."

"A lot you know, tea isn't for another hour. Give me one second, I'll be right there. Let me put a note on the door for the guests."

Geena and Bob's bed and breakfast was just a couple of doors down from us. Our two girls, Katie and Lindsey, were growing up together, and had become best friends. Geena and I were much the same. We banded together early on to keep our cantankerous neighbor, Mr. Breecher, from curbing his obnoxious white and black Jack Russell Terrier on our lawns. We meticulously saved over a month's worth of "Richochet's" constitutions, and redistributed them, in full, on Breecher's front porch setting his morning newspaper amongst his darling's droppings. Breecher now carried a pooper-scooper around with him on his outings, and avoided our side of the street with a passion.

I emptied a bag of Chewy Chips Ahoy on a plate, and was pouring two glasses of milk when Geena walked precariously through the kitchen door in her bare feet, carefully balancing on her heels. I looked down to find cotton balls between each of her toes, slaving to save her hard-earned pedicure.

"This had better be good. It took me over an hour...oh my god, what happened to you?" Then even more horrified, she pointed straight at my feet, "I can't believe you went out in public with your toe nails looking like that!"

By the time I'd recounted my day, we'd all but eaten the plate of cookies and had refills on the milk.

"That's unbelievable," Geena said, wiping the crumbs from the corner of her mouth. "You're like a crime magnet. Remind me not to go anywhere with you for the next few days." She added, "My guests will have a fit if they find out about this. We'll have to start locking the doors at night, and giving them keys. What an exercise in pure drudgery! You see, our lives are already changing!" She gave me one of those "I told you so" looks.

"Could we get back to me here for a minute? Why do you think I was his mark? What made him pinpoint me out of the crowd? And why did he take my satchel and not my wallet?"

"Maybe you were the mark because you were the only pinhead still around after everyone else had left. And have you looked at your wallet lately? If I'd had a choice, I would have gone for the satchel too. At least I could have gotten something for that at the pawnshop." Geena examined her toes for imperfections. "He obviously thought the satchel was more valuable," she said, appearing satisfied with her work.

I couldn't help but laugh at both the simplicity and truth of her statement. Anyone who knew me was aware that I carried only the most basic necessities in my wallet: a stick of gum, some lipstick, driver's license, insurance information, press card, and a comb for my few moments of vanity. I never had cash, always using the ATM's in the stores, and I didn't carry credit cards, believing that a good night's sleep was the best cure for impulse buying.

"Do you think he 'thought' or 'knew' the satchel was more valuable?" I wondered out loud.

"Like it could have been someone you know? Why would you even think that? You would've had to do something pretty drastic to someone to have them attack and rob you. Are you keeping some nasty little secrets from me?" Geena raised her eyebrows.

I sipped the last of my now warm milk and contemplated life. "Writing for the paper makes me a sitting duck for one thing or another. But it's not like I get death threats or anything. The last thing I remember getting was that mean-spirited note from Mrs. Nelson who was very disappointed about my review of their annual Beach Art competition."

Geena nodded. "I remember. That didn't make you too popular."

"That's all I can think of. If it's something else I'll have to claim child-induced senility." I played dead and dropped my head over the back of the chair.

"Well, you might want to clear out the cobwebs, and get some of those cells synapsing." Geena tossed the cotton balls into the trash on her way to the door. "What if this lunatic is still in town, and decides he wants more than your satchel? He's got your name, address, and phone number. You wouldn't be too hard to find."

That thought had never entered my mind.

Chapter Four

September 14, 2001

"Mom, you look so cool!" echoed my two children as they raced into the kitchen for a sample-n-dash breakfast.

"Mom, you know we've been studying about first-aid in health class. Could you come in and be my 'show and tell' mannequin?" Katie asked, dead serious.

Before I could answer, a flash blinded me.

"Kevin! What in the world are you doing?" I rubbed my eyes.

"This is great, Mom! I can use these for my theater make-up class. No one else will have anything this good!" my fourteen-year-old son said excitedly.

"Take them and go!" I handed each of them a lunch bag and shoved them out the door into the patchy, morning fog to catch the school bus.

"Katie, did you feed Fitz this morning?" I yelled down the driveway.

"Yeah, Mom, he's fine!"

I peeked my head around the corner of the house just to be sure Fitz was alive and kicking. He seemed quite happy gobbling down his last few baitfishes.

Fitz was our resident Brown Pelican for the next few months. He was an attractive young male with a yellowish crown, white head and neck, and gray-brown body plumage. He had a traumatic experience with some fishing line and broke one of his wings. He was rooming with us on the back patio until it healed.

As far as roommates went, he wasn't so bad. He kept to himself most of the time, was rather quiet, and never complained about the cuisine. Sometimes I'd lie on a lounge chair in the backyard with the radio on and talk to him. It didn't seem any stranger to me than people who talked to their plants, and he seemed to enjoy our time together. He'd hop from foot to foot on his perch in time to the music, and preen himself...a compliment I liked to think.

We'd had unusual animals in our home since Katie was three and brought home her first lizard missing his tail. She was so intent on doctoring it back to health, I didn't have the heart to tell her that he probably dropped his tail in fear when she picked him up and that it would grow back on its own.

Of course, she was quite pleased with herself when the tail did grow back. Once that happened, there was no stopping her love for doctoring the animal kingdom. My only ground rules were: nothing poisonous; nothing larger than a St. Bernard; one animal at a time; and everything had to be named after an author of a book she had read. This kept her reading at a feverish pace to maintain a log of potentially suitable names. Fitz was named after F. Scott Fitzgerald; she chose a young reader's edition of *The Great Gatsby*.

My friends thought I was nuts, but having an array of unusual animals around the house was actually a plus. Everyone seemed a bit more cautious when they approached our house; we rarely had unannounced visitors; and it kept the in-laws at bay. Whenever we invited them over, their first question was "What do you have living in the backyard?"

Fitz started preening himself, reminding me that I should be doing the same.

Pulling myself together this morning was going to take a little work. I used a headband over my straight, short, blond hair to hide the goose egg on the side of my head. Pulling my hair back so tight made me realize it was time for another dye job. I spit out the gauze. Satisfied that my tooth wouldn't come tumbling out, I dared to chew a half piece of spearmint gum on the other side of my mouth.

Luckily, I had lived long enough in Florida that getting dressed was no longer the main event of my day. I lived the reality of "optional ironing." I once again thanked the great retail God for the no-nonsense, design brilliance of two of our local ladies, Liz and Jane. They created a comfortable, artistic, versatile line of everyday, anywhere style of 100 percent natural clothing for women. I lived in it, and hoarded my pennies for their semi-annual sales.

Selecting a long, cotton, bright tangerine skirt, white short-sleeved top, and beaded sandals, I decided the ace bandage had to go and stored it in the closet for the next person who tripped over a hose and fell into the bay.

A quick look in the mirror confirmed I hadn't forgotten any strategic piece of clothing, but also verified the obvious: I was getting older, and couldn't hide it any longer. Forty sucked. I didn't think getting older would affect me the way it had. I hated judgmental people, yet found myself comparing my body parts to other unsuspecting women at any given opportunity.

Every day seemed to bring the birth of new wrinkles, bumps, and gray hairs. Plus, my body didn't hesitate to let me know when I'd broken some cosmic rule regarding eating, drinking, or exercising.

Reaching for my array of vitamins, I realized the medicine cabinet looked more like a plea for help from a health food junkie than a place to store aspirin and antacids. The fridge wasn't much better. It was stocked with green vegetables to boost my immune system, soy products for those damn hot flashes I'd started having, and filtered water to keep "the body hydrated and supple." I washed down the vitamins with concord grape juice wondering if all this effort was worth the trouble.

Outside, I rolled up the remains of Fitz's breakfast in newspaper and took a quick walk to the trash can at the end of the driveway. Breecher was across the street sweeping off his steps and walkway. He turned his back to me.

I refused to let the little rodent ruin my day. I grabbed my sun hat from inside the house and took off in my new, yellow VW Bug...compliments of my loving husband, the son-of-a-bitch.

Chapter Five

I arrived within minutes at the sheriff's office: a lovely, sky-blue, one-story cottage with a few judiciously placed Adirondack chairs on the front porch, projecting an aura of a friendly constable's establishment. A simple white rectangular sign read "Sheriff's Office."

I tried hopping out of my Bug, only to be sharply reminded of my bumps and bruises. Opening the door to the office, I was relieved to feel a breeze blowing from the fan overhead. It was already starting to get humid, or was it just me?

I looked around the office. Betty, the person who did everything but chase down the bad guys, wasn't in yet. I was disappointed. I'd known Betty for years. She was a real spitfire. With five kids, ages three to eleven, she was a miracle of motherhood. A few years back, her husband had an accident at work and had to go on disability. Betty didn't miss a beat. She got a job organizing Andy and still kept her house and kids in working order. She made Martha Stewart look silly.

"Andy, are you here?" I raised my voice in case he was in the kitchen getting coffee.

"OUCH! You stupid machine. Stop! Stop!" he yelled from the back room.

"What's going on back there, Andy? Something *too hot* for you to handle?"

Andy walked from the kitchen, his forearm wrapped with a dishtowel. The corners of his mouth took an obvious turn south.

Andy Hagen was one of the most eligible bachelors in town, a fact that rarely escaped him. He had a good job that seldom kept him out beyond six o'clock. He was educated and literate. He owned his own home. He still had all of his own hair, and he wore a uniform that he filled out quite nicely. Not that I paid much attention to that sort of thing.

"How did I know it was you?" He grabbed tape from his desk to secure the towel on his arm. "I guess you'll be wanting to file a report on that market incident yesterday?" He sat on the edge of his desk and winced as he crossed his arms...playing up the hurt big boy look a little too much for my taste.

"Well, yes. I hate to be the bearer of bad news for our community crime statistics," I said, circling behind him, "but I think robbery and assault is just-cause for you to earn your paycheck."

He jumped off the desk and turned abruptly to find me leaning back in his chair, legs crossed.

"Robbery and assault?" his voice almost squeaked, as the weight of his body forced his hands on to the desk. "Are you off your Prozac?"

"Let me see." I stood, spit my gum in the trash can, and leaned towards him, nose-to-nose, over the desk. "No. I'm also not pre-menstrual, post-menstrual, peri-menopausal, paranoid, or pregnant! And I think I'm capable of knowing if I've been robbed and attacked or not!"

Andy and I had a history of one-upmanship. We'd been at it for years, so I didn't see it stopping anytime soon. His professional credentials had been adequate enough to make him the first Sheriff of Paradise Pointe. The most important credential being he'd take the measly salary we could afford to pay. He also jumped at the opportunity to be the "big guy." This was the part that didn't settle well with me.

He came from a job in a small Alabama town where he had been number two since the beginning of his career, and it didn't look like that would change for another twenty years. I couldn't blame the guy for wanting a little bit more than what he had, but he really played it up.

The part that killed me was that the women in town just loved it. He was their Superman in disguise. I thought it was disgusting. He ate it up.

Andy backed down. "Now Tess, calm down. I didn't mean to imply you were one round short of a full clip. But, don't you think you might be over exaggerating just a bit?" He held back a grin.

His voice was so condescending, I bit my tongue until I couldn't stand it a second longer. "A raving, foreign lunatic purposely attacks me on the docks and steals my satchel. I don't think that's terribly imaginative on my part, do you?"

Coughing into his hand to keep from chuckling, Andy straightened his face and answered, "More like a drunken transient mistook you for someone who owed him money." He walked over to the water cooler to get a drink.

"If he took your satchel, it was probably to hock it for his next bottle of Tequila. I'm not condoning behavior like that, mind you. We can't have that kind of unruliness going on around here. Besides, I'm havin' more than my fair share of trouble keepin' this exotic animal group under control and within the limits of the law. Word spreads about your encounter, and we'll be front-page news over in Panama City. Before you know it, we'll have every drunken activist in a 100-mile radius booking reservations." He crushed the white Dixie cup in his hand and tossed it into the recycle bin.

His indifference was driving me crazy. "I think I know the difference between a drunken panhandler and a deliberate attempt at subterfuge." I felt belittled and defensive.

"I know you've got a number of years of police experience behind you, but it's been a while since you used it, Tess." He used a bent paperclip to clean some dirt out from under his nails.

I could feel my brain boiling.

He tossed the paper clip into the trash can. "Why don't we both compromise a little? How about I consider the possibility that you were attacked and robbed by a foreign national, and you consider the possibility that you were rolled by a drunken transient? We'll both sleep on it tonight and see if we don't have a better basis for discussion tomorrow?"

"Andy Hagen, you're impossible! I know what I saw, and I know what I heard. This wasn't a case of mistaken identity. I want to file a formal complaint, and I want the paperwork in my mailbox by the end of the day."

As an afterthought, I turned in the doorway and smiling sweetly, added with my best southern drawl "by the way, if you'd use the coffee pot to measure the water instead of filling it from the faucet, you wouldn't have that overflow problem." I shut the door quietly behind me, abstaining from my urge to rip it from its hinges. I was very pleased with myself. My victory was short-lived.

******

I didn't have to shift out of second gear before rolling into the parking lot of the *Paradise Gazette*. Our small-town paper was housed in a bright yellow building that resembled an old time train depot. My blood raced a little each time I pulled into its parking lot. I felt like a train would pull into the station at any minute and whisk me off to some exotic destination. Michael and I had always intended on traveling, but the time got away from us. The kids came along, and the rest is "history" as they say.

Paradise Pointe wasn't such a bad place to live. There just wasn't a lot around. Pensacola was two hours west. Panama City was forty-five minutes east, and Atlanta was six hours north if you didn't take into account the time change. Due south—the water, for as far as your eye could see. I'd come to understand what people meant when they talked about having "island fever."

Push come to shove, I suppose Paradise Pointe was better than a lot of other places. I'd been here so long, I couldn't imagine being serious about moving anywhere else. But then, I used to be more content. Everything seemed to be changing. Lately, I just wasn't a hundred percent sure of anything. It was an unsettling feeling.

I pulled in next to Edy's gray Volvo liftback. She kept it meticulous. Edy Davenport was our ultra-efficient secretary. She was a retired executive secretary from up north that had taken to wearing purple outfits and floppy hats. She had given in to her whimsical nature and decided to embrace her interest in unusual hobbies. This month, it was learning how to greet and welcome people in nine different languages. I never knew exactly what to expect when I walked through the door. I found that comforting.

Our Editor, Tom Daily, owned the gold Nissan Pathfinder. Tom was a transplant from a large East Coast paper where he was vying for the number two spot and a heart attack, all before age fifty. His doctor told him it was time to relocate and reassess the stress factors in his life, or the only thing he'd be planning for was his estate. It took one frightful trip to the emergency room, with a near-death experience, to convince him of the seriousness of his situation. He got rid of his condo in the city, the red Miata, and all the other boy-toys he'd acquired, including his second wife Heidi, who was just as happy to be released from her love contract. Tom appreciated where he was, what he was doing, and the person he'd become. He enjoyed each day, as if it might be his last. He was prone to occasional stress backslides, which he overcame by chanting his mantra "let go and live life."

The third car raised my blood pressure ten points. My nemesis, and food critic for the paper, Carlisle Witherspoon, owned the black BMW Roadster. His father had donated the money to start the paper, a point that "Spoony" was always bringing to our attention. As much of a sour note as that was to our ears, it was also a painful reminder to him of his living "condition." Spoony worked because he had to. His father, an insightful man, had seen to that by attaching a stipulation to his son's trust. In order to receive his monthly stipends, Carlisle had to work twenty-five hours per week either at a paying job or volunteering for the community. I smiled each time I tried to imagine Spoony volunteering anything but his opinion or profile for a picture. So he worked for the paper doing what he did best...complaining about mediocrity and attesting to his superiority.

"Meowwww!" chastised the large calico cat perched on the front porch railing.

Hemingway was the *Gazette's* office cat. He adopted Tom a few short weeks after the paper opened. Tom thought is was good Karma and refused to take the cat to the Humane Society regardless of Carlisle's remonstrations and allergies to cats.

Hemingway and I got along notoriously well and had struck a deal early on. In return for leaving his predatory prizes on the hood of Spoony's Beemer, I provided him all the liver treats he could consume. It was the best deal I'd ever made.

Spoony was certain it was the local kids pulling pranks on him and spent most of his time infuriated to the point of paranoia. He couldn't sit at his desk for more than a few minutes without going into surveillance mode...poking his fingers between the slats on the blinds, pressing his nose to the window, and scanning the surrounding area. This lasted a short time, as his breath began to fog the window, stealing him of any potential victory.

I figured I was doing the community a public service by keeping him busy. Overall, I thought the whole thing was a hoot. I mean, how superior could you be with a half-eaten lizard lying on the hood of your car?

"Hey ol' man, how ya doin?" I asked while giving the cat a few long strokes and slipping a handful of treats between his paws. Looking up, I saw two fingers bending the slats open, then a "ping," as they snapped back into place. "Well, let's get to it, eh?" I popped a couple of Chiclets into my mouth.

Entering the office was a spiritual experience—literally. Tom had an expert in Feng Shui identify the energy of the building and help balance that natural energy force around and within the building, to promote our good health, prosperity, and well-being. I didn't understand exactly how they went about doing that, but it did feel nice when you went inside. There was no clutter so that the energy could enter and move about freely. A few potted trees and plants were strategically located in the corners, and a fountain with ceramic dolphins on a table near one of the windows. There was full spectrum lighting, to energize you more because it's the closest match to natural sunlight. The air temperature was always just right, even though use of the fans was discouraged. Evidently fans get the energy all in a frenzy and send you running for the door, which I almost did anyway this morning.

"Buon giorno, Tess! Io sono Edy. Piacere!" Edy said, as she rushed around her desk, kissed me on both cheeks, and shook my hands.

Her accent reminded me of the man at the dock.

"Tess! Tess! Are you still with us?" Edy snapped her fingers in front of my eyes.

"What? Oh, yes, yes. I'm guessing we're in Italy this week, and you didn't just propose to me?" I took a deep cleansing breath, and added, "That's a great shade of periwinkle you're wearing today," as I emptied my mailbox onto my desk.

"How nice of you to notice! I found this little creation in a shop on one of the bayous west of here; it was love at first sight. I just had to have it."

"You and your bayou shopping. You're braver than I am." I flipped through the mail.

"Oh, I seriously doubt that. By the way, I love the article you wrote about Nell. Her friendship with the Contessa, and their escapades in Paris after WWII...ohhh la la! She certainly has led an interesting life. I love the part of how you're named after the Contessa. What a great story to be able to tell to your grandchildren one day. I did take the liberty of editing a few spots, here and there. I hope you don't mind?" Edy looked hesitantly over the top of her wire-rimmed glasses.

"I never do, Edy. If it weren't for you, I'm afraid my readers would be sorely disappointed at my untidy use of the English language." I tossed all but two pieces of the mail into the trash.

"Well, I'm not surprised at the shortcomings of your education," interrupted Carlisle. "It takes quite an effort to get a good education in the United States, particularly in the south. There are exceptions, of course. Though I'm afraid your school isn't one of them." He went to get a cup of water from the cooler.

I tried to will the hot water to come rushing out instead of the cold, but to no avail. I must have walked counter-clockwise in the room, according to Feng Shui that can screw everything up.

Spoony was sporting his normal attire: bright yellow golfing pants that were too short for his lanky frame; a long-sleeved, red paisley shirt; and a red ascot wrapped inside his collar. He topped off this fashion statement with a safari hat.

Carlisle had been dumped from one prep school to the next. He lacked any sense of empathy or familial closeness. From a distance, it would be easy to feel bad for him. But, up close, there was no mistaking the breeding of an uppity S.O.B.

Edy flipped her ionizer on to full, a warning sign that a lot of nasty ions were going to need to be wrestled back to a positive state, and went back to her typing.

"Thank you for your insightful comments, Carlisle. I'll be sure to share them with Congressman Howell next week when I have that interview with him about the successes and failures of our nation's educational system." I casually picked up the copy in my in-box, replacing it with my mail. I noticed a piece that was running about the visiting exotic animal group. I folded the copy and put it in the side of my purse.

Spoony's back stiffened.

I knew it fried his ass senseless that I'd pinned down that interview instead of him. Victory over Spoony wasn't that difficult, since he devoted his life to the theory that he didn't need to work for success, because he'd been born into it.

He threw his crumpled cup at the trash can, missing by a long shot.

"Say, Carlisle, isn't that giggling I hear outside?" I cupped my hand over my ear and nodded my head towards the door.

"No, no, not again!" He ran to his desk and grabbed a pocket camera. "I'm going to catch those little delinquents red-handed this time!" He straightened his hat, and raced for the door, slamming it behind him.

"I imagine the only thing he'll catch on film is his thumb," I said to Edy.

"I think he needs more fiber in his diet," Edy snorted.

We both broke out laughing.

"What's so funny?" Tom said, poking his head out from his office. "Anything that will help lower my blood pressure?"

"Sorry, not today," I wiped tears from my eyes with the back of my hand.

"Well, I'm glad to see your brush with disaster didn't break your funny bone." He waved me into his office. Once the door was shut, he put both hands on my shoulders, and looked directly into my eyes.

"Now, all joking aside. How are you really?"

"Really? I'm in a state of denial." I sat on the overstuffed loveseat. "Physically, I feel the bumps and bruises, but mentally, my mind keeps trying to tell me I fell out of bed and hit my head on the treadmill. I'm just as happy with that explanation right now. The truth is too hard to believe. Believing what happened will only piss the hell out of me, and make me do things I'd rather not. Besides, with Michael out "finding himself," I can't let myself fly off the handle with the kids around. I won't do that to them."

"You're a brave woman, Tess. Always have been. But you've got to stop trying to do and be all, especially when it comes to your kids. I know it's not easy being on your own right now, but you have to reach out for some help now and again. That's what family and friends are for.

"Speaking of family, what did your mother think about all this?"

I shifted uneasily on the sofa.

"Tess, tell me you called her?"

I shook my head guiltily. "I started to a half dozen times, but there didn't seem much point to it. I don't expect her to come running every time my life runs amok."

"Have you spoken since the 'Michael' incident?"

"The dueling mother-in-laws you mean? His mom accusing me of sucking her Mikey dry of his creative juices, depriving him the coddling and adulation he so thrived on, and refusing him family and companionship during his trip abroad. And then my mother, happily gloating and wagging her finger at me in her 'I told you so' fashion."

I could see that Tom was going to try to convince me otherwise, but I didn't give him the chance. With a quick breath, I added "No, thank you. That was just about as much unsubstantiated drivel as any sane person should have to endure in a lifetime. This incident would just add kindling to somebody's fire. Trust me, Mother will find a way to turn this all around and make it my fault, even though she's been waiting for this day since Michael and I were first married."

"I thought she adapted to Michael fairly well," Tom said.

"Adapted, yes. Accepted, never. She was furious that I didn't accept Dick Dashel's proposal. She always dreamed of having a doctor in the family, and I ruined it for her. But then, bursting her bubble seems to be my role in life."

"You never know, maybe she'd surprise you with some wise, supportive, caring gesture."

"We are talking about my mother, right? I don't even know how you managed to say that without laughing. I don't need *her* kind of help now. I don't need all that extra baggage. I can handle this on my own. I can, really." *Why were my palms all sweaty?*

"It's your life, sweetheart. Just remember..."

"I know, I know, it's hard to move forward, when you don't recognize your past, savor your present, or trust your future."

"Do I really say that? How nauseating. What have I become?"

"A good friend who never fails to tell it as he sees it. I wouldn't have you any other way." I smiled.

"No other way, huh? Maybe that's what's ailing you, not enough variety," he joked, as he made his way behind his desk into his big, blue, cushy chair.

"Very funny. Now did you want to talk about my column, or have we given up on having any copy for the paper this week?"

"Yes, yes. I loved it. Who wouldn't? Nell's life has enough twists and turns in it to write a hundred columns, and you still wouldn't scratch the surface. I can't wait to see your pictures. What have you got?" He reached over the desk towards me.

"Yeah, well, I can't wait either. That's what I wanted to talk to you about. I have some good news, and some bad news. The bad news is that the pictures were in my satchel that was stolen during the attack. The good news is Felix forgot to make the second set. I'm supposed to pick them up after lunch today. I forget the exact time. It was written on a yellow sticky on the outside of the photo envelope. I remember the copies of Nell's older prints from the '50s looked fine, but I didn't get a close look at the recent shots of Nell, I hope there's something we can use."

"Right, like you don't get a winning shot every time. I keep telling you, you have an eye for the lens. Don't worry about it. Pick up the other set after lunch, and drop off your selects later this afternoon. I'll start judging the white space we've got left to fill this evening. Everything's copasetic, right?"

"Right. Thanks Tom, I'll drop by later." I rocked back and forth to gather some momentum to get myself off the sofa.

Shoving my edited copy into my purse, I decided a bite of lunch at Josie's was just what I needed to raise my morale. I waved to Carlisle, who had circled the block looking for collaborators in crime. I couldn't help myself from pulling up to the curb next to him.

"Carlisle, did you get a new hood ornament? I thought I saw something headless on your car," I said innocently, as I pulled away, flaunting my license plate behind me...INTHENO.

Chapter Six

Josie's is one of those places you can't find on a map. It isn't a mistake that you never see the name on a tourist itinerary. Josie's is ours. A local place for people who love fresh seafood, a cold beer, and a little friendly conversation or anonymity.

Josie's husband, Rick, is a primo fisherman. His catch-of-the-morning is written on the bar blackboard at 11:30, by 11:45 it's erased.

The restaurant is built on the end of a short, shallow-water pier in "Smuggler's Cove." There are ten-or-so tables and chairs on the front deck and seating for another twenty inside. The outside is the best. There are twinkle lights tacked along the roof overhang. They're used after sunset, year round. Free bags of crackers and breadcrumbs are given to the kids to feed the fish while the parents enjoy a drink or two. Neon colored caddies keep the menus, napkins, and sugar packets from blowing around the tables.

As its name suggests, the cove was used during the Prohibition Era to smuggle hooch. The restaurant had been around back then, and Rick was always ready to share one of the colorful stories that had been passed down to him.

It wasn't unusual to see a diver's flag bobbing about in the water. The cove was a diver's paradise, containing the remains of many ancient unsuccessful launches and landings in its shallow waters.

I went inside right away to see what was on the blackboard and to place my order.

Josie was behind the bar cleaning glasses.

"Well, look what the dog dragged in!" Josie said, as she stacked glasses. "Haven't you been the talk of the town?"

"Yeah, I guess anonymity isn't my strong suit." I pulled the barstool a little closer.

"Hey, Toots, need a sugar daddy?" cackled the red macaw in the corner.

"Give me a break, will ya, Bugsy?" I said over my shoulder. "I see he's as introverted as ever."

"Yeah, we've pretty much given up trying to change his ways. His previous owner left quite an impression on him. Besides, Rick loves telling people we've got a bird with connections." Josie laughed as she put a paper placemat and fork in front of me. "What can I get you?"

"How about a cold Michelob and one of those Amberjack sandwiches with slaw before you're wiped out and save me a piece of key lime pie."

"You got it." She placed the cold beer and a glass in front of me before disappearing into the kitchen.

I turned the stool around, leaned my back against the bar while coddling the cold beer between my legs. There were a couple of construction workers talking about the new sewage lines being laid; a few court reporters talking about the latest murder trial; some moms talking about the plans for the new high school; and the mandatory fisherman or two huddled in the corners seeking refuge from their wives. The place was starting to buzz.

"I could go for a dame like you. Nice chassis, babe," squawked Bugsy from his perch in the corner.

My cell phone vibrated against the side of my purse. "Hello? Oh hi, Felix. Yeah, thanks for calling to remind me. I'll be over to pick up the prints in about forty-five minutes. I'm over at Josie's eatin' lunch. Okay, see you then. Thanks." I put the phone back in my purse, and noticed the folded paper in the side pocket. I sipped my beer and read the copy being prepped for the next issue.

The Citizens for Ethical Treatment of Exotic Animals (CETEA) is having their September meeting at the Village Green Conference Center. Over seventy-five locals and out-of-towners are expected to attend. Bea Wanamaker, President of the Southeast District, will be attending the meeting and speaking on September 19 for the group's luncheon being held at the Water's Edge. Miss Wanamaker will also be attending the local meeting of the Gardening Club to share her latest information on indigenous flora and fauna of Florida. For information about the conference, please contact Wendell Breecher at 235-8900.

My beer almost came back up. There was a picture of Miss Wanamaker running with the article. It was Breecher's lady friend. I guess he'd run through all the local women, if he was hitting on the conference speakers now. There wasn't a word about the recent riot in front of the veterinary clinic. I wasn't surprised. The town Commissioners probably turned the thumbscrews on Tom to keep things quiet for a while. It was a well-known fact that the community was looking for ways to diversify the town's economy. Conferences could be one of the answers, unless locals made the visitors feel unwanted. I could already see another committee underway, one that would select conferences that 'meshed' with the community concept of Paradise Pointe.

I turned to find Josie sliding my lunch plate in front of me. On the edge of the plate were a few mussels smothered in butter and garlic.

"Fresh as that bump on your head. Thought you could use a pick-me-up today."

"You're a gastronomic angel, Josie." I savored every buttery morsel. It took me twenty minutes to clean my plate, including the key lime pie. I was enjoying my last few sips of beer while doing some neighborly eavesdropping. If people didn't want you to listen, they should speak softer, I always thought. Or they should sit in one of the dark corners, and be incognito.

It was easy to imagine the shady characters and unsavory alliances that were made in these very corners. People closing questionable deals, exchanging money for favors, and testing the validity of the commandment "thou shalt not kill."

"Hey Tess, you keep staring at Crazy Luke over there, he'll think you're smitten." Rick chuckled as he slid the check over to me.

"Oh! I didn't even see him there. I mean I guess I saw something, but I wasn't really looking. Oh forget it, you know what I mean." I shoved my empty beer over to him.

"Ya know, Rick, I've never thought of corners having histories, but if they did, I bet these would have some incredible stories to tell." I reached for my wallet to pay the bill.

"No doubt about that. Our north corner even has a bit of a mystery to it. One tale in particular bin told around here for as long as I can remember. It had to do with a sly ol' rumrunner name of Slippery Sam

Slater. He was the best. But bein' the best gits you noticed. The Coast Guard and the Feds were always tryin to catch ol' Sam, to make an example of him. One time, they thought they had him cornered here in the cove. He'd anchored his sloop in the bay and rowed his dinghy here to the pier. He was sittin' over there in the north corner, chair leanin' against the wall, enjoyin' a couple shots. He yelled out 'give um a round, on ol' Sam Slater'! The Feds had staked out the doors and went to move in on him. But the bar thugs crowded their way, and by the time they reached the corner, he was gone. Vanished. Really ticked the Feds off. Never did find ol' Sam. Rumor has it, he doubled back and sailed south to the Tortugas where he lived a rich and full life."

"Yeah, I bet 'ol Houdini stiffed the bartender for all those shots too. Rick, why is it that all your stories end with the rebel sailing into the sunset to live a rich and peaceful life on some remote Caribbean island?" I popped a piece of Dentyne into my mouth.

On that philosophical thought, my cell phone did another vibrating dance. "Hello? Yes, this is Tess Titan. I understand. Of course, I'll be right over."

I closed the phone, and looked up at Rick "It's the school. Kevin was in a fight."

******

I shifted into third gear and sped towards the junior high school. I couldn't imagine the circumstances that would make my son use physical force. Fighting! Kevin had never hit anyone, as far as I knew. He wrestled with Katie, and they both took swings at each other occasionally, but nothing overly nasty. Kevin had never been disruptive in school. Good grades didn't come easy to him, but he worked hard and always made us proud.

I parked the car in a visitor's space and headed for the principal's office; a place I was too familiar with from my own educational escapades. I nearly ran into the school nurse as she was leaving the office.

"Now keep that ice on your eye for the next half hour. It'll keep the swelling down," she said exiting the office.

I slipped in before the door closed and saw Kevin sitting in one of two chairs opposite the principal's desk, holding an icepack to his right eye. No one else was in the room.

I walked over to him and put my arms around his shoulders, giving him a small hug. "Are you okay?"

"Yeah, I'm fine. Nothing to worry about."

"So...what karma did you blow to put yourself in this situation?"

He looked at me for a second like I was crazy, then chuckled. "You're spending too much time at the office, Mom. I almost believed you for a second."

"Is that what this is all about? Am I not home enough for you guys?"

"No, no, Mom. Nothing like that." He looked around the room for a minute, avoiding eye contact with me. "It's kind of embarrassing to talk about." He paused for a few more seconds before the words came tumbling out "They were pushing me around. They started saying things. I kind of lost it, and before I knew it everything was over and I was brought here."

I was just getting used to the topsy-turvy thought processing of teens, and couldn't help but wonder how my dad ever got through those years with me. "Well, let's start back at the beginning. Where were you? Who was there? And what were you arguing about?"

He waited a minute, got up from the chair and started walking around the room. "I'd just finished my theater make-up class and was heading for the john to wash my face when a couple of guys stopped me. They started calling me names like 'pansy,' and 'faggot.' It wasn't anything I hadn't heard before."

He turned to me, and trying to raise my spirits added, "Liking theater is almost as bad as being in the chess club."

I smiled back reassuringly, understanding all too well.

"They started shoving me back and forth between them. The larger guy grabbed me by the shoulders, and said 'What happened? Your dad find out you were a fag and couldn't take it? Had to leave the country to avoid the embarrassment? Maybe it runs in the family, in the genes and all. Hell, he's probably not even your real old man. Mor'-an-likely, you're just a bastard boy.'"

"After that, I dunno what happened. I started swingin' and just kept swingin' until Principal Sanders pulled me off him and brought me here."

Kevin sat back down, and stared out the window. "Mom, I knew what he was saying couldn't be true, but it bothered me. It bothered me like nothin' has before. I know things aren't great between you and Dad, but he is coming back, isn't he, Mom? We'll see him and he'll still be Dad, won't he?"

My eyes were stinging. I could feel them filling with tears. I tilted my head back to keep them from rolling down my face. A sharp pain in my chest told me my heart was breaking. It was easy to remember the awkwardness and cruelty of growing up. The wounds were always there, fresh for the licking. I could understand the precarious balance of truth and reality that I had chosen to deal with every day in my life. But, I could never understand how God's littlest angels could live with such happiness and joy one minute, and such pain the next. Children would be children, and boys would be boys. But this was *my* child, *my* boy. How could I stop the pain? How could I erase this moment from both of our lives?

There were no answers, only the responsibility. I couldn't cry now. Kevin deserved more. He deserved an explanation from his father. But that wasn't going to happen anytime soon. The very thought ignited my pain into fury. I could feel the blood pumping to my temples, banging against the inside of my skull fighting to get out. *Michael Jonathan Titan, I hate you with every drop of blood that flows through my veins. I'll never forgive you for making me lie to my first-born!*

I stood up and gulped back the truth, feeling the air of guilt quiver between my tongue and vocal cords. "Yeah, he'll always be Dad, Kev, and he's comin' back. He just needed some time away, some time to think. Your dad loves you guys more than anything in this world, and he'd be furious about what happened to you today. *Boy, is that an understatement.* I can't change what happened, but I'll do everything possible to make sure those boys are punished."

"That's certainly correct," Principal Sanders said, pushing his way through the door. "I will not allow this kind of bullying and intimidation tactics in my school. These are little people with little minds. By the time I'm finished with them, they'll have a new appreciation for the world we live in."

I felt better already. *Yeah, right.*

******

"Kevin, I have to make a quick stop at the photo shop before we go home. Are you up to it?" I asked.

"Sure, Mom. I'll wait in the car for you." He hedged for a few seconds before adding, "Mom, I've been thinking I'd like to take some self defense classes. You know, Karate, Tae Kwon Do, that kind of thing. I'm pretty sure they have a class starting up at the Institute in a few weeks. What do you think?"

I wanted to say, "You're safe. You don't have anything to fear." I wanted him to believe that fighting wasn't the answer to his problems. I wanted Michael to be here to reassure me, and say, "it's a stage of life, this will pass too." But none of that seemed remotely plausible.

I looked over at his young face. But it didn't seem so young anymore. When did I miss the transformation? His chin was squared, his face firmer. His eyes were set deeper in his brow, the mischievous look of youth gone. His shoulders looked broader, and for a moment, I thought I saw his shirt pull across his chest.

"I think it's a good idea, Kev. But it's a real commitment, you know? It takes time to learn something like that right. It takes a lot of responsibility, and you can't abuse what you learn. Do you understand all that?"

"Yeah, Mom, I do. But I'd like to give it a try. I think it will help me feel better about what's going on."

I knew what he was getting at. He needed to feel in control. He needed to believe in himself and his ability to overcome whatever life had to throw at him.

I pulled into the Village Green parking lot and grabbed a spot in front of the hobby shop. I knew Kevin liked to look at the car models in the windows. "Be back in a flash." I waved as I hurried around the corner to the photo shop.

I was running a good hour behind schedule, but it was after lunch and things were usually dead this time of the afternoon.

The bells rang on the door as I pushed it open. Everything was quiet.

"Felix. Hey Felix, its Tess!" Felix was nowhere to be seen. I looked above the darkroom door to see if the red light was on, warning patrons processing was going on and to stay out. No light. That's odd, I thought. It's not like Felix to leave the store unattended. My stomach cramped. I hoped it was the garlic on the mussels.

"Felix? Are you here? Is everything okay? My hand settled nervously on the darkroom door. My head felt funny. I opened the door, fumbling to find the light switch. "Felix?" I whispered. My heart jumped as the light flashed on. I looked around the room, no Felix.

I shut the door and had to lean up against it. My head bounced off the wood harder than I'd anticipated. I gulped some air, trying to catch my breath. *What was wrong with me? Was I having a panic attack? Get a hold of yourself!*

I walked towards the counter on the other side of the shop, the dizzy feeling got worse. Bile rose in my stomach. My head felt like a brush fire burning out of control. My hands shook uncontrollably.

I turned to make my way back towards the outside door. It felt like I was in a dream. The door was at the end of a long tunnel. The harder I tried to reach the exit, the longer the tunnel became. I tried to run, only to find myself moving in slow motion, until my feet weren't moving at all.

I fell forward, my fingers reached to meet the door handle. My attention was drawn to "Kodak," Felix's yellow canary in the corner. I tumbled to my knees in front of the cage. My eyes went in and out of focus. Fingers clawing at the metal bars, I pulled myself up high enough to see into the cage. I remember focusing one last time on the canary before the floor fell out from under me and the darkness closed in. *Poor Kodak, he was deader thanna lobster in high season.*

Chapter Seven

I had visions of lobsters dancing in my head when I awoke in the ICU at Paradise Pointe Medical Center. There were tubes running in and out of my arms, and an annoying beep in the background that certified I was still alive. My head felt like someone had used it for basketball practice, and a strange taste lingered in my mouth. I was hoping it wasn't residual puke.

I turned my head to find Nell sitting in a chair by the bedside. She was resting her eyes. It was calming to know she was there.

She'd always been there for as long back as I could remember. When our family moved around from place to place, she helped me see it as an adventure. When Mom went through her "spells," Nell was there to take care of me. When dad left, Nell gave me support and hope for the future. She was there for my college graduation, my wedding, and for the births of both the kids. If you looked up "Mother" in the dictionary, I'm sure her picture would be there. At least in my mind, that's what I envisioned a mother to be. I always felt if I could be half the person to my children that she'd been to me that I could never fail at being a mother.

"It's not polite to stare, Tess, I'm not dead yet." Nell opened one eye then the other.

"If anyone's supposed to feel dead, I think it's me. I can't tell you why. Just a sneaking suspicion though, since I'm the one in the bed."

"Well, just remember 'people die in bed,' and the rate you're spending your life in one lately, I'm surprised you don't have bedsores."

"Leave it to you, Nell, to get me up and moving before I even know why I'm down and out." I laughed.

As if in anticipation of my questions and concerns, a nurse came through the door. "Hello, Mrs. Titan. We're very glad to see you awake. I expect you must be having a whale of a headache about now. Let me increase your IV drip a bit to help the pain. The aftertaste you're experiencing will bother you for the next couple days. I'll put a cup of water by your bed in case you want to rinse and spit."

Nell rose to leave. "I'm just in the way here. I'll go down to the cafeteria and get some dinner. You talk to the doctor and get yourself situated. I'll be back for another visit before I head over to your house to help with the kids for the night. Now, don't worry about anything, I've already packed my bag and moved into the guestroom. I'll be staying until things settle down a bit." She scooted out before much of anything had registered. The harder I tried to organize my thoughts, the messier things became.

The nurse's badge read "Miranda." She was tucking in the corners of the bed and smoothing out the sheets. I felt like a little girl again, warm and safe. Then it struck me, *why was she wearing gloves and a mask*? It had been a long time since I was in the hospital, but I didn't think they wore those unless you were having a baby, or some kind of surgery. I quickly raised the bed sheet and scoped out the situation. It looked like everything was where it was supposed to be.

Relaxing a bit, I decided it was time to find out what was going on. "Excuse me...umm Miranda?" I said, interrupting her humming rendition of "I Could Have Danced All Night." "Can you tell me what happened? Why I'm here? And why you look like I'm Typhoid Mary?"

She looked a little startled. "Oh my, Typhoid? Oh, no. These are just a precaution. We always wear them when we're in Contact Isolation Units. Don't look so worried. You'll be just fine. I know you have lots of questions. I'll let the doctor know you're awake," she said, making a quick escape.

Contact Isolation Unit? That didn't sound good. I practiced moving my toes, legs, arms, fingers, neck...everything seemed to be in working order. The metallic taste was getting stronger in my mouth. I reached for the water on the table and started rinsing. As I leaned over to spit in another Dixie cup, Jack slid through the door acting like a cat burglar sneaking into someone's apartment. Just my luck, I was sure I had spit hanging out the corner of my mouth and no tissue in sight. I grabbed the edge of the pillow and did the deed.

"Well, Titan. You've really done it this time," Jack mumbled from under the mask.

"I feel like an amnesia victim waking up in a biological M.A.S.H. unit. What's going on? What happened to me?" Then terror struck. "Oh, no! How long have I been out? Are the kids okay?"

"Don't worry, it's only been a few hours, and the kids are fine. They're at home with your mom. She came right over when I called her."

I lay back in the bed wondering how things could get any worse.

Jack pulled up a chair and handed me a cup of water, bending the straw down to meet my lips. "I know you've got a ton of questions, but it's important that you take it easy, and not get your blood pressure on the rise. I'll fill you in on things, if you promise to lie back and take it easy."

Looking into his eyes, I realized they were green. Green in the middle with this amazing splash of aqua blue around the outside of the pupils. Funny how you can know somebody for so many years and yet, not know the color of their eyes.

He pulled the chair closer and leaned his head toward me. "It's complicated, Tess. But I'll tell you what we know so far."

His face took on a serious expression. He hesitated, apparently not knowing how to start. He rubbed his chin for a minute, let out a long sigh, and then launched into the facts.

"Felix died of an airborne pathogen approximately thirty minutes before you arrived. He was poisoned, Tess. You're a lucky girl. Ten minutes earlier and you wouldn't be worrying about much of anything right now."

The water went down the wrong way, and I started choking.

"Are you all right?" He patted my back a little harder than necessary.

In between coughs, I croaked, "Poison? Felix was poisoned?"

"Yeah, we don't know yet if it was something with the processing chemicals, or maybe the air coolant. The coroner is doing an autopsy on Felix. He'll send tissue samples up to the toxicologist. We should know somethin' in the next week or so."

"Poor Felix. And Kodak! He was killed too, wasn't he?"

"Yeah, the bird was probably the first to go. Felix collapsed behind the counter. You arrived and must have looked around for a few minutes. The remains of poison started affecting you. You made your way to the door, opening it a bit before collapsing, pulling the birdcage down on top of you. You were smart to head for the door. The air circulating around you decreased the side effects of the poison to your system."

Yeah, I was feeling like a real Einstein right about now.

"Kevin got bored when you didn't return and came looking for you. He found you in the doorway and dragged you out onto the concourse. He called me, and the ambulance brought you here at 2:15 p.m. It's now 5:00 p.m."

"Kevin found me? He must have been terrified. Did the poison hurt him? Is he here?" I sat straight up in the bed, spilling the remaining water down the front of my gown.

"No, no. He's fine. He wasn't in the air long enough for it to affect him." He handed me some tissues to sop up the spill. "He made his calls from a cell phone outside. He's a smart kid. Once he saw you and the bird, he knew something was wrong. He didn't go back inside."

"He is smart, isn't he?" I said smiling.

"No doubt about that, though from the looks of that shiner of his, he needs to work on his upper cut."

"Yeah, he's working on that." I lay back on the pillows. "So that's why everyone is wearing masks and gloves. They think I may still be contagious?"

"It's just a precaution until the doctor finishes running your blood tests. As soon as they determine the poison is no longer a danger to you or anyone else, you'll be free to go." He patted me on the arm in a reassuring way.

"So the headache and funny taste in my mouth...?"

"Yeah, those are side effects of the poison. You're probably not going to feel so great for the next couple days." He pushed his chair back. "The doctor should be here soon to fill you in on the details. The hospital will call me when you get released. We can talk more then, in case you think of anything else."

I felt the whoosh of a breeze as the door closed. Someone had been standing in the shadows listening.

"I'm afraid you were a victim of circumstance," said a deep voice from the dark.

Jack's back stiffened. "I think that's still to be determined."

The figure moved from the shadows toward the end of my bed. *It* was a he, and he looked like something straight out of a *Godfather* sequel. He was in his young forties, maybe 5'10", and 200 pounds. He was a big boy. But I didn't see an ounce of fat on him. His dark pants, black shirt, and hair below the collar tied back in a ponytail were eerily alluring. He had a take-control attitude that was easy to admire, but my woman's intuition told me to run and not look back. He checked the chart hanging on my bed, flipping the pages like he understood what they meant. My head began to pound.

"I don't think there's any reason to alarm Mrs. Titan unnecessarily, Jack," he said.

Jack stood and looked like he was ready to dismantle the guy, one piece at a time. "Don't call me 'Jack,' we're not friends."

I watched them position themselves against one another. Friends or not, it was obvious they knew each other.

He lowered the clipboard and raised his chin. I almost gasped at the scar that ran from the top of his left cheekbone down to the corner of his mouth. Instead, my head began to pound harder. The guy stood motionless staring at Jack like he was looking at himself in a mirror. He finally breathed. On the last part of his exhale, there was a choking laugh...like someone who'd been smoking for too many years.

"Well, Mr. Daniels, I'm sorry you feel that way. I was hoping we could be of mutual help to one another." He returned the clipboard to the bed. "But it appears that chip on your shoulder is causing a dangerous case of shortsightedness."

"Better a chip than a stick up my ass, you sonnafabitch."

"Pardon me," I said, totally exasperated. "As much as I'm enjoying watching this sequel to *Planet of the Apes*, if the two of you don't stop this male positioning shit, my head is going to explode."

They both looked taken aback, and at least momentarily speechless.

Jack looked over at the monitor and checked out my blood pressure readings. I could tell from the tightness in his lips that the numbers were too high.

He sat back down and rested his hand on my arm. "Don't worry about this asshole, Tess. You just lie there and try to relax."

Out of the corner of my eye, I could see him pushing the emergency call button by the bed.

I *was* relaxed. At least I thought I was. My head felt fuzzy.

Jack moved into the background. I saw the nurse hovering over me, and felt the shot. The last thing I saw was Doctor Dick making his entrance. Darkness came more quickly this time.

******

September 15, 2001

An extra day of bed rest without visitors fixed me up just fine. The forced rest gave the bump on my head time to heal, and the ache in my head and ankle were barely noticeable. I enjoyed a few tasty hospital meals of mystery meat, starchy vegetable, green salad with Thousand Island dressing, roll, butter, and the mandatory chocolate pudding. Obviously, no one was watching cholesterol around this place.

I was given walking papers and a personal ride in Andy's black and white back home. I lingered in the car, not ready to face the music in my own home.

"Thanks, Andy. I appreciate the ride."

"No problem, Tess. What would the Town Council think if I didn't take care of one of their founding members?"

"Right. Wouldn't look good to lose ol' Tess, now would it? Thanks again." I got out of the car and headed for the kitchen door. Once I was sure Andy had pulled away, I sneaked around the corner and lay back in one of the lounge chairs. I felt a hundred years old. Thank God, Tom had called from the paper and put me on vacation. He was pulling the article about Nell until things calmed down and cleared up.

"How ya doin, Fitz? Tasty breakfast?" The pelican turned his head and eyed me for a minute, and then, seeming to recognize my voice, gurgled and did this bubbling thing with his neck. I'm fairly sure that's Pelicaneeze for "Where ya been? I missed ya." I shut my eyes and lifted my face toward the rising morning sun.

There was something magical about the warmth of the sun's rays. A few deep breathes of the clean, salt air and I almost believed I was in another place. A place where people were happy, free of burdens. A place where fear didn't exist. I didn't want to be greedy; any place except where I was right now would be fine. But that was too much to wish for, and I knew it. I was merely postponing the inevitable.

Then I heard it. Her knuckles tapped a staccato death march on the window above my head. The kitchen door slammed, and the clicking of Ferragamo slingbacks echoed on the terra cotta stepping-stones until she stopped in front of me. Her shadow blocked the sun, draining the warmth from my sanctuary. I opened my eyes.

"Hello, Mother."

"Good Lord! Is that all you have to say? Hello, Mother! You're attacked by a transient at the market, almost killed picking up photos for your job, your son is being bullied at school, and the best you can do is, hello Mother?"

I took a deep breath and started again, "You're right. Thank you for coming and staying with the kids. I appreciate your being here when I needed you." *Well, that didn't kill me.*

She looked at me a bit quizzically before continuing her tirade. "Well, I should think so! You're the talk of the town, and I, your own mother, have to find out the gruesome details during my tennis lesson at the country club. Do you have any idea how that made me feel? I looked like a complete idiot!" *I'm not going to touch that one.*

"That must have been embarrassing, Mother. I apologize. Everything has just happened so quickly. In the beginning I didn't want to worry you needlessly. Then before I knew it, the situation got out of hand. I never thought things like this would happen to me."

"Things like this wouldn't happen? Well, you must have lost all your senses. I've told you for years that job of yours was nothing but trouble from the very start. You don't need to work. I don't know why you bother, when you could be doing something more constructive with your life." *Now there's a new argument.*

She started pacing around the patio, hands gesturing toward the sky. "And being attacked at the market! You must not have been paying attention to anything going on around you. You probably made yourself a target and didn't even realize it." *Take a deep breath.*

Her hands settled on the patio table. Disgusted at the build up of pollen and dust, she clapped them together in mid-air and shook her head. "And Kevin...brawling at school! He's obviously displaying feelings of anger and inadequacy because of Michael's departure. He's at a very dangerous age, very impressionable. You need to be here to pull in the reins, and teach him the facts of life." *Yes, Mother Theresa.*

She eyed a prickly vine growing in the Begonia hanging basket and started ripping at it until the basket swung precariously from its stand. "And all of this happening in the aftermath of Michael's exit. Couldn't you have let the dust settle from that fiasco before making another spectacle of yourself?"

That did it. I stood up from my seat of consciousness and took a stand. "A spectacle of *myself,* Mother? Or rather an unwanted spotlight that casts a shadow on your social high stepping?"

The plant was swinging on its own accord; the vine piled lifelessly on the ground.

"Well! Is that gratitude for you? I leave my candidacy dinner early to race over here for the children. I find Kevin in a state of shock from dragging his own mother from the clutches of death. The boy will probably never be the same. Katie wouldn't stop insisting that she could nurse you back to health with her tonics and bandages. The phone is ringing off the hook. And all the while, I'm tiptoeing around the fact that you've been poisoned, by God only knows what, and may never be the same again! So, I'll pretend I didn't hear that, young lady. I don't know who taught you to speak so disrespectfully. I know I didn't raise you like that."

You didn't raise me, mother.

She stood in front of Fitz's cage. Her hands rested firmly on her hips, accentuating her slim, but aged physique. Her lips pursed, she looked ready to take on the world.

I didn't feel like taking on the world this morning, much less my mother. But before I had time to acquiesce, Fitz took things into his own hands, or shall I say "beak." He was none too happy about all the ranting and raving going on so close to his home and let Mom know about it, unequivocally. He snapped at her butt and regurgitated his breakfast down the backside of her pants.

"Aghhhhh! What has he done? What has he done to me?" she screamed, looking over her shoulder trying to see down the back of her pants. "Oh! What a repulsive animal! How could you let him do this to me? How horribly disgusting!" She tried pulling the wet, fishy-smelling fabric away from her backside.

"Mother, come here quick and let me hose you off. You don't know if he upchucked any gastric acids that will eat through those pants and leave you with a pocked butt."

Well, that got her attention. She ran over and shook her butt in front of me, like a stripper desperate for rent money. I sprayed her better side with the hose on full blast, enjoying every second. I guess life does have its moments.

She grabbed a towel from the patio basket, wrapping it sarong style over her blouse and pants. The Ferragamo's were looking a little worse for the wear, sputtering a little as they snapped back across the stepping stones to the driveway. Mother was furious. I was surprisingly content. For a moment, life was picture perfect.

Pictures. I never did find the pictures. *What was it about those photos that seemed to wreak havoc on my life?* My stomach muttered a steady song of dissension. I hoped it was the physical duress from the family dispute, but I knew life wasn't that simple.

Something was wrong, and I'd put my family and myself in danger pretending it didn't exist. I was attacked in the market and then almost killed at the photo shop. Victim of circumstance? I don't think so. Jack always says, "Coincidences are for fools and the faint of heart." I'd already broken two cardinal rules of police work, listen to your body and don't believe in coincidences. It was time for me to face reality.

Chapter Eight

I spent the rest of the afternoon with the kids. Katie wrapped me in gauze bandages while soothing me with aroma therapy and Mozart. Kevin kept watch, pacing around the house as if he expected some madman to come dashing through the front door any minute. I let them work through their insecurities and find some semblance of normality before announcing that "Life would now go back to its previously scheduled craziness."

They seemed relieved to let go of the unexpected catastrophes, but cautious of the unknown plight of life to follow. They loved having Nell around. Her presence made it easier for them to make the transition back to normal life. She had a way of lifting the spirit in a room. No one could be depressed around Nell. She wouldn't have it.

I signed permission slips, made lunches, and updated my calendar. There were clothes to be washed, floors to be vacuumed, and dishes to put away. As usual, no fairies had converged on my house to do good deeds while I was gone. We settled in the living room to watch our favorite shows. Everything seemed right as we started to argue about the television line-up for the evening.

There was a knock at the front door. Everybody looked a little uneasy. I smiled reassuringly, and checked the peephole before opening the door.

Andy was standing there in a pair of black Docker pants and a red golf shirt. "Hi, Andy. What's up?" I tried to sound upbeat.

"Just driving by and wanted to check in on you all. Everything all right?" He raised his eyebrows and motioned towards the kids.

"Thanks, yeah. We're all recuperating fine. A good night's rest and we'll be back to normal. Whatever that means."

He leaned back against the porch rail looking like he was ready to set a spell. "Boy, isn't that the truth? Seems like a nest full of killer bees has been dropped into Paradise recently. Don't understand where it's all coming from. Never seen anything like it around here before."

I decided it was time for me to make my move. I hated to ask Andy for anything, but I wasn't going to get anywhere without his help. "Andy, I hate to bother you. I know you must have your hands full, but I need to ask a favor. Is it safe to go back into the photo shop?"

"Photo shop?" He crossed his arms in a defensive move. "Why in the world would you want to go back there? Figured you'd steer clear of that place and get your photos delivered by mail."

"Normally, yes, that would seem the most logical thing to do. I'm afraid logic isn't one of my stronger points." I tried sounding a bit helpless. "I was in the shop in the first place to pick up some copies of some prints Felix had forgotten to make for me. Your "transient" stole my first set with my satchel. I really need that other set for an article I'm doing. Can you help me out?" I tried to bat my lashes and look like a lady in distress.

He looked at me a bit too long, probably deciding if I was trying to pull a fast one on him. I guess his need to save the damsel was too strong. "You and your articles. I've never seen a woman dig her teeth into something the way you do." He shifted his weight from foot to foot. "I know it's useless to argue with you. You'll just find some way to go around me."

"Andy, I wouldn't do that." I tried to sound indignant.

"Save it for someone who doesn't know you. I'll give you a call in the morning and let you know if the crime lab is finished with the scene." He looked me straight in the eye, and pointed his finger at me, "And don't get any grandiose ideas about going there by yourself. I'll meet you at the café and we'll go to the photo shop to look for your pictures together. Capish?"

"Every syllable, sir! Will I need special battle gear, or will pedal pushers and Keds be adequate?"

He rolled his eyes. "Just remember who's doing whom a favor here." He drummed his fingers on the door. "I'll meet you at the café nine sharp." He turned to leave then turned back around. "Be sure all your windows and doors are locked, and use the sliding glass bars and deadbolts, okay?"

"That sounds very ominous, Andy. Let me ask you. Do you believe

I'm a victim of circumstance?"

"Circumstance or not, things tend to happen in threes. And at the rate you're going, the third one will be here before sunrise." He waved over his shoulder as he walked to his car.

"Thanks for that vote of confidence. I'll see you at nine sharp. Latte in hand."

I watched him walk back to his patrol car. I could see my neighbor, Breecher, and his female friend getting ready to go somewhere. Seemed late to me to be going anywhere. But then I was a mom, anything after 9:00 p.m. counted as late for me.

I shut the door, and locked the deadbolt. Why did they have to call the stupid thing a "dead" bolt? If something were meant to provide added protection for your life and valuables, you'd think they'd come up with a more upbeat name, something with a more positive outlook. Maybe a "Guard Bolt," or "Rest Easy Lock," or better yet a "Live Long and Prosper Device." Now that was catchy, something that didn't make you think twice about turning out the lights at night, and even provided a bit of encouragement that the sun *would* rise tomorrow and you *would* be there to see it.

I turned and facing myself in the hallway mirror did my best Mae West imitation. "Ah, another moment of advertising brilliance in an otherwise ho-hum existence, and no one around to appreciate it." I forced my chest out and pushed my hips from side to side.

I caught Katie out of the corner of my eye. "Mom, I'm really glad you're feeling all right now, but promise me you'll never do that in front of my friends."

"I wouldn't dream of it, sweetheart." I winked to myself in the mirror and uncrossed my fingers from behind my back.

"Mom!"

******

September 16, 2001

Nell, Geena, and I sat powwow style around the coffeepot and bagels. The kids had taken off for school, and I had a good hour before I needed to get dressed to meet Andy at the café.

"I don't like it, not one bit," Geena said as she spread cream cheese

66

on her toasted garlic bagel. "If something is going on, you'll be caught right in the middle of it and with your proverbial 'pants down.'"

"Well, if you are, please make sure you're wearing good underwear. None of that thong stuff," smiled Nell, as she put the finishing touches of butter and marmalade on her cinnamon and raisin bagel.

"I'm not planning on getting caught with my pants down. I've unknowingly ended up in the middle of some dangerous business, and I'm tired of being a sitting duck."

"Better a sitting duck than a roasted duck," added Geena, while turning her bagel in a complete circle, tongue extended, to even out the cream cheese all the way around the edges.

"Thank you, Madame Cliche."

"You're quite welcome, Madame Poirot."

"I wish. I'm going to have to work up to that title. Right now, I'm tired of being caught off guard, and I don't think hospital gowns suit me. Worst of all, if Andy's right, it won't be long before "Murphy's Law" catches up to me and delivers my third blow. I suspect running or hiding won't stop it from happening, so the best I can do is be better prepared, and try to figure out what I'm going up against." I spread some apple butter on top of my plain bagel.

"Well, I'm all for it." announced Nell. "I don't know what's going on around here, or even *if* anything's going on, but I've visited the hospital enough this past week to last me a lifetime. What's the first step, Miss Marple?"

"I think you two are taking a long walk on a short pier, but someone's got to be there to throw you that ugly orange and white buoy. I guess I'm in too," Geena added.

I looked at both my friends and felt stronger than I had in a long time. "Good. Three minds are better than one any day."

"We'll have this case cracked wide open before the sun sets." Nell lifted her coffee cup high over the center of the table, and in her best three musketeers' voice, said "One for all..." Geena and I joined in by clunking our coffee mugs together with Nell while we all chimed in unison, "And all for one!"

"If we've finished with the pomp and circumstance, perhaps it's time to move on to the important stuff, like whose Cheerios did you pee in?" Geena asked.

I picked up the paper plates from the table and scrunched them down in the overflowing trash can. "I can't think of anyone who'd want to do me bodily harm, at least not the permanent "write your epitaph" kind. I certainly have a well-rounded short list of people who'd like to see me in a number of uncomfortable positions, but none of them are dirty enough to want me six feet under."

"What about your patrol days?" Geena asked. "Is there anyone from that part of your past that could be looking to cause you trouble?"

The question caught me off guard. I was so detached from that time in my life, I hadn't even considered that a possibility. I thought seriously about her question, remembering the promises made by any number of angry men and women that I'd carted off to jail. "I can't be absolutely positive, but no one sticks out in my mind. I can't think of anyone that made open threats to me." I lied.

Nell poured everyone another half cup of coffee as she pondered the question before committing to her answer. "There are two things you can surely depend on, first—that appearances are deceiving, and second—that people are very unpredictable."

"I know exactly what you mean," Geena said as she made her way to the trash can to empty it. "People are just like those nice, powdery white donuts at the bakery. You see them all the time, they look so perfect, and you know they have a filling, but you can't see it. You expect cherry, and then you get something gross like coconut cream. Yuck! What a salivary disaster." She reached under the cabinet to get a new bag, snapped it open and fitted it into the open can.

"I'm not so sure about these jelly filled people you're so profound about, so let's go over what we do know." I picked up my coffee mug and leaned against the wall oven door.

"I was pepper sprayed by a man I think was Italian. He took my satchel, which had some odds and ends in it from the paper, as well as the pictures I was going to run with my column about Nell. He didn't take my wallet. Then, I go to the photo shop to pick up the extra set of prints only to find Felix and Kodak dead. We know that Felix was poisoned from an airborne substance. I think that about covers it."

Nell added a lump of sugar to her mug, "Well, let's start with the mysterious stranger in the parking lot, dear. What did he look like?"

I bit the side of my mouth for a minute trying to think. "You know, he looked a little like an out of season Snowbird. His clothes were nice, but obviously not from around here. They were darker, and he had soft looking leather loafers. He was dressed more like a casual businessman, in nice slacks, a jacket, and dark tee shirt. I remember thinking 'he must be hot in that get-up.' His hair was dark, as were his eyes. He hadn't shaved for a day or two. He looked tired and ill-at-ease."

Geena was looking at me, her jaw hanging open. "You saw all that in the seconds it took for this screaming crazy to attack you?"

I stirred a little uneasily, rubbing my fingers along my temples. "Police training. I guess it never really leaves you."

"Well, I for one am glad all that housecleaning, PTA meetings, and car pooling didn't dampen your senses any." Geena gushed as she reached for a napkin to wipe her lipstick off the edge of the coffee mug.

Her accolades left me feeling more than a little awkward.

Nell twirled the ring on her finger. "Your description of the attacker at the market sounds very much like the man they pulled out of the Pirate Ships' nets."

I was stunned at the obvious. "You're right Nell. They looked far too similar for it to be a coincidence."

"You see Geena, your confidence in me is misplaced, contrary to popular belief, I'm way out of my element here."

"Well, let's not ponder our shortcomings, dear." Nell took a few sips of her coffee. "Is there anything else that sticks out in your mind about the attack in the parking lot?"

I nodded, "Yes, the way I was attacked. It was odd. Pepper spray is easily available, but I've never heard of anyone using it around here, for robbery or otherwise. Then there's that airborne poison that killed Felix and Kodak. Again, probably not difficult to obtain, but it's not your everyday choice of murder weapon for our sleepy little town.

Nell poured more coffee into her mug and motioned to Geena to ask if she'd like some more. "So our perpetrator appears to use commonly available items to perform his unsavory deeds."

Geena walked over and topped off her mug. "You keep talking about Felix like this wasn't an accident. We don't know that, right? "

"We won't know for sure until the lab report comes back. But let's think of it this way, if it was an accident, then I have nothing more to worry about. But, if it was a premeditated murder, then it's important for me to figure out anything and everything I can for my own protection."

Geena nodded. Her eyes looked spooked.

Nell stirred another lump of sugar in her coffee. "Well, if we're talking premeditated murder, I guess we need to ask, 'Who was the murderer trying to kill and did he succeed?'"

I paced back and forth in the kitchen, "I have to think his main target was Felix since he was exposed to the highest concentration of the poison. It's unusual for Felix to leave the shop that time of day; he would have just gotten back from lunch. So someone was expecting him to be there at that time."

"And what about you, dear? Could the murderer have been expecting you? Could he have known you would be coming when you did?" Nell asked matter-of-factly.

"This is getting scary. You two are worse then an *Outer Limits* rerun." Geena wrapped her hands around the mug.

"You're right. It is scary. That's why it's important to ask these questions." I turned back to Nell. "Good questions. Let's see if I can answer them."

"How could he have known if or when I was coming?" I thought out loud. Pacing a few more steps, my eyes lit with recognition. "Of, course!" I brought my fist down on the countertop. "The satchel."

"Would you like to fill us in on what your brain is doing?" Geena plopped down in the chair next to Nell.

"Sorry. The satchel is part of the key. I can feel it in my gut. I know I'm right." I started pacing in small circles. "I'd just picked up the pictures from the photo shop. Felix had put a yellow sticky on the front of the envelope to remind me to pick up the extra set the next day at lunchtime."

"That would have been quite a risk on the murderer's part. 'Lunchtime' could cover quite a bit of time. He couldn't be sure exactly when you would be there," Nell said.

"Yessss...too risky. How did he know?" My mind raced as my fingers drummed the countertop. "Oh my God! He did know. Or at least he thought he knew."

Geena started turning pale. "I hate to even ask. How could he have known?"

I looked straight at Nell, "He knew because Felix called me on my cell phone at Josie's yesterday when I was eating lunch to remind me to pick up the extra set of prints. I told him I would be there in about forty-five minutes. That was before the phone call from Kevin's school! By the time I'd finished up at the school, I was running a good hour behind schedule. The murderer must have been standing right there in the photo shop listening to our conversation."

"Well, there's irony for you," Geena said shifting uneasily in her seat. "Your behind was saved while your son was getting his whipped."

Drinking the last of her coffee, Nell added, "It also makes your Italian mugger a primary suspect for the photo shop catastrophe. He would have known when and where to expect you because of the note on the envelope."

I bit the side of my thumbnail and shook my head. "But if he wanted to kill me, why mace me and make it look like a robbery? Why not just kill me right there on the docks?"

Geena squeezed her eyes together, forcing the words to follow. "Maybe he needed it to look like an accident?"

"Or maybe it's not the same person," I said rubbing Geena's shoulder for reassurance. "The mugger could have ditched the photos and anyone could have picked them up."

Geena relaxed for a moment before her eyes popped open in frustration. "Anyone? But then we don't know anymore than we did before!"

I could see the doubt in Nell's eyes. She wiped up her coffee drips from the table with her napkin and got up to put her cup in the sink. "I don't like this, Tess. Probably "nothing" has a real possibility of being "something." I think you should tell Andy all about this when you see him this morning."

The doubt in Nell's eyes had turned to genuine concern.

"I will, Nell. I'm not the heroine type. When the time is right, I'll let him know what we talked about."

"Find the right time, dear, and find it soon. Before it becomes too late."

Chapter Nine

I dressed hurriedly for my morning rendezvous with Andy. My pedal pushers and shirt were already laid out and ironed. My open toed black sandals reminded me once again that I still needed a pedicure—badly. I coated my toenails quickly with "A Breath of Burgundy," before carefully slipping on my sandals.

I looked down at my toes. "There, that's better."

I ran a brush through my hair and tied a handkerchief around my neck; a knee-jerk reaction just in case I needed something to cover my mouth.

Nell was showering and planning to go over to her house this morning to collect the mail and water her plants. I poked my head into the steam-filled room, and said a hurried "goodbye" before rushing out the door.

I'd decided to walk to the café and save on the gas. I took the most direct route staying on the main thoroughfares. This also provided me the most shade. The large Sugar Gums and Oaks were still holding onto their big leaves, and dropping nuts and seeds everywhere. A few areas were so dense that the Spanish moss had taken hold, connecting the trees, and making it like a tunnel.

The smell of Jasmine was so strong that I had to stop and find its source. It took me a few minutes to discover its hideout, because the flowers had already bloomed and disappeared into the bushes where the vine had attached itself. Many of the azaleas were still blooming, and probably would for months to come. It wasn't unusual to get a particularly warm week in the fall and see azaleas blooming. They were easily confused with the weather around here, blooming at unseasonable times.

I got to the coffee shop just in time to order two lattes and wrestle the cardboard handgrips on so I wouldn't burn the tar out of my hands.

Andy met me at the counter. "I like mine hot," he said over my shoulder.

Without turning around, I answered, "Oh, I'm sure half the town's aware of that. But after your recent 'coffeepot accident,' I thought you might need these cardboard training wheels." I turned and walked outside, leaving him to doctor his own brew at the counter.

He followed me in a few minutes, holding the door for a number of ladies who couldn't resist chatting and batting their eyelashes at "Mr. Eligible."

"Betty holding down the fort?" I settled myself down at one of the wrought iron tables meant for two.

"You bet." He winked at one of the girls passing by. "Don't know how I ever got things done before without her."

I couldn't take it any longer. "I don't know how you stand that," I quipped, tearing off the coffee breathing hole and blowing inside.

"Stand what?" Andy said with a boyish grin.

I took off the lid and blew some air into the milky brew. "Don't act all prim with me. You know exactly what I'm talking about. Don't you get tired of all the mindless chatter, the giggling, the appearances at your office for 'no reason'?"

Andy tried to look solemn, "I don't know, Tess. I rather like the mating rituals of our species. Of course, the rituals have been around forever, but there's something comforting in knowing what to expect from a woman."

"Expect? You're really out there in left field, aren't you? Have you ever heard of the black widow? Her behavior is probably truer to form for the female of our species than anything else I can think of. And I should know, I'm one of them!"

"Don't have much faith in your gender, do you?"

"Oh, I have plenty of faith because I accept the truth of who we women are, as opposed to you, living in some *Loveboat* rerun."

"Well, rerun king or not, I've never had any complaints." Andy smiled and sipped a little latte in with a lot of air.

"You really are impossible."

"Yeah, you are, too."

I waited until we'd drunk a reasonable amount of coffee before trying to move him along. I knew I was in his territory now and needed to tread lightly. "So, are you ready? Did the lab give the okay for us to go in?"

"Yeah, everything's been cleared. That is everything except your head. I think that bad air is muddying your thinking."

"Unfortunately, it doesn't get much better than this. So just call me "impaired" and let's get this over with."

We walked the short block to the photo shop, trashing our coffee cups in the receptacle provided out front.

We stood in front of the door for a minute as Andy untangled the "crime scene" tape and jostled the keys on his chain looking for the right match. I stared blankly through the large picture window into the darkened shop. It didn't look right. It didn't look real. The reality of what I was about to do had finally caught up with me. I turned my back to Andy and took a few deep breaths. I couldn't let him see my fear.

He tapped me on my shoulder, "Are you ready, Lone Ranger?"

I straightened up and forced the pictures of Felix and Kodak from my mind. "Let's do it, Tonto."

Andy turned the handle on the door. We walked in quietly like we were entering a church. I showed Andy my movements within the store the other morning, shuddering again when I turned the light on in the darkroom. I shut the door and leaned back against it, feeling a shortness of breath.

"Are you okay? You don't look so good." Andy looked concerned.

"Yeah, I'm fine, just a little déja-vu. Is it all right if I go look for the pictures?"

"Sure. Why don't you start in the front desk drawers, and I'll look back in the darkroom. What am I looking for?"

"Pictures of Paris in the 1950s, and people dressed in clothes from that same time period. You might recognize Nell. She was just eighteen." I thumbed through the picture envelopes in the drawers.

I searched every drawer. No pictures. I stood helpless for a minute behind the counter, before seeing the clipboard dangling from a string beside my leg. I picked up the board and realized I was looking at log sheets. They showed the date an order was received, the date the order was completed, a space to note that contact was made with the customer, and the date the order was picked up. I ran my finger down the sheets looking for my name. It wasn't there. On a hunch, I checked the pages. They were numbered....23,24,25,26,28. *"Damn it"!* It was gone. Page 27 was missing. I was beginning to suspect we'd never find those extra prints.

Photos, prints, reprints. It finally dawned on me. *What if killing me was secondary? What if the killer's primary purpose was to retrieve the photos? But he already had one set from my satchel, why did he need another?*

My mind drifted back to the shop. This person was good. He found the reprints and still had the sense and time to dispose of the log sheet.

I hollered back to the darkroom, "Anything back there yet, Andy?"

"No, I got a couple more places to look. Be done in a minute."

"Take your time." I rummaged through the paperwork on the counter. I found it. The yellow sticky pad by the phone. I took a pencil and gently rubbed the lead over the surface. It read, *Send Messenger, 3:00 p.m., Nell's.* I tore off the top sheet and put it in my pocket.

I stared blankly at the wall for almost a minute before I saw the message light on the phone blinking. I pushed rewind. It seemed to take forever. Then the voices began. I recognized the first few as friends of Kevin's from school, then some long-winded tourist giving specifics on his reprints. Finally, there it was—Nell's voice. "Felix, this is Nell. Sorry to be calling so early, I got your message about my photos being ready. Could you please have them delivered to my house this afternoon about three o'clock? If I don't hear from you otherwise, I'll expect the messenger. Thanks again, I can't wait to see them."

I stood motionless trying to put the pieces together. Suddenly, it all came to me. I searched frantically for the trash can. Grabbing the can, I threw the garbage on the floor and fell down on my knees looking for the original yellow sticky note. It wasn't there.

"Hey, I'm not paying for a cleaning crew to come in here and pick up after you," Andy said as he came out of the darkroom.

"Andy, quick, look around the rest of the store for other trash cans."

"Well, what's got you so excited? Calm down, maybe we'd better go outside and sit down."

"Andy! Please do what I say, right now. It's very important." I ran around the room looking for anything that might have trash in it. Andy came out of the darkroom with one large can. I emptied it hurriedly on the floor and searched again.

"Are you going to tell me what we're looking for, or would you prefer for me to just stand here looking deaf and dumb?"

I was sitting on my knees amongst the scraps of paper and film debris. "The original yellow sticky. It's not here. It should be. The murderer must have seen it and taken it with him when he was here. He didn't think anyone would notice it missing. He didn't remember to check the messages on the phone."

"Yellow Sticky? Murderer? Phone message? Okay, Tess, I think you've had enough of this. I shouldn't have let you come in here. That was stupid of me. It's been too soon after the accident. Come on, let's go outside and sit down on that nice park bench out there and get some air."

I blocked out his condescending remarks, and tried talking some common sense through that dense head of his. "Don't you get it, Andy? The murderer was here in this shop looking for my reprints. He found them and noticed a message on the yellow pad that Nell's photos were to be delivered to her at 3:00 p.m. He assumed they might be another set of reprints so he took the yellow sticky with him, as well as the log sheet. He's trying to make it look like the pictures never existed."

I could tell he hadn't heard a word I'd said. He was helping me up off the floor when reality struck me hard.

"Andy, quick, we've got to get over to Nell's right away!"

"Now hold on, Missy. I think you just need to sit down and rest for a minute."

"Did you hear me? NOW, Andy! Don't you see?" I dragged Andy by the arm out the door and over to the parking lot to his car, explaining along the way. "Nell hasn't been home since my accident. She'd already picked up her bag before she visited me at the hospital, and then she went straight to my house. She was heading over to her house this morning while I was meeting you. She hasn't been home since the pictures were supposed to have been delivered."

"Excuse me if I don't understand a word you're saying, since you're rambling on like a crazy person." I pushed him into the driver's seat, and jumped in on the other side.

He looked at me questioningly. "I don't think it's a good idea for us to be going anywhere, except maybe the hospital to have you checked over again. I think you're experiencing some after effects and don't realize it."

I was about to burst. Running to Nell's would take too much time. His car was the fastest way to get there. "Andy Hagen, if you don't start driving this car as fast as you can to Nell's house right this minute, I will hold you completely responsible for her DEATH!"

Chapter Ten

We pulled up in front of Nell's home. Everything looked serene.

"Oh no, please don't let me be too late." I jumped out of the car and ran to the front porch. I turned the handle on the glass Victorian door. It was locked.

"Nell! Nell! Are you in there?" I frantically banged on the door. Swinging around, I searched the front porch for a hard object. Spotting a large potted geranium on the porch railing, I grabbed it, and started to pitch it through the glass door.

"Tessa, dear, I have the key if it will make things any easier." Nell dangled some keys from her hand.

I caught the pot at the last second, letting it crash to the floor. Dirt and flowers covered my feet. Broken shards scattered over the entranceway.

I turned around and saw Nell standing beside Andy on the walkway. I ran to her, hugging her as tightly as I could. "Oh Nell, Nell. You're all right." Tears formed in my eyes.

"Yes, dear. I'm fine. I got here just in time, it appears. I stopped at the store to get some fertilizer for the geraniums, which may be a moot point now," she said stroking my head.

"I was so worried about you. I heard your message at the photo shop about having the photos delivered here yesterday afternoon, and then Felix made himself a message on a sticky pad about the delivery time, but the original was missing!"

"I see. Well, not exactly. But I understand your concern. It has to do with those pictures, doesn't it?"

"Yes, the pictures. For some reason, they're very dangerous. Then I thought you got here this morning, and the...the..."

"Murderer was waiting for me?"

"Yes, I thought he might still be here—waiting for you."

"Well, let me calm your nerves. I'm just fine. As a matter of fact, the pictures were delivered while I was away at the hospital with you. I let Emma next door know that the delivery would be coming and gave her the key to let him in. She called when I was at your house to let me know that he had come and left the package on my desk. Why don't we go take a look at these old pictures, and see what's causing such a fuss?" Nell walked around the pitiful geranium and put her key in the door.

"Nell, let's have Andy go in first and take a look around. Just humor me," I said warily.

"Oh, so now it's time for the masked avenger," teased Andy. "You go first, Andy. Look for the bad guy, Andy. Make sure everything's safe, Andy."

We could hear him mumbling as he made his way through the house. Then everything got quiet.

"Ladies, I think you'd better come in here."

We hurried into the house, and found Andy standing in the middle of Nell's study or what was left of it.

Desk drawers were lying overturned on the floor, the contents strewn across the room. All the books had been pulled from the built-in shelves and were scattered in piles. Her sewing box was upside down; dozens of colored threads had rolled in all directions. The love seat was lying on its back, and pictures had been ripped off the walls.

None of us said a word. I could feel the weight of Nell's body leaning on my arm.

"This is the worst of the rooms. Everywhere else is in fairly good order. They seemed to have concentrated on book cases and drawers," Andy reported.

I put a protective arm around Nell and pulled her in close to me. "Come on, Nell, let's go to the kitchen and sit down. I'll make you some tea," I said, fearing she might collapse.

"Yes," she answered weakly. "Maybe that would be a good idea."

I got Nell settled in the kitchen and hurried back to the den to take a closer look.

"Don't touch anything," Andy directed. "I've called the lab. They'll be here in a few minutes to dust for prints. That includes the back porch. It looks like the intruder gained access through the back door.

One of the window panes was busted."

I was a little surprised at his professional attitude. I'd never seen this side of him. I started scanning the debris. "Do you see a photo envelope anywhere, Andy?"

"A photo envelope? Your Aunt's home has been rolled, her privacy violated, and all you can think about are your photos for the paper? You really had me fooled with that hysterical female act you put on back at the shop. You had me going good." He shook his head in disgust. "You really are a piece of work, Tess Titan. Excuse me while I go outside and check the perimeter."

I stood dumbfounded in the middle of the room. He still didn't get the connection between the pictures and everything that had been going on. I guess it's true what they say, "A wink's as good as a nod to a blind mule."

All I could do was raise my arms and let them fall to my sides in exasperation. I closed my eyes and took three deep breaths. When I opened them, Nell was standing in the archway balancing a cup of tea and a plate full of brownies. Her color looked much better.

"Chocolate, dear?" She offered me the plate. "Why don't we retreat to the kitchen and raise our endorphin levels a bit? Once we're stuffed with pleasure and guilty beyond belief, we can start looking for those photos."

"That's the best offer I've had all day. I hope you've got more brownies back there. I may be vying for a Guinness record." I took the brownies in one hand while placing the other around Nell's shoulder. "Are you sure you're not my Guardian Angel?"

******

We waited for the lab to finish dusting before rummaging through the mess. After a few unsuccessful hours of searching, we uprighted the sofa and plopped ourselves on top of the cushions.

"Well, Tess dear, we can't be certain until this mess is cleaned up, but I'd venture to say that those photos are no longer here."

"I just don't understand it, Nell. The photos were in clear sight. The intruder must have seen them right away. Why tear up the rest of the house?"

"I'm no mind reader, of course, but it looks to me like he was looking for something else in addition to the photos."

I got off the sofa and started putting books back on the shelves. "Just when I thought I was getting my hands around this mystery, it takes off in another direction. I feel lost without those pictures. I was hoping for a real breakthrough when we got to look at them."

"Don't worry, Tessa. You'll figure it out, pictures or not. And stop worrying about this mess. I called the gals from my Poker Club. They'll be over first thing in the morning to help me with all this. It'll be put all back together by noon, and we'll play a few quick hands at lunch to boot. Who can beat that?"

"Sounds like a plan to me." I set the books on the shelf. "Andy put a piece of wood over the broken pane. The glass shop will be by tomorrow morning to fix it. Are you sure you won't stay with the kids and me a few more nights? We could use the company, and it'd make me feel a lot safer."

"Oh my, no. Thank you, Tessa. But there's so much to do here. I want to be up early tomorrow to get ready for everyone. Plus, Sheriff Hagen will be patrolling the street and house. I couldn't feel safer. Really. Now you go on, and start doing whatever it is detectives do. You've got quite a job for yourself, so stop dilly dallying and get to it." She shoved me towards the front door.

"I'm going. I'm going." I walked around the geranium on the porch. "Nell?"

"Yes, Tessa?"

"Do me a favor? Don't bet the house drawing into a straight."

I could hear Nell chuckling as I started back home. It was hard to believe anything had happened by the looks of the neighborhood. I cut down one of the many footpaths that criss-crossed the community. Looking over the short, white picket fences into the quaint backyards of homes, I found everything to be in order, no strangers.

The paths were barely big enough for two people to walk side-by-side. People grew trees and plants over and through the fences on purpose to provide a little backyard privacy. Some of the trees came together over the path, closing out the sunlight. It didn't take much imagination to believe you were walking back in time, or into a magic garden. The kids loved to ride on the paths with their bikes, and probably knew them better than most of the adults.

The path offered me a number of walkway options. I decided on the scenic route past the croquet field and tennis courts. I took a right at the bicycle rental cottage, and walked a short distance before I connected with one of the main roads. A few more twists and turns and I was standing amidst a circle of Victorian beach homes. Each home displayed the individual taste of its owner. They all had to adhere to strict rules as to style and size, but they were free to choose their own color, amount of gingerbread decoration, and number of porches.

Everything looked peaceful and quiet. An outsider would have thought they'd walked into paradise. I guess that's what Paradise Pointe was all about. I'd been so busy trying to live a normal life that I'd forgotten to stop and appreciate what I had. I found myself smiling as I made my way past the homes reading the names identifying each abode; "Mellow Yellow," "Dreamsicle," "Catch of the Day."

It reminded me of how much trouble Michael and I had coming up with a name for our house. We couldn't agree on anything for months. Then Katie had been born and I left the patrol. I came home one day to find a sign in front of our home. Michael had chosen the name "Destiny." He believed everything was predestined. I thought it was romantic at the time. Now I think it's a crock.

I heard familiar voices and looked up at one of the porches to see Breecher and the exotic animal lady talking. What was her name? Wanna...something. It would come to me later. Anyway, she was talking with Mrs. Davenport, the owner of the home. I knew Lydia Davenport owned an exotic pet that looked like a flying squirrel. I supposed they were trying to recruit her for the upcoming meeting. I took the long way around the circle and continued on my way home.

Our home borders the eastern end of Paradise Pointe. The lots are older and larger, leaving more space for a backyard, and breathing room between neighbors. Two stories are commonplace, and we'd added a Captain's Nest with room for a small table and chairs. In our romantic days, we would sit up there with a bottle of wine and watch the sun set over the Emerald Coast. We'd made love countless times up there. I smiled remembering how we used to pull up the moveable staircase so the kids couldn't surprise us. That was a long time ago. I couldn't remember the last time I'd been up there. The only thing fornicating up there now was squirrels and seagulls.

I tried to erase that picture from my mind as I picked up the newspaper from the driveway and went in the side kitchen door, throwing my keys on the table. I took the paper and disappeared into the sunroom on the side of the house. It was one of my favorite spots. There was just enough room for two overstuffed lounging chairs, a coffee table and some large plants. A small bamboo and glass desk was in one corner. I did most of my thinking and writing here.

I lay back on the lounge chair and closed my eyes for a few minutes. Feeling more relaxed, I opened the paper to see what was happening in this little snow globe I called home. Let's see, another illegal gill net was found about fifty yards from the beach. *The 200-yard long net was full of skipjack, catfish, Spanish mackerel, crabs, and at least three sharks.* Jack had been quoted *"The real tragedy is that a net like this will stay intact and just keep killing and killing."* The big headline was *"Cannibalistic JellyFish Visiting Our Waters."* All right, that got my attention. *"Gulf Coast waters are again playing host to alien jellyfish. First came Australian hordes, now it's pink and slimy Caribbean cannibals. The creatures grow to three feet in diameter and their tentacles can reach seventy feet. On the good side, they are solely jellyfish eaters and are consuming quite a few of our bothersome local moon jellyfish. They likely drifted from the Caribbean into the northern Gulf on a current."*

"Well, that's enough of the spectacular," I thought as I turned to the local section. My eye was caught by another robbery. *"Ms. Elaine Jacob's exotic coatimundi was stolen from her home yesterday. "Jasper" is the size of a large housecat and is a member of the raccoon family. He resembles a cross between a fox and a raccoon. Please contact the Sheriff's department if you see any sign of the animal."*

That was enough bad news. I quickly scanned the pages to find *"Paradise Events." Story time, Magic Show, Oriental Fairy Tales*...ah there it was *"Paradise Amphitheater." Free concert featuring a variety of ethnic music, Friday, September 17, 7-9p.m.* I ripped out the announcement and put it on the fridge with my favorite Disney magnet.

Retreating to my sunroom desk, I pulled out my laptop and checked for mail. I usually checked every morning, just in case some incredible force was trying to reach me and could only do it via the Internet, but I had gotten behind and hadn't checked for days. While waiting for the sorrowfully slow connection, I stared out into the yard watching some redheaded woodpeckers enjoying one of my hardwoods. My mind snapped back to attention when I heard, "You've got mail." There was something exciting about hearing those words. I realized I hadn't checked my mail in days and loathed to think how much of it would be spam.

I scanned down the ten messages, deleting the annoying advertisements as I went. There was a note from the PAWS Christian Ministry wondering if I had any suitable pets available for visitation to the local hospital and nursing home. I didn't think Fitz was quite ready for a yard pass. A reminder from the Town Council on the upcoming meeting, an emergency request from the PTA for baked good donations, and what was this? "Photos.com" It didn't sound like a virus, so I opened the file.

I couldn't believe it. Sitting in front of me were copies of Nell's pictures.

Chapter Eleven

Felix had been trying to convince me to receive my pictures on my computer for months. Being the techno-dweeb I was, it took his offering to download the prints free the first time for me to even consider doing it. I'd completely forgotten, and now here they sat. I spent the next hour printing out the photos and making a copy on disk.

Seated in the sunroom with a glass of sweet tea by my side, I searched each of the photos, over and over, looking for some clue to what was happening to me and why. There wasn't an easy answer. I touched the automatic dial on the phone.

"Nell? It's Tess. You'll never believe what happened. I found a set of those pictures on my computer. Yes, it's amazing what they can do these days. Anyway, I've printed copies out and was wondering if you'd like to come over for dinner tonight and take a look at them? Maybe the two of us can see something that I'm missing. Great. How about six o'clock? See ya then."

I hung up and carefully hid the pictures in a brown envelope behind the bookcase in the living room. Now, for my next "Master Mom" feat of the day...what to cook for dinner?

＊＊＊＊＊＊

We all pushed back from the dinner table, full, if not completely satisfied.

"That was...ah, creamy and crunchy, dear. What an unusual treat," Nell cleared the dishes from the table.

"Nice dodge, Nell, but no score." I balled up the recipe I'd torn from the magazine and tossed it into the trash can. "Don't worry with those dishes, Nell. The kids will finish up."

"We will?" Katie moaned.

"What's with this "we" thing? It's Katie's night, Mom," Kevin echoed.

"I need your help tonight while I'm doing some work with Nell. Katie can't do the pots and pans and I don't want her wiping around the stove. So you've been volunteered." I placed the dishtowel over his shoulder.

"Oh, all right. But I should get extra this week in my allowance for this." He stacked the pots off to the side.

"I got a better idea, how about I don't charge you for forgetting to put the trash out yesterday morning, or for emptying your sandy tennis shoes on the bathroom tile, and we just call it even?" I said over my shoulder as Nell and I headed for the sunroom with coffee cups in hand.

"Awe, Mom."

We set our cups on the table in between the lounge chairs and went over to my desk. I pulled out a folding chair for Nell, placing it near the bright reading lamp. It was still light outside, but I didn't want to miss any details on the pictures. I pulled out a magnifying glass from the desk drawer and placed it between the two of us.

I took the pictures from the envelope and handed them to Nell. She thumbed through them quickly, then started back at the first one. "I don't see anything unusual. These are the pictures you decided would go well with the article you're writing."

"Let's try something else. Look at each photo and describe it to me as if I've never heard any of the stories. Tell me what each picture shows and what was going on. I'll keep some notes as you're talking."

"All right, dear. Let's see, this first one is of mother, father, and me standing at the Colleville-sur-Mer, the American cemetery where over 10,000 casualties of the D-Day invasion are buried. That's why we were there in the first place—for father to attend the tenth anniversary of D-Day. It was his first visit back since the battle on June 6, 1944. There were ceremonies, banquets, testimonies, and medal presentations, but the greatest part of the trip was all the people he met and the stories they shared. I think it was a very cathartic trip for him."

Nell stared out the window as she continued. "We visited the beaches where the invasion began. It was easy to see why the forces had so many casualties; they were sitting ducks coming in off the water. Hundred foot cliffs overlooked the beaches, and the elite German infantry division they encountered was far stronger and better trained than they'd expected. Father had been part of the Army Rangers that scaled the cliffs to take out the guns guarding the coast. It was a miracle he lived through it all. That trip struck home with me. I was lucky to have had a father at all." She looked back in her lap, turning to the next photo.

"This photo is of the Contessa and me people watching at the Café Guerbois, one of the leading literary cafes situated at the beginning of the Avenue de Clichy. In the late 19th century, Monet, Renoir and Bazille were regulars at this café. It was right next door to the legendary restaurant of Pere Lathuille."

"Let's back up a second. How did you meet the Contessa?" I asked.

"We met at a banquet that was being held one evening. We were sitting at the same table and hit it off immediately. She was a few years older and recently widowed, but she decided to take me under her wing and show me the 'real' Paris." Nell's eyes looked dreamy, and the blush in her cheeks blossomed.

"I had lived a rather sheltered life up to that point. Oh my, the things she showed me. The places we went...the Theatre des Champs-Elysees, the Moulin Rouge, and Maxim's! She opened my eyes to the world, and I've never shut them since."

She turned the photo over and held the last few together in her hand.

"These next few shots are pictures of a dinner party she held for me at her summer residence in Paris. Oh, the food was exquisite. And the wine flowed like a waterfall during the rainy season.

This one shot was taken in the library. She gave me one of her favorite books that evening as a token of her friendship. You can see I'm holding it in my hand. There was music and dancing until the late hours of the night. She delivered me back to the hotel where we said our goodbyes, and I left with mother and father the next morning to return to the United States."

She laid the last of the pictures aside and smoothed her skirt with her hands.

"Okay, we've got the story. Let's lay the pictures out like a mosaic and see what we see." I laid the pictures out on the desk.

"What can we tell from them?" I picked up the magnifying glass for a closer look.

Nell ran her index finger across the pictures. "Well, all of these pictures were taken during that trip I took with mother and father almost fifty years ago. I guess that means all of this trouble has something do with that trip."

"Is it possible your father was involved in something you didn't know about? He was an Army Ranger. Could he have had some secret business dealings? Or perhaps there was an old vendetta from the war or debt that needed to be repaid?"

"I couldn't say positively, but it wouldn't seem likely. Father was focused on the planned activities during most of the trip, and he and mother stayed very close to each other the entire time."

"So you weren't aware of any unusual meetings or conversations that took place?" I looked at the banquet picture. "He looks at ease in this picture, almost smiling."

"I think the banquet was the highlight of the trip for him. The Contessa made him feel quite welcome. She was so gracious and appreciative; she seemed to lighten his load. She had a way of making you laugh, when all you wanted to do was cry." Nell wiped a small tear from her eye. "She was quite a person."

"I wish I could have met her. She made such an impact on you. I can only imagine the effect she had on so many others during her lifetime." I put my hand on top of Nell's.

"Oh, that would have been a sight to see! She would have loved you and would have ruined you for life! I never would have seen you. She would've had you bouncing around the globe until you couldn't tell what was north and what was south. No, I think the good Lord knew what he was doing keeping you two apart." Nell patted my hand and focused the magnifying glass on the pictures.

"I'll try to forget that my life could have been totally different, and that I might have been a royal adoptee!" I got up from the chair and started roaming the small room.

"What about your mother? Anything unusual there?"

"Mother?" Nell giggled. "Sorry. It's just that mother was—well—she was mother. You have to remember this was the fifties. She was a housewife and a very good one at that. She did it all and smiled while doing it. I can't remember her ever losing her temper or arguing with father. She was a saint."

"She was probably on Valium."

"Tessa!"

"Sorry, I was having one of those *Leave It To Beaver* flashbacks. Well, if we take your mother and father out of contention that would leave you, the Contessa and her friends. Since the trouble is taking place here and you're the only person that we know of who lives here that was also in these pictures, we have to assume the clue lies within the photos where you were present."

"That would seem to make sense." Nell placed the first picture of her and the Contessa at the outdoor café in the middle of the table. Next to it, she placed the group picture taken at the dinner table. Next to that, she put the picture of her and the Contessa in the library.

We both stared bullets at the photos, but they didn't reveal any secrets. We moved over to the lounge chairs and took "the" position—head back, legs straight out, hands resting by our sides.

"Nell, what did you know about her?" I picked up my coffee and took a sip.

"Who, dear?"

"The Contessa. Did she ever talk about herself? Where she was born? Who her parents were? How she met the Count? Did she like being a Contessa? That sort of thing." I laid my head back against the cushion.

"Oh yes. She shared quite a bit with me. I was like the younger sister she'd never had. Her life sounded like a romance novel. Whenever she spoke of it, I was quite enthralled and honored. I'd never had anyone trust in me as much as she did."

"Trust in you? That sounds a bit ominous. Did she have secrets?" I opened my eyes and turned my head toward Nell.

She held her hands in her lap, fingers intertwined, thumbs twiddling. "I wouldn't call them secrets. More like 'rumors' that were never confirmed."

"You should've been a lawyer, Nell." I shook my head. "So what kinds of rumors were circulated about her?"

Nell didn't appear any more comfortable with this line of questioning, but she continued.

"Well, I was never one to put much validity in the rumor mill. But give me a second to collect my thoughts. Let me see what I can remember. It was a long time ago. I'd hate to get the sequence of events out of order."

She played with the beads on her necklace before she was ready to share the details with me. She took a sip of coffee and began.

"Her parents were Swedish Internationalists. They were very active in the Swedish Red Cross. I believe her father was president of it at some point. It was "implied" that he was involved in the evacuation of Danish and Norwegian prisoners from German concentration camps. The Contessa was very sketchy about those days in her life. You see, her parents sent her to America to live with relatives during the war. They felt she'd be safer there."

Nell raised her eyes to the ceiling. "She must have been about fourteen at the time. Yes, that seems about right. She spoke quite fondly of her time in New York. She loved the hustle and bustle of the big city, and she loved the music!"

Nell's eyes began to dance and her hands swayed back and forth to a tune only she could hear. "She would sneak into the bars to hear all the great jazz musicians play." Nell rested her hands back in her lap. Her voice lowered and became sedate.

"When the war ended, she was to return to her parents. But her father had taken a post as a UN Mediator and was assassinated by extremists before she returned home. Her Mother was devastated and plunged herself back into work for the Red Cross. She thought it would be best for her daughter to go directly to Switzerland to begin her studies at the University. She spent a lot of time with family friends who lived nearby. It was through them that she met the Count."

She took another sip of coffee. "I know she finished school with a degree in Art History and shortly thereafter married the Count. They lived in Italy, but had homes in other countries as well. The Count's business affairs took him to many places. I remember her telling me how she used to love to travel with him, but that after a while she no longer cared for all the dashing about and hobnobbing that had to be done. So she chose to stay at the various homes while he traveled and spent her time visiting art galleries and the theater. The Count died in a flying accident a few months before I met the Contessa. She told me she was saddened by her loss, but that they'd grown so far apart, she felt she'd lost an old acquaintance instead of a husband."

She finished the last drops of coffee and held the cup in her hands. "It was her interest in art and the memory of her father that brought her to the reception we were attending that evening. There was a poignant photography exhibit of pictures taken by soldiers and families during the war that was unveiled at the banquet. A portion of the exhibit showcased the humanitarian efforts of the Red Cross. She was quite taken with the display." Nell brushed some strands of hair away from her face and placed the cup back on the table.

"We corresponded for a few years after that. She said she was involved in doing research work that took up all her time. She spoke of visiting, but never made the trip. She was very sketchy about the details. Over the years, the letters were fewer and fewer. I know she lived with a poet and after that a French painter. Then we lost touch, until I received notice of her death." Nell started rubbing the beads on her necklace again.

"There had been an accident on a ferry crossing the English Channel. Her body was never found, but the waters were so cold the authorities presumed her dead.

They notified me because I had been included in her will. She gave me a few pieces of jewelry and a remembrance of her card-playing days. She was quite good at playing games. She taught me most of what I know today when it comes to poker. The home in Italy, its contents, and any money passed on to historical societies and charities. I never imagined I might be included in her will. Even in her death, she managed to surprise me."

Nell managed a faint smile.

"That story is so fantastic. Her life really was like a fairytale."

"Yes, well, I used to think the same thing. I envied her and the life she led. But then I realized how lonely she was later in life. She had no living relatives. She lived for art and music and the few friends she had made along the way. I came to realize how lucky I've been to live the life I have surrounded by people who love me."

I held back the tears forming in my eyes and reminded myself to take a breath.

Kevin peeked his head through the French doors. "Mom, the garbage disposal ate a spoon, and I can't get the dishwasher to start."

I looked over at Nell, "Do you think the aristocracy has troubles with their major appliances?" I got up to tend to that part of my job description referred to as "other."

I returned with the coffeepot to find Nell holding one picture in her hand, looking off to nowhere in particular.

"What is it Nell? Have you found something?" I set the pot on the table, and looked at the photo. It was the one of her and the Contessa in the library.

"Tessa, do you think it's possible someone wants this book?"

"What book?"

"The book I'm holding in this picture. The book the Contessa gave to me as a momento."

I looked more closely at the picture. Of course, it made sense. Whoever ransacked Nell's house seemed very interested in her bookshelves, or in places books could be stored.

"What was the book about? Could it be valuable?" I tried to see the title in the picture.

"Nothing exotic, I'm afraid. It was an art history book with a few comments written in the borders by the Contessa."

"Where's this book now?"

"Well, that's what got me thinking about this in the first place. You see, I sent it out of town a number of weeks ago to be repaired. The binding was in terrible shape, and the inside pages were starting to break loose from the cover."

I sat down on the chaise and faced Nell. "I need you to think carefully. Does anyone else know you sent the book out to be repaired?"

"No, Tessa. I don't believe I thought it important enough to even mention, until now. I got a notice recently from the bookshop letting me know they were almost finished and were preparing to mail it back to me." Nell got up and started picking up the dishes.

"If you're right about the book, the mail may be the safest place for it to be right now." I got up and started pacing again. I didn't want to scare Nell, but she needed to be aware that she might be in danger. If they wanted the book that badly and thought Nell had it, I doubted they'd stop at breaking and entering to get it.

"It's probably nothing. But I don't think we should take any chances at this point. Why don't you pack a bag and stay at our house until this all blows over?" I took the dishes from Nell's hands. "Humor me. Please?"

"I see what you're getting at, Tessa." She picked up the pictures and put them back in the envelope, then got the coffeepot and walked towards the kitchen. "Thank you dear for the offer, but I intend to stay in my house. I won't allow some crooked deviant to scare me from my home."

So much for tact, I thought. I laid the cups on the counter and counted to five before I spoke again. "Nell, I can understand your point of view, but I think it's important that you not be alone until this case is solved. You may be in danger, and I couldn't live with myself if something ever happened to you."

Nell set the pot down and picked up her sweater from the chair. "Well then, you'd better hurry up and get this case solved, Tessa. I have no intention of hiding like some ostrich with my head in the sand." She stopped at the back door and turned to me, "And stop fussing so much. I've lived quite a bit longer than you have, missy, and am quite capable of taking care of myself." The admonishment turned into a smile. "Thank you for dinner, dear, it was...crunchy."

I stood in the middle of the kitchen. The sun had set, and the last rays of light were disappearing behind the hedges. I had no clue what to do. I felt very alone. Then the phone rang.

"Hello?" No sound, just an open line. "Hello?" Silence. Then came the click, and a disconnecting buzz sound.

Chapter Twelve

I looked into the hand piece, waiting for an explanation. Hoping a better one would prevail. I heard the kids racing to the top of the stairs.

"Was that for me?" Kevin yelled.

"Kevin's got a girlfriend, Kevin's got a girlfriend," Katie sang in the background.

"I do not, you little twerp. Why don't you keep your little munchkin mouth shut! Mom?"

I put the phone back on the hook. "No, Kev. Wrong number," I yelled back from the kitchen.

I wanted to believe with all my heart that it had been a wrong number. I wanted to believe Kevin had a girlfriend, but naiveté wasn't my forte. Whatever was happening wasn't over. Whoever was terrorizing my town and family hadn't finished.

It was obvious the criminals weren't from around here. They were big time, big town trouble. The kind of trouble Jack would know how to deal with. Or he'd know someone who could.

When it came to Jack, I never asked too many questions. Whenever I did, I usually walked away with more questions than answers. He had a way of rubbing people the wrong way, but you wouldn't want anyone else watching your back.

He'd taken two or three leaves of absence during the ten years I'd worked with him. No explanation, just needed to take some time. His mother had died when he was a teenager. He rarely spoke about his father, and he didn't have any siblings.

He'd been married for five or six years to one of the commissioner's daughters, an unlikely pairing most of us had felt from the start. She left him a couple years back for a Golf Pro on a winning streak in the

94

circuit. He'd never quite gotten over her.

That's what I'd learned after being his partner for ten years. Besides the fact I knew he had friends in strange places. Friends that came in handy when you needed a favor, and I was ready to ask him for a doozy. But first I needed to get some insurance.

******

September 17, 2001

"Tess, how're ya doin? We haven't seen you here in ages," said the man from behind the display cases filled with guns.

"Not much reason till now," I answered as I window-shopped.

"Lookin' for anything special?"

I put my nose a little closer to the glass top. "Nah, just checking out the competition."

"Not a bad thing to be doin these days. You can never be too safe, I always say."

"By the looks of your cases, I'd say most other people believe the same thing."

"Can't complain. This rash of nastiness about town has brought in some new business. One of the writers from the paper was in just the other day. Real strange lookin' fella. Not the kind of guy you'd think would carry. He wasn't happy about the waitin' time, but he still wanted the piece."

I stopped looking and dropped my leather bag on top of the counter. "Did he look like a human flamingo with an ascot and safari hat?"

The big guy chuckled. "Yeah, that's him."

I rolled my eyes and held my head in my hands. "Tell me you didn't register him."

"What can I say? I don't make the rules, just follow them."

I stood there for a minute thinking about the implications of Spoony owning a weapon. Nothing good could come from it, I was sure of that. I picked up my bag. "Well, now I really feel like I need to hit the range. Anyone else back there?"

"Nah, quiet as a whorehouse on the night before pay day."

It was my turn to chuckle.

"Ya still got that Glock?" he asked, handing me some earplugs, protective eyeglasses, and targets.

"Yeah, comfortable and dependable. At least that's what I remember."

"Do ya need any rounds?"

"No, I'm fine. But stick around, I may change my mind if these targets start doing the electric slide."

"Nah, don't even think that. It's like breathin'. Ya never forget."

"I'll try and remember that." I put the headphones around my neck and picked up the targets.

I was surprised how easily I found my way through the dark maze back to the shooting range. It was humid, and the air smelled like gunpowder. I dropped my bag on the floor and pulled the line in to set my target. I could feel my adrenaline building as the target moved out twenty-five feet. I was glad no one else was there to see this. I'd be lucky if I could hit the paper at all.

I loaded the Glock and took the standard position to shoot, legs spread, left hand gripping the right wrist to support the shooting hand. *It's just like riding a bike. You never forget. Nice and easy. Don't think about it, just do it.*

I took a breath, started to squeeze the trigger, and the memory came crashing through.

I heard the click of a 12-gauge being pumped from behind me. It was dark. Jack and I were in his Jeep out in a field. There was a drug bust going on five miles down the road at a farmhouse. We were at the end of the property. If anyone came running from the field, we were supposed to cut them off. No one had anticipated any dealers being outside the property, but it looked like someone had underestimated them.

Jack whispered, "On the count of three, you shoot right, I'll shoot left. Then I'll floor it into the field." I nodded and lifted my weapon. I heard the dry grass crunch under his feet before I saw him in the side mirror. By then he was close enough to take out both of us with one shot. I slid down on to the floor and pointed the gun toward the back. Sweat was dripping down the back of my neck. I thought about my baby at home and how he'd grow up without a mother. The trigger felt wet and sticky. I tried to squeeze it slow and easy. But then I saw it, that side-by-side 12-gauge barrel pointing right through the back side window of the Jeep. My breathing stopped, my finger fell away from the trigger.

Someone was screaming at me, there was a slap across my face. My small body hit the floor. But it wasn't the car floor. I was on carpet, shag carpet. I was crying, "I promise I won't touch it again, I promise."

Then the thunder came. My ears were ringing and I was being thrown around on the hard floor of the Jeep as Jack shot through the field. He had seen the guy in his rearview mirror and got off a shot over his shoulder before the son of a bitch had time to squeeze off that 12-gauge.

Jack drove until he was sure we weren't being followed. He stopped the Jeep, and called in the shooting. It was dead quiet.

"You all right?" He asked.

I pulled myself back up into the seat, glad it was dark so he couldn't see me shaking. "Must have froze," was all I could say.

Jack grabbed a blanket from the back seat and wrapped it around my shoulders. "Could have happened to anyone," he said wiping his forehead with his shirtsleeve. "It was a tough shot, a tough call. You must have been thinkin' pretty hard. What was it you were promising me?"

"Promising you?"

"Yeah, right before I took my shot, you were promising me something."

I thought about the child being thrown to the floor. The promise she was making over and over again. Was it me? What was I promising? Who was I making the promise to?

I pulled the blanket tight around me. "I don't remember. I was totally out of it. If you hadn't shot, we'd be six feet under right now. It'd be my fault you were dead, and my child would be growing up without a mother."

Jack shook my shoulder. "Don't ever think that way, Tess. You're a good cop. Next time you won't hesitate. Next time you'll be the one having to write out the report in triplicate."

"You're a good man, Jack. A good partner. But I'm not willing to bet your life on another 'next time.'"

I could hear my own words ringing in my head as the paper target came back into focus. I wiped the sweat from my hand, held my breath, and squeezed gently until the first pop sounded. I exhaled, and shot another and another. It gave me a pretty good kick, but each round came easier and easier.

The word "promise" faded with each shot and was replaced with a surge of adrenaline. I was light headed from the endorphin rush. I felt like I'd just lost my virginity, and there was no turning back.

Before I knew it, I'd shot two boxes of ammo. The smell of fresh gunpowder surrounded me. I smelled my shirtsleeve. The powder had permeated the material. "Oh great," I thought, "more laundry."

"Was it as good for you?" a voice said from behind me.

I gasped, almost jumping out of my skin. "Jesus Christ, Jack! You scared the shit out of me." I grabbed my heart and tried pushing it back into my chest.

"Nice language for the former PTA President." He took the gun to check the sight. "Come on, pull the line in and let's see how ya did." Jack laid the Glock on the counter and turned his back to the target. "Promise I won't look before you do."

I was angry and embarrassed, but damned if I was going to let him get the better of me. The pulley squeaked as I tugged on the string. Within seconds my moment of truth was staring me in the face. I accepted what it had to tell me, gracefully. I snapped the target down, thrusting it into Jack's chest. "Read it and weep, sweetheart."

I got my bag and started packing up. Jack looked at the target and couldn't help but grin. He was staring at fifty rounds, all within the target parameters. Most were in the chest area, a better percentage kill zone than the head.

"Hope you weren't picturin' me as your target." He folded up the target and slipped it into my bag.

"Don't flatter yourself, Bubbles. I was thinkin' more about a cook who gave me a bad casserole recipe."

He smiled, having been a culinary guinea pig many times at my house. He checked to be sure the clip was empty, then handed it to me.

"I heard about the trouble at Nell's. Thought it was time we had a chat and turn this game around. Thought you might be thinkin' the same thing since you freed the Glock from captivity this morning."

I didn't give him the satisfaction of asking how he knew I'd been at the bank this morning to get my Glock from the lock box. "Yeah, I decided the insurance policy could take care of itself. Besides, our opponent's been holdin' all the cards lately. That bothers me."

"Agreed. I think it's time we started playin' a little more aggressively. You happen to know what the game is?"

"Poker. Up till now the odds haven't been in our favor. But then, our selfish little bastard doesn't know we're holdin' a wild card."

"Wild card, huh? I like wild cards. So, ya goin' to clue me in on our ace in the hole?"

"Well, Nell and I got to talkin' last night and lookin' over some pictures. We think there's a connection between one of the pictures and a book she received."

Out of the dark came the sound of a metal casing rolling under foot, running footsteps and the sound of air "whooshing" as the door closed.

"Stay here! Don't move until I get back." Jack pulled his weapon and disappeared into the dark corridor.

I reached for my gun, only to realize I didn't have any ammunition. I felt like a deer in high season. Poking my hands in my pockets, I found a melted piece of Dentyne. I unwrapped it and shoved it into my mouth. I grabbed my 9mm and flattened myself against the inside wall of the cubby. If I swung low with the gun, hitting the asshole's shins I'd have a good chance of bringing him down.

The air from the outside door "whooshed" again. Someone was coming. My heart was racing. The footsteps came closer. I closed my eyes and held my breath. I could hear heavy breathing on the other side of the wall, smelled the muskiness of a man. I opened my eyes and prepared to swing. I could see the toes of two size eleven black tennis shoes right beyond my reach.

Come on, you son of a bitch. One more step. Just one more step, I thought.

"Tess, its Jack. Where are you?"

I stood up. Doing a half turn, I faced him head on in the doorway. Adrenaline rushed through my body. I tried to sound cool, but only heard stuttering coming from my mouth. "You're a lu-lu-lucky man, Bu-Bu-Bubba Bubbles. One more step and you'da been wearing knee braces for a ve-ve-very long time." I couldn't catch my breath. I was hyperventilating.

Jack grabbed a chair and me at the same time. Next thing I knew my head was between my legs. When I came up for air, he handed me a leather-covered flask.

"Here, take a little of this. It'll help slow down the rush."

I reached for the flask. My hands were shaking big time. I used both hands to steady the flask and bring it to my lips. The liquid went down easy. The burn didn't come till seconds later. A few sips and the shaking started to subside. A few minutes later, I felt I could stand.

"Did you see anyone?" I asked reaching for the counter to steady myself.

"Just a car pulling away—a black BMW roadster. Can't be too many of those around here."

"That's funny. I know someone who drives a roadster." I thought about Spoony.

Jack looked serious. "Friend or foe?"

"Neither, I'd say. Just one of those road bumps of life. How about the guy up front? Did he see anything?"

"Nothin'. He's nursin' a pretty good goose egg. Someone hit him from behind."

Jack picked up my bag and offered his arm to me. I took it gladly. "Well, one thing's for sure, we just lost our ace in the hole, if we even had one to begin with."

"What do you mean?" Jack asked as he helped me through the maze back to the front of the store.

"Nell figured out last night when we were looking at the pictures that the book might have something to do with all this. If she figured it out, our friend probably did too. That explains why he tossed her place. He was looking for the book."

Jack helped me out the front door. "So, he really doesn't know anything more than he did before. All you did was confirm that the book might have something to do with all this. We're still one-up on him."

"How do you figure?"

"He knows there's a book. He knows it isn't at Nell's house, which hopefully will take her out of this equation for a while. That's gotta really be pissing him off." Jack unlocked my car door and quietly stared at me.

"What are you looking at?" I tossed my bag into the passenger's seat.

Jack kept his hand on my door. "I'm waiting for you to tell me that you know where the book's at. I'm waiting for you to tell me we still have an ace in the hole."

I sat there smiling. "We still have an ace in the hole. That's all I'm tellin' you."

"That's enough for me." Jack started to shut my door.

I stopped him for a second. "You know, it just dawned on me that our friend is rather rude."

Jack nodded. "Miss Manners would be appalled."

Chapter Thirteen

The house felt refreshingly safe as I sat in the sunroom reviewing the current complexities of my life. It was definitely time to take a break from reality. I took down my note from the refrigerator and decided the musical event on the lawn at the amphitheater was just what I needed to feel part of the "common" community again. I showered, ordered chicken delivery from the Colonel, and rounded up the kids to join me in some quality down time.

We walked together the short distance to the amphitheater staying on the main streets. The sun had started to set, and the heat of the day had ebbed to a manageable temperature. The humidity was still bad. A number of people were carrying spritzers and mini-fans to beat the heat.

The houses looked quiet and inviting with outdoor porch lights illuminating the paths. Spanish moss hung from the trees, emitting warmth and familiarity that might seem eerie to an outsider. Looking down the last street before we crossed over to the amphitheater, I could see a flock of pelicans gliding low over the water hunting for their dinner. They came so close to the water I often imagined what they'd look like tumbling bill over wing into the Gulf?

The hillside was parched in a few spots from the lack of rain, but that didn't seem to bother the locals and tourists looking for an evening out on the town. We spread our old beach blanket on the manicured lawn and started making ourselves comfortable for the evening...just like simple folk.

"Well, howdy neighbor." Geena sat down next to us. "I wasn't sure you'd be here tonight with the way things have been going lately."

"I think that's why I have to be here." I helped Geena unfold her pristine patchwork quilt. "Where's Bob and Lindsey?"

"My picnic pack mules, you mean? They're unloading the wagon with our essentials." She smoothed out the wrinkles and secured the corners with some new fangled device she'd acquired that staked the corners of the blanket into the ground without damaging a thread on the quilt.

I watched in amazement over the next several minutes, as our simple campsite became an advertisement for *Town & Country* magazine. Bob placed their caned beach chairs, complete with removable footstools next to my humble abode. Geena proceeded to "set the table" complete with real flatware, glasses, and a four-course gourmet meal of cold strawberry soup, stuffed chicken croquettes, asparagus, and a fruit tart.

My chicken leg, done up just right with the Colonel's secret recipe was beckoning me. I bit my way into the plastic bag holding the recycled plastic ware, spitting little pieces of plastic into my hand before I gagged on them. I took the plastic lids off the Styrofoam containers holding the potato salad and coleslaw and divvied up the little dinner rolls and butter pats. The kids split a root beer, while I chose to indulge myself with a small bottle of Chardonnay I'd slipped into the basket.

The music was starting. I settled back, balancing my glass of wine between my legs, while sucking the chicken out of my teeth and wishing I'd brought toothpicks. I could feel the tension leaving my body as I listened to the Irish fiddle and dulcimer.

My eyes began to drift around the lawn, checking out the attending patrons. Many were regulars, some were residents from nearby beach towns, and as usual a few tourists had stumbled onto our delightful event.

Edy sat high on the hill in an unmistakable lavender pantsuit. Her granddaughter was dressed in a complementary sundress. Tom was relaxing in one of those new camping chairs, and Andy was surveying the perimeter while making moves on the single women. I saw Betty way down front with her husband and all the kids. High on the hill, distancing themselves from the masses, were Breecher and Wanna-whatever, his lady friend. It looked like he was feeding her strawberries. I had to turn away before I lost my appetite.

After a few minutes of scoping out the crowd, my eyes settled on two figures talking at the outside coffee bar. They were sitting on stools with their backs to a ten-foot panoramic mural painted by the latest art class. They were well behind the crowd. No one would have taken special notice of them.

I pinched Geena on the arm. "Look across the green at the coffee bar, and tell me who you see."

She turned her head and squinted a bit in the direction of the two men. "Well, I couldn't be certain at this distance without my glasses, but isn't that Jack? I've never seen the other guy, but he looks pretty urban to be from around here. Why do you ask? Can't you see from here?" She gave me one of those smirking looks. "You haven't gotten that prescription filled for those glasses the doctor suggested, have you?"

"No, I haven't. And yes, I can see them from here just fine. I merely wanted a second opinion before I mosey over there and eavesdrop unobtrusively."

"Do you always eavesdrop on people you know? Why don't you just go up and join the conversation?"

"Be-cause," I said, accentuating the 'cause', "these are two people who under normal circumstances would never be sharing a cup of coffee."

The light bulb finally came on. "So you're thinking maybe some extraordinary circumstance has brought them together?"

I patted Geena on the head. "Good girl. Now sit back and enjoy the show and act like you don't know what I'm doing." I grabbed a piece of bubble gum from the picnic basket and popped it into my mouth.

"You got it, Carmen Santiago. Be careful."

I smiled at Geena's reference to my daughter's favorite cartoon detective as I made my way through the back of the crowd to the end of the buildings that made up the semicircle of businesses on the quad. The semicircle split in the middle to provide pathways back to the residential section. The coffee bar was the last shop before the split. I scurried around the backside of the buildings and crept along behind the mural. Walking slowly on the thick St. Augustine grass, I inched my way up the side until I heard two male voices on the other side. A part of me felt like a complete fool. *What was I doing spying on the only person I would trust with my life?*

I recognized Jack's voice.

"I don't care why the hell you're here. This town is off limits. Tess

Titan is off limits, and that goes double for her family."

"Save your knight in shining armor act for someone who gives a damn, Daniels. No one gives a shit what you think. You got no jurisdiction on this one. It's so far out of your hands, you couldn't touch it even if you did know the right people—which you don't."

"Who're you working for this time, Romeo? Do they know you butter your bread on both sides?"

"Shut up, Jack."

"What's so big that someone would actually hire your sorry ass and bring you into this country without a leash?" Jack shot back.

"No comment."

"How're we supposed to have a mutually satisfying détente here when you don't want to share any information?"

The voice sounded angry and frustrated. "This isn't a détente. I thought I'd give you a heads up since I'm in your town and figured we'd end up crossing paths." The voice became way too nice. "There's no reason anyone needs to get hurt. Talk some sense into the girl. Have her get the book. We'll decide on a drop spot, and all will be right again in Oz, Auntie Jack."

There was a long pause. Jack's voice sounded strictly businesslike. "Whose guarantee do I have on that?"

"Why, Jack. You cut me deep. You know you have my word and the word of the family."

"I want more." Jack's voice sounded matter-of-fact.

There was an angry grunting sound. "You want too much. You never did know when to cut your losses."

Jack sounded real cool. "My mistake. I thought this book was a necessary addition to your family's library. No big deal. I'm sure the other buyer's still interested."

I heard a Styrofoam cup crackle. "What other buyer?"

"Oh, did I forget to mention someone else is interested in acquiring the book as well?"

"You're bitin' off more than you can chew, Daniels."

"You may be right, but after this sale, I can afford to have someone else do my chewing for me."

There was another long pause, then a hideous chuckle that turned into an ugly cough. "Maybe time has changed you, Jack. I never thought I'd see this side of you."

"Don't get all choked up over it. I want the pictures, any copies, and the negatives. Tomorrow, deliver it to the central post office on the Village Green. I'll bring the book."

"Tomorrow? Jack, you know I can't get my hands on them that quickly. They're not even in this country. It'll take at least a week."

"Hey, I got all the time in the world. But with Tess workin' on the case now, I don't know how long the book will be available."

"All right, three days. But I'm depending on you to take delivery of that book and have it in your possession. No screw ups."

"Romeo, would I screw you?"

"Don't mess with me, Jack. It won't be pretty."

I could hear the two men push their stools back. I took my ear away from the mural and stood there wondering if I'd just heard what I thought I'd heard? *Was it possible that Jack was selling me out for some insignificant trinket? Had I misjudged him all these years? Was he nothing more than a five-and-dime con artist?* I felt betrayed. I felt lonely. I felt an incredible stinging and burning between my toes. I looked down to find red ants crawling all over my feet and ankles.

"Ahhhhhh!" I let out a low scream. Kicking my sandals off, I swatted the little buggers into oblivion. The more I moved, the more they bit. I danced around from foot to foot, then spied the fountain. I dashed over to the water and hopped in. A few ants' remains floated to the top. "Aha! I got you, you little piss ants." I stood there a few minutes with my eyes closed, hoping to be spared the pain of the puss-filled welts.

"We have the Gulf for that kind of thing," a familiar brusque voice commented.

I opened my eyes to find Andy Hagen standing in front of me writing a ticket. I was so at a loss for words, I didn't know where to start.

He held his hand up. "Don't even try, Mrs. Titan. I'm not in the mood today." He pointed next to me. "The sign says, 'No Wading,' and that's obviously what you're doing."

He ripped off the ticket, handed it to me, and walked back towards the concert.

I stood there in the fountain, red welts forming on my feet, holding a ticket for $25, and feeling sorry for myself. I hobbled over to the coffee shop, picking my sandals up on the way.

Grabbing some packages of mustard and taking a seat at the nearest table, I tore the tops off the packages with a vengeance, not caring where the mustard squirted. After a few minutes, I had my feet and ankles coated with yellow mustard. I got a few odd stares from the other coffee patrons. "Old family remedy," I said, as I made my way back over to the concert.

I was about to beeline-it back to safety when I remembered the BMW Roadster in the parking lot. I did an about-face and made my way over to the car. It looked like Spoony's, but the license plate wasn't right. I took the well-chewed bubble gum from my mouth and stuck it under the chrome bumper. It wasn't exactly a homing device, but who said hi-tech was better?

I took the long way back to the blanket. People probably thought I was just being nice, not blocking anybody's view. Truth was I didn't want anyone seeing my yellow feet. I sat cross-legged on the blanket and ripped open one of the Colonel's tasty apple crisp desserts. It was luke-warm, just about how I felt.

Geena looked over at my feet. "I told you, you should just go up and join the conversation, but noooo, you had to eavesdrop."

I didn't have the energy or the heart to tell Geena what I'd overheard. I sat quietly the rest of the concert, Katie sitting between my legs, and Kevin sitting above me on a chair. I used the time to think. *What was I going to do? I'd always counted on Jack being in my corner, and that was looking iffy about now. Andy Hagen was barely talking to me, and Nell and the kids were not getting any safer.*

We collected our few meager items and started the short walk home. The kids were running ahead trying to catch lightning bugs. Geena and Bob had taken the car back home.

I walked alone with the blanket draped over my shoulders. Usually, I would have found the darkness a comfort. Tonight, it felt spooky. The sun had set, and the porch lights casted long shadows into the streets. The Spanish moss hung low from the trees reminding me of an old horror movie I'd seen as a child. The bushes seemed taller and able to hide an intruder. I didn't think anyone would attack us, not this soon. "Romeo" had told Jack three days. I hoped I had those three days.

We walked up the driveway. The kids went in the side door to the kitchen and started fighting over the remote. I went around the corner to the back patio and sat down in one of my comfortable wicker rocking chairs. It had a big fat cushion. I double-checked the mustard to be sure it had dried, then tucked one leg under me, and put the other to work rocking the chair.

The sky was clear, the stars plentiful. I recognized a few of the summer constellations, and made a couple of selfish wishes on shooting stars. I sat for a while, until the numbness was replaced with resolve. I was finally ready to talk.

"So Fitz, what do you think about all this?" It was dark on the patio. I couldn't see our resident pelican, but didn't deem that necessary for an evening chat.

"I know, I couldn't believe it in the beginning either. But it is real, and it's happening to us. That includes you, pal. Anything happens to us and your buffet of bait fish comes to a crashing halt."

I listened for some movement from Fitz's side of the patio, but all was quiet.

"You're awful quiet this evening, Mr. Brown Head. I hope you're busy figuring out who's causing this commotion in our lives. Just between you and me, I could use a little insight into that question." There was no answer.

"No ideas, huh? I was hoping one of your migrating bird friends might have stopped by to give us an inside line." Still quiet.

I switched feet. The one under me was going to sleep. "You know, Fitz, I'm havin' a hard time believin' Jack would roll over for that scum, Romeo. I don't know what his family has on Jack, but it must be big for him to even consider dealin' with the dirtbag." I could hear the anger rising in my voice and paused to take three deep breaths.

"I don't know if I'm angry at the low-lifes who put Jack in this situation, angry at Jack for turning on me, or if I'm just angry at myself for feeling guilty and inadequate."

I took two pieces of gum from my pocket and chomped away. "Whatever, I figure I got enough raw emotion to cover all those bases." I lifted my foot up and sat Indian style.

"I envy you, Fitz. A few fish, a little sunshine, some nice friendly wing action from the opposite sex every once in a while. You got it made."

I looked over in Fitz's direction, waiting for a response. Nothing came.

"Fitz, old boy, are you feelin' okay tonight?" No response.

I uncrossed my legs, feeling the stiffness in my knee joints. It took me a few seconds to reckon with the pain as I stood up and stretched my legs. Walking towards Fitz's cage, I expected to see him asleep on his perch. I have that effect on man and beast.

"Fitz, what's up bud?" I didn't see him on his perch, and he wasn't in his cage.

I hurried back to the side of the house and turned on the patio light and the motion sensor lights up in the trees. The lights shown bright, and made one thing unmistakably clear—Fitz was gone.

Chapter Fourteen

"That sonnafabitch!" I stomped down the driveway and across the street. "He's the lowest form of a creature that was ever made. No! He gives those creatures a good name! The little waste of a weasel, I'd never thought his cherry-pit-sized balls were big enough to do something like this," I muttered to myself all the way to Breecher's front porch. It was dark. His porch light wasn't on.

The animal robberies in the area crossed my mind, but only for a second. They were exotic animals. The last time I checked Fitz didn't fit into that category. He wasn't stolen for his value. He was stolen for spite.

I banged on Breecher's brass knocker as hard as I could. The lights flicked on. I heard commotion and scuttling about inside. Breecher opened the door a crack with the security chain in plain view. His little black beady eyes squinted through the crack.

"Wh...who is it? What do you want?" He had the backbone of a jellyfish.

"Listen here, Breecher. If you gotta problem with me, then stand up like a man and deal with me. What kind of spineless creature are you that you'd steal a wounded animal and break a little girl's heart in the process?" I knocked my fist against the door for emphasis. The chain stretched to its limit.

I could hear Breecher sucking on his inhaler. He tried to close the door, but my middle aged figure had a good twenty pounds on his skanky little bod. He pointed his finger at me through the crack.

"Now you listen to me, Mrs. Titan. I have no idea what you're talking about. You bang on my door after dark going on like a crazy person. But good riddance I say if that filthy animal is finally gone."

I heard a growl coming from my throat.

"You leave me alone and get off my property or I'll call the police and have them take you away. I'm sure they'll be happy to oblige me."

"Why you troublemaking, little snot of a man." I was interrupted by a shrill, barking voice coming from inside the house.

"Wendell? Who's down there? Do you need me to call the police?"

He turned his head toward the stairs. "No, Flower Face. Everything's fine. Just a solicitor. I'll be done in a minute."

"Flower Face? You have that exotic animal lady in your bed don't you, Breecher? Is that how you all get your kicks? First you steal other people's pets, then you let loose on each other while the adrenaline rush is still fresh?"

He took another quick breath on the inhaler, pulled back his shoulders, and tried to look like he meant business, an impossible feat with him wearing his shorty pajamas. "We're done, Mrs. Titan." He shut the door.

I stood on the porch fuming. I kicked the door with as much hatred as I could muster. It would have sounded pretty convincing if I'd been wearing steel-toed boots, but it seemed I'd left those at home. Instead I was wearing my open-toed leather sandals. The outcome was pain, lots of it, straight up my leg. I hopped around cursing under my breath while holding my foot in the air. It was the same foot I'd hurt earlier falling off the pier.

When hopping seemed no longer possible, I leaned against his porch railing, resting my foot on the top step. My toe was throbbing. I hobbled back across the street, and back to the house to lick my wounds.

I ate three Creamsicles so I'd have enough Popsicle sticks to tape to my toes. I was fairly certain I'd broken a few of my digits.

I lay down on the living room sofa. After two glasses of wine, my brain was finally able to function on facts instead of emotions. Fact: Breecher was a weasel, but I couldn't see him manhandling Fitz into a bag or cage. He needed an accomplice. The more I thought about it, the clearer the kidnaping became. I definitely needed to talk to the Sheriff before any more animals were reported missing.

My call to the Sheriff's Office reporting Fitz's disappearance rewarded me with a recording. "We are unable to take your call at this time. If this is an emergency, please dial 911. If this is not an emergency, please leave a message and we will contact you during working hours, eight a.m. to six p.m." I set the phone back in its cradle and pondered if a missing pelican was a 911 emergency.

My inside voice was telling me to make some hot chocolate, go to bed, and deal with this problem tomorrow. For once in my life, I listened. The kids were fast asleep. I figured the bad news would keep until morning.

I slipped into my oversized tee shirt, diverting my eyes from the full-length mirror. It'd been six months since Michael's departure. The weightlifting, aerobics, and power walking were low on my list of priorities. First, I was too angry to exercise. Then, I was too depressed. Now, I just didn't give a damn. I'd been packing on the pounds. I knew it all had to stop, and soon. There were enough changes going on in my life and in my body that I didn't need to sabotage myself. Mother never seemed to gain an ounce. But all I had to do was just think about something deliciously sinful and it would push my scale into the next times table.

I propped myself up in bed, took a sip of hot chocolate, and switched on the late news. I recognized the evening anchor, not an easy feat. It seemed most of our "more mature" local celebrities had decided to move on and up, leaving us with a number of pop-n-fresh twenty-somethings delivering the local politics and happenings of our town. Big city polish, our local station would never have, but it served its purpose and was always good for a few chuckles. I enjoyed checking out the bad haircuts and babbling ad-libs when the teleprompter broke down. I saw a picture of the Pirate Ship in the corner of the screen and raised the volume.

"The Medical Examiner has listed probable cause of death for the John Doe found entangled in the lines of the Pirate Ship as death by marine poisoning. Authorities believe the visitor could have fallen off a boat, undetected, and was stung by a Scorpion Fish. The venom from the fish could have paralyzed the victim leading to his drowning. It's hoped that in this scenario, the man left his valuables and identification on the boat for safekeeping. The police are asking anyone who may have these items to contact the Sheriff's department. The body will be buried this weekend at the Greenwood Cemetery. An anonymous donor provided the plot and monies to cover the deceased's expenses."

I muted the volume. *What was a Scorpion Fish doing this far*

north in the Gulf? The sting paralyzed him and then he drowned?
That didn't sound right. I knew the fish was poisonous and that its
sting could cause a bad reaction, but paralyze a 180-pound man?
And what good-hearted soul is paying the burial expenses? I was
having some serious doubts about the cause of John Doe's death.

I watched the pregnant weather girl do a sort of mime dance on the
screen trying to detail the upcoming week's weather to me. It's not
that I didn't trust her, but I tended to think she had "short timer's"
disease. I mean, what did she care if she got it right or not? It wasn't
like someone was going to fire her. Besides, what's there to get right?
The September weather in Northern Florida was very predictable. It's
gonna be damned hot and humid, followed by an occasional late
afternoon thunder storm during which some idiot will go strolling on
the beach and get struck by lightning. It never failed.

I clicked off the television, and rolled over onto my stomach. I
sensed the sandman was near and gladly surrendered myself to his
boyish advances.

******

September 18, 2001

I awoke early, my dream still intact. The weather lady was having a
litter of Scorpion Fish. She was spinning in circles faster and faster
until she became a waterspout shooting fish into the sky and onto
land. People were running around trying to avoid getting stung by the
fish. Those that got stung turned into stone statues. *I gotta cut back*
on that nighttime cocoa. I threw back the sheets on my bed checking
for Scorpion Fish. You can't be too careful.

I got dressed and downstairs earlier than usual. The kids were
suspect right away, when they were met by a hot breakfast that didn't
come out of a box. I told them about Fitz, minus my run-in with
Breecher.

Tears rolled down Katie's cheeks. "Mom, who would do something
like this? Who would want to steal a pelican? What did he ever do to
them?"

"I don't know, honey. These things never seem to make sense." I
poured extra syrup on her pancakes and shoved the clear plastic cap

back on the messy, sticky top.

Kevin had already devoured two pancakes and was reaching for his third. "Tell you what, Katie Matie, how about you and me go lookin' for Fitz after breakfast? We can check out the vet, and the pet store, and call down to the State Park and see if anyone brought in a pelican to release this morning."

Katie's tears slowed to a fine misting. "You'd do that for me, Kev? You'd help me look for Fitz?"

"Sure I would. What are brothers for? We can even put up some posters around town. Maybe someone's seen him. It wouldn't be real easy to hide a pelican, especially around feeding time. You know how grumpy he gets when he's hungry!"

Katie smiled. She wiped the last tears from her eyes. "You're right. We're not doin' Fitz any good sittin' here. We need to start lookin' for him. I'll run upstairs and get my shoes. I'll be ready in just a minute."

She shoved her plate aside and took off for the stairs.

Kevin shoveled down his last pancake and finished his glass of O.J. I tossed him a wet towel to wipe his face. "Thanks, Kev. She really needed that."

He opened his hand, palm up, towards me.

I reached into my pocket and gave him a twenty. "That has to cover the whole day...posters, lunch, ice cream, and anything else that can affordably brighten her day."

"No problem, Mom. I got it covered."

At least he could still be bought. I'd hate Katie to think her brother didn't really care about her. I was hoping that my purchase today would come freely sometime down the road. Just another one of those wishful moments in a mother's life. All I had to do was live long enough to see my son's true nature break through that guise of inherent male machismo.

They trotted out the door to scout the neighborhood and put the word out on the streets...a dangerous pelican napper was loose in our community.

******

"You're notifying me of what?" Andy blurted at me.

"I want to report the theft of our pelican, F. Scott Fitzgerald." I was very precise.

Andy paced in circles, rubbing his hands through his hair. "I can't believe you even came out of your house today. Do you know what kind of trouble you're in?"

"Me? What do I have to do with all this? It's Fitz that's in trouble."

"Will you stop worrying about that stupid fish-guzzling bird! We're talking about you here. Breecher woke me up from a dead sleep demanding I get a restraining order keeping you 100 feet away from him."

I couldn't believe my ears. On the one hand I couldn't believe the little weasel had the balls to go to the law; on the other hand, where do squealing pigs go when they get scared? I figured that thought was better kept to myself.

"I don't know what you're talking about. The man is obviously overreacting to a simple misunderstanding."

"A misunderstanding?" Andy's hands went from his hair to his hips, then folded across his chest. He looked incredulous.

I tried to sound convincing while taking a seat across from his desk.

"Yes, a misunderstanding. When I found Fitz missing, I was at a loss for whom to turn to. It was late, and I knew you were off duty. Then I remembered Mr. Breecher was friends with the president of that exotic animal group visiting town. I was hoping he could give me some idea where to start looking for Fitz. I mean, who in the world would steal a pelican?

It just so happened that she was with Mr. Breecher when I went to his house. They seemed uneasy to be seen together and didn't want anything to do with helping me find Fitz. I was disappointed. I tried to convey how upset Katie would be, but they didn't want anything to do with it. They didn't seem to care who was affected by our loss."

Andy dropped his arms. "I didn't even think of Katie. She must have been heart broken."

I put on my sad face for his benefit. "Yes, she took it pretty hard. Kevin is keeping her busy today. They're putting up posters and talking to some of the community businesses."

Andy shook his head and leaned back against his desk. "I can't believe they were so unhelpful. By your account, they seemed downright belligerent."

"I think they were caught off guard. My stopping by made them very uncomfortable. If I was of a suspicious nature, I might think they were trying to hide something." I looked at my nails, trying to make it seem that I could care less what they were trying to hide.

Andy walked around the office. "So Miss Wanamaker is cozy with Breecher?"

I pushed back my cuticles, one by one, with one of my longer nails. "Well, I'm not one to start rumors. But this, Miss Wanamaker, seemed quite familiar with him when I saw them. He referred to her as Flower Face."

"Flower Face? That's pitiful."

I folded my hands into my lap. "I know. Let's not even go there. I got weird enough dreams as it is."

He looked at me for a second as though he was going to ask me about my dreams, but thought better of it. "So, you think Breecher is in cahoots with Flower Face, and they stole Fitz?"

I spied a bowl of candy on Betty's desk, got up, and walked over to it. "As much as I'd like to believe that, I think he's being used by Wanamaker." I grabbed a handful of M&M's, dropping one by one into my mouth.

"Used? What in the world does Breecher have that she'd want?"

"I don't pretend to know the whole story. But, I do know that Breecher met this woman on the Internet. They've been corresponding for the last six months and worked together to bring her exotic animal folks here for their regional meeting. Breecher's a wealth of information when it comes to this community and its animal population."

I picked out three of the yellow M& M's and popped them in my mouth. "I imagine she's been playing Breecher all these months collecting information that could be acted on once she got here for the meeting."

"Acted on?" Andy looked puzzled.

It looked like I was going to have to spell it out for him. "I think Wanamaker uses her position as president of CETEA to case out communities with exotic animals. She warms up to the animal leader in the community to acquire valuable information about the animals and their owners. Then, she plans to hold the CETEA meetings in these locations and steals the animals during her stay at the conference."

Andy's eyes widened. I could see the truth was sinking in.

He nodded. "I hate to agree with you, but I think you may be on to something." He coughed into his hand, but I could have sworn I heard him say 'beginner's luck.'

Luck or not, I knew it was killing him to admit anything I proposed was remotely possible. I didn't want to rub salt in the wound, so I tiptoed around the salt flat. "She's probably nothing more than a common thief dealing in the unlicensed sale of exotic animals. Since she's bunking down with Breecher, I suspect there's some information she wants pretty bad. My guess is you find out the latest information Breecher's passed on to Wanamaker and you'll find her next mark."

Andy headed for his desk. "I'm going to check out the last few places CETEA held their meetings and see if they had any unusual thefts during that time. If you're right, I'll be one step ahead of her this time." Andy was getting revved up. He pumped one fist into the other. "I can't wait to see her face when I catch her red-handed."

I couldn't help but notice how quickly things went from "we" to "I," but I could let this one slide. I had bigger fish to fry. "Happy to brighten your day. Maybe you can let me know if she accidentally picked up Fitz on one of her shopping sprees?"

"You bet. I'll call you as soon as I hear something." He sat down at his desk and started pulling papers from different files.

I pulled a tissue from my pocket, licked it, and tried wiping the melted, candy rainbow from the palm of my hand. "By the way, did you hear anything back from the lab about the poison used at the photo shop?"

He looked up from the papers. "I was wondering when you'd get to that. You know that's confidential. I can't share information with you on an active case."

I saw Betty, his office assistant, pulling into the parking lot. "Well, you can't blame a girl for trying." I waved goodbye as I hurried out the front door.

I met Betty as she got out of her Suburban. I couldn't help but laugh. "I don't know how you manage that beast on the streets around here."

She jumped off the seat, her five feet, neat little frame bouncing on to the cobblestones. "Oh, it's not so bad after you get used to it. The space is so wonderful. It's the only car we've ever owned that can manage all the kids, their friends, and sporting equipment." She opened the middle door and got some folders from the seat.

I shook my head in amazement. "Better you than me. By the way Betty, did you happen to hear anything about the type of poison that was used at the photo shop?"

She smiled and looked towards the office. "Andy holding out on you again? Well, I did happen to see a little something on that very issue cross my desk this morning." She shut both the doors and looked back at me. "But, it'll cost you."

I looked down the long side of her Suburban imagining it plastered with love bugs. "As long as it doesn't have anything to do with cleaning your car, we should be okay."

Now it was her turn to laugh. "Nothing that easy. I'm chairing the silent auction committee this fall for the PTA. I need you to guarantee me thirty items for the auction."

"Can they be the same thirty things?"

"No. And they have to be really good things, not just passable."

"Boy, you're tough. How much time do I have?"

"Until mid-December."

"All right. You've got a deal. Now Barter Betty, what have you got for me?"

She glanced towards the office to make sure Andy wasn't looking and pulled me behind the back of the Suburban. "When I was making copies of the report this morning, I couldn't help but notice some of the finer details. Not that I'm nosey."

I nodded in agreement with her.

She leaned up against the car. "It was very unusual. I couldn't believe it when I saw the details. I mean we've had those things in our backyard lots of times. They stink like hell, and I tell the kids to stay away from them until I can dig them up and throw them away. But who would've thought they could kill somebody?"

"That's very interesting, Betty. But what the hell are you talking about?"

"Oh, yeah. Sorry. We're talking about Phallales."

"Phalalalala's?"

"Stinkhorns."

"Stinkhorns?"

"Mushrooms! You know those orange, stinky ones that are poisonous and grow around here, especially in mulch, when we get too much rain and humidity?"

My eyebrows rose. "Sure, the ones they tell us to keep the pets and kids away from?"

"Yep, those are the ones. Remember when we had that electrical outage a couple days ago and some of the businesses didn't get their electricity back for days? Well, there was a coolant leak at the photo shop, and mold started to grow in the drip pan. The coolant was laced with the poison from the mushrooms. The combination was deadly. Once the air went back on, it only took a couple minutes for the poison to become airborne and contaminate the shop. The report said a person would lose consciousness within a few minutes. The place was a time bomb."

I shook my head back and forth. "Who would've thought something like that could ever happen?"

"Made me go home and check my drip pan and throw some bleach down there."

I smiled. "Just what I need, another way my mother can prove I'm a bad housekeeper."

Betty peered around the bumper. "Well, I'd better get in there. Andy will start wondering what's keepin' me."

I headed over to my car. "Thanks, Betty. I appreciate it."

"No, thank *you* for those fabulous auction items." She gave me a thumbs up.

I hopped in my car, blasting the air conditioning. The humidity was killing me. I sat back with my head against the rest. *If this guy wanted to take me out, why didn't he just do it with a gun, somewhere quick and easy? Why go to all the trouble to make it look like an accident? One thing was certain, I must be on the right track.* My mind began to wander. *Where was I going to come up with thirty auction items? More importantly, where the hell was my drip pan?*

Chapter Fifteen

It was my lucky day. I found a parking space under the only shade tree at the Marine Fisheries Lab. Grass was sneaking up through cracks in the black asphalt, and the lawn around the main building looked like it was two weeks overdue for a mowing. A couple of catbirds sitting on the flagpole lines were perturbed that I was passing their way. A number of people, old and young, dressed in shorts and tee shirts passed me in the parking lot. They were talking excitingly about samples they were planning on collecting today.

I was more than familiar with the lab. Katie had served as an intern the year before, counting plankton and documenting the age of fish by counting the rings in their ear bones.

The building was a typical, single-level government building that had been erected in the early seventies and hadn't been touched since. The bricks were an out-dated yellow color and the landscaping was native Floridian, which meant anything that would grow on its own with very little maintenance. The ten-acre facility sat right on the bay. In the seventies, it was probably considered off the beaten path. Today, it sat across from multi-million dollar homes and an award-winning golf course. The Federal Government owned this property, like much of the other waterfront real estate. The lab fell under the auspices of the Department of Commerce, though it did cooperative research with scientists from other agencies and universities. It also participated in a number of symbiotic programs with colleges and universities and had a county partnership agreement with the area middle schools.

The five-tiered, slatted wood sign providing the lab's name had seen better days. It looked like it was being held up by the three-foot shrubs tightly surrounding it.

By the time I reached the front door, sweat was dripping from my hairline. It felt cooler inside, but not as good as in my car. I took a right and passed by the secretary's desk. No one was there. I made my way to the library passing a number of people talking in the hallways. No one paid me any attention.

The building is over 13,000 square feet, holding numerous offices, labs, conference rooms, and storage areas. Though it doesn't look like much from the outside, it's a fully equipped, modern science facility. There are always over two dozen projects in the works. Katie had been involved in a study of the age and growth of reef fishes. There were programs on fish reproduction, shark population dynamics, marine mammal stranding, turtle nesting, bottlenose dolphin studies...and on and on.

I'd spent many an hour waiting for Katie in the marine library. Professionally, Mary Beth was known as the Technical Information Specialist, but to me she was the Librarian. She had spent many afternoons educating me about our local marine life, ecology, and the on-going work at the lab.

I didn't see Mary Beth at her desk, so I sat down and decided to wait. The space was crammed full of aisles of books. Posters were taped on the end of each aisle: *Know Your Florida Fish, Saltwater Fishing License Fee Revenues, Marine Fishes of the Gulf and South Atlantic*. Her desk was overrun with reference materials. She had a "mongo size" tape dispenser, glue bottle, and stapler. Her Rolodex was overflowing.

"Well, look what the dolphins threw back." Mary Beth maneuvered her way to a table with an armload of books and papers.

"Hi, it's good to see you." I jumped up to help her balance the stack, and managed to drop a book on my foot instead.

"Thanks. It's just reference materials for the shark guys. Everyone's trying to figure out why those three hundred black tips died last week at the west end of the bay."

"Any clues yet?" I divided the books into two stacks so they wouldn't fall over.

"They found some red tide residue in tissue samples, but nobody believes that would have killed them all." She took some papers from the top of the books and headed to her desk.

Mary Beth did not look like your typical librarian. She was

probably 5'8" and had a knockout figure. She wore her straight chestnut hair in a blunt shoulder-length cut. Her skin was perfect. "In the genes," she told me. Her only imperfection was a pair of dark rimmed eyeglasses she kept pushed up on top of her head. I'd never actually seen her use them and wondered if they weren't just a prop.

"Another marine mystery for the books?" I took a seat across from her.

She laughed. "Yeah, it's looking more and more that way. So, what made you decide to finally drag your sorry ass over here?"

I loved it when she talked dirty. "Sorry, I guess it has been a while."

"No problem. I know what it's like to have to change your life around unexpectedly. It takes a while to get back on track."

Mary Beth had gone through a nasty divorce. The judge found it in his heart to give her custody of her son, but forgot where he put his balls when it came time to set alimony and child support. Meanwhile, her husband took off for the Bahamas with a margarita waitress.

"Thanks for understanding. Maybe one day I can share the details with you." My eyes looked awkwardly around the room. Anywhere, but directly at her.

"No sweat. When the time's right, you'll know it."

I pulled a small notebook from my purse.

Mary Beth's eyes opened wide. "A notebook? Well, this is a first. You really have my interest piqued now."

"Ha, ha, very funny. I just want to be sure to get the facts straight. I figured I might need this when you start talking that librarian lingo."

She pursed her lips a little. "I'll do my best to keep to the English language, the butchered American version, of course."

"Thanks. Now the reason I'm here has to do with that John Doe who was found in the bay last week."

"I heard about that. You were right there, weren't you?"

"Too close for comfort. Anyway, the news said last night that the Medical Examiner suspected marine poisoning by a Scorpion Fish. What do you think about that?"

"I heard that on the news, too. It's not impossible, but highly improbable. There are a couple of species of Scorpion Fish here in our area, but they aren't deadly. Don't get me wrong, you'd know if you were stung by one, and you'd never forget it, but it wouldn't kill you. Besides, he was found in open water. The natural habitat for these guys is rocky areas."

"Couldn't he have been stung near shore, then his body pulled out with the tide?"

"Anything's possible. I think they're reaching a bit, but maybe they have more information then they're letting on to."

I sat there twiddling the pen between my fingers. "Do you have any idea how much poison it would take from one of these guys to kill a man?"

Mary Beth shook her head, "You mean like if he fell into a school of them and got stung repeatedly?"

I nodded.

"Not realistic. Plus there'd be multiple stab marks, and the toxins would have left discolored marks around the wounds. If I remember right the guy was fully clothed, so he had some protection."

I tapped the pen against the notebook, trying to think of another possibility. Mary Beth got an idea first.

"Now, there's an even further remote possibility." She got up and disappeared down one of the aisles, returning with a massive textbook. "This is the bible of *Poisonous and Venomous Marine Animals of the World*." She turned the pages to the index, running her finger down the list under Scorpion Fish. She turned to the middle of the book.

"What are we looking for?" I asked, looking over her shoulder.

"Here we go." She settled her finger on a nasty picture of a Stonefish.

"The Synanceia Verrucosa, better known as the Stonefish, is a member of the Scorpion Fish family. He's the most venomous member of the family, some believe one of the most venomous fish in the world." Her index finger skimmed down the page. "The venom is contained in twenty six glands lying below the skin. Ducts lead away from the glands to thirteen sharp spines on the creature's back. It raises its spines at the slightest disturbance. The venom is involuntarily expelled when the spine is pressed upon. The spines have been known to penetrate sandals."

I stared at the ugly little bugger. He was greenish-brown and looked like a big stone. His eyes were deeply set in bony hollows of the head. I read down the page, my eyes catching on the phrase, "hypodermic-like projections capable of piercing a shoe."

"This is one bugger you wouldn't want to mess around with." Mary Beth shut the book.

"So, why couldn't he have stepped on one of those?"

"He'd have to have mighty long legs. These guys are found in Australia."

"Do you ever find species in this area that don't belong here?"

"Sure. It's not unusual for eggs to get swept into the Gulf Stream and deposited into our area. You ever notice the variety of tropical fish we get over at the inlet swimming area in the summer months?"

"Yeah, that's a great place to go snorkeling."

"Well, most of those aren't indigenous to this area. They live in the warm waters through the summer, but unless they manage to migrate farther south during the winter months, they die off."

"So, you think something like that is possible for a Stonefish?"

"No."

"Just, no? Not, maybe? Or could be?

"No, just no. It's too far off base for me to believe."

I closed the notebook, and grabbed my purse. "I guess that's that then."

"Do you mind me asking, why the intense interest in the death of a John Doe?"

I took two pieces of gum from my purse and handed her one. "When the time's right, I'll be sure to tell you."

Chapter Sixteen

I hated going to the morgue at lunchtime. It's not like I go to the morgue every day or that I'd even been once during the past ten years, but I'd been there enough times during my Patrol days. It's not something you easily forget.

The morgue and Medical Examiner's Office were located in a simple square looking building that used to be a fish processing plant. The huge lock-in freezers made it a no brainer for the county to purchase and renovate for the morgue facility. The property was on high ground and didn't have many residential neighbors, both important criteria for selecting a morgue location.

The road wound around for a few miles, running along property owned by the airport. There were a number of warehouses and commercial manufacturing offices lining the sides of the road.

I pulled into the black asphalt parking lot and took a space near the decorative plank fence. The Crepe Myrtles were bulging with new growth, and the tall pines were green against the blue sky. I was hoping for a little shade from the trees, and opened the windows up front to keep the air circulating. It wasn't unheard of for car windows to crack from the intense summer heat.

This was a newer building with tidy landscaping. I looked a little closer at the grass and saw dollar weed growing. A nemesis to any grass connoisseur, it was nice to know the ME's Office wasn't immune to the same trials and tribulations of us ordinary Harriette Homeowners.

The building was a one story tan stucco with wheelchair access. A porch covered one side of the building where a solitary picnic table sat. There was a loading dock farther down the side of the building. In the far back, I could see a tall, wired fence and a mobile home on the other side. I often wondered who had the guts to live behind the morgue? Probably the same guy who forced the county to put up a "No Skateboarding" sign by the loading dock.

A large, rectangular stucco sign designated this building as the location of the Medical Examiner's Office for the Fourteenth District. I happen to know that the Fourteenth District is no walk in the park. The District is made up of thirty-nine hundred square miles of property, populated by 260,000 permanent residents, and another 240,000 tourists during the summer season.

The current ME, Hunter Taggert, had been around since my days in the Patrol. He had a tough job. I remembered when he first started. He'd been the Acting Director for over a year and was waiting for his appointment to Director. Until the title change came, he worked twenty four/seven as the only full time ME for the district. That meant handling about 400 bodies a year. He was director now and had some part-time help, but the body count and the hours hadn't changed much.

I headed for the front entrance, and buzzed just once. That was the secret handshake. If you buzzed more than once, the staff thought it was somebody dropping off a body at the dock, and they went rushing for the back door leaving you standing at the front. Allie Wade, the Director of Operations, met me at the door.

"Why, Tess Titan, haven't seen you in this neck of the woods for quite a time."

"Hi ya, Allie. No, I haven't been in the business of corpus delecti in quite some time." I walked over to the records window and signed in the Visitor Log Book, noticing a couple of local law enforcement officers had been by earlier. The book was more a resource tool than a precaution. If a body was diagnosed with Meningitis, everyone in the facility had to be put on antibiotics, including visitors.

I took a quick look around the outer waiting area. Nothing had changed. It was still decorated in retro sixties...Naugahyde sofa and chairs, two tables with white, Formica tops, a fifty-gallon fish tank growing someone's science project, and the best magazine collection in the county...*People, Yachting, Coastal Living, Smithsonian, Highlights, Nickelodeon, Glamour, National Geographic.* If the ME's office didn't have it, it probably wasn't worth having.

I followed Allie through the double doors and down a hallway to her office. I peeked into Hunter's office as we went by. He wasn't in.

"He's finishing a case in the suite. You want to wait in my office until he's done?"

"Yeah, I think I'd prefer that. Thanks." I took a seat opposite her desk.

Allie was a tall, fit, red-haired tomboy. Her hair was her signature mark. At first, I thought she had a dressing table full of wigs. But I came to know through the grapevine that it was all her own hair. She would change the color a couple times each year, always keeping it red, but changing the tone darker or lighter. I suppose it was her way of brightening the workplace.

"So, what brings you to our humble abode?" Allie moved a pile of reports from the center of her desk over to one side.

Her hair was straight now, shoulder length, sporting that purplely undertone that was so popular. "I have some ideas about that John Doe brought in from the Pirate Ship that I wanted to toss around with Hunter."

"That was an odd one. I imagine the body will be sittin' here on ice for the next couple of months before the county buries him."

"Oh! I thought I'd read something about an anonymous donor providing all the money for the burial. Wasn't he supposed to be buried this weekend?"

"Well, the television got part of it right. There was an anonymous donor, but there won't be a burial for a few months."

"No burial? Does that mean Hunter thinks it was a suspicious death?"

"I don't think he has any doubt about it being suspicious. He just can't get his hands around this one. It's really bugging him. He won't let go of it. He's in there now checking over the body again."

I sat forward in the chair and swallowed deeply, kicking myself mentally for what I was about to say. "Do you think he'd mind if I joined him?"

Allie chuckled. "Tess, my friend, if you think you can stand on your own two feet in there and have a conversation while he's elbow deep inside that guy, be my guest." She waved her hand toward the door.

I stood to leave. My legs felt like they might collapse underneath me.

"Remember if you can't take it, get out of there. I was working painting the outside of the house yesterday, and my back is killing me. The last thing I want to do is drag your sorry ass out of there."

I laughed. "No problem, it's like riding a bike, right? You never forget?"

I walked up to the double doors, and took a deep breath before I pushed through them into the autopsy suite. Hunter was on the other side of the room leaning over the body. I slipped on a protective suit, pair of gloves, and a paper mask. Finally exhaling when I couldn't hold my breath any longer, I waited a minute to be sure I wouldn't faint from the smell of formaldehyde and antiseptic.

I walked slowly across the room, reminding myself to put one foot in front of the other. I tried not to look around, but the glint from the stainless steel pulled my head from side to side. There were four stations. Each had its own sink, set of tools, and various scales. I knew the stainless steel gurneys were in the back room. Bodies transferred from the EMT vehicles to the gurneys were rolled into the suite and weighed before examinations were given.

My gaze fixed on the gurney in front of Hunter. I couldn't help but notice it was permanently slanted toward the sink. This was done so body fluids drained directly into the sink. There were no fluids today, so I knew he'd completed the autopsy. But I still had to blink back the image from my brain a number of times before I could take the final steps.

I stood next to Hunter, averting my eyes as best I could. He wasn't what you'd expect. Because he was six foot four, my head barely reached above his armpits. His dark hair was pulled back into a pigtail, sporting a bit of gray. From under the apron, I could see his Nike tennis shoes and Hilfiger pants. He turned and looked down at me. I could tell he was grinning behind the white mask.

"I can't believe my eyes. Did Hell freeze over when I wasn't looking?"

I was glad I had to look up to talk to him. It kept me from having to look at what his hands were doing.

"A bit shocking, I know. I even surprised myself."

"Must be something pretty important to bring you back to this side of the business."

"Unfortunately, you're right. This is really close to home, close to family."

His eyes blinked a few times and he nodded. "Let me get these organs put back and we can talk." He took plastic bags filled with organs and started placing them back in body cavities.

"Actually, I think this 'unknown' may have played a part in my recent troubles."

Hunter stopped moving the bags and looked at me with increasing interest. "I'd like to hear what you have to say. I haven't had much luck. This guy makes no sense. He has no identification. His clothes and haircut are foreign, probably Italian. His fingerprints aren't on file, and I haven't found any dental comparisons on his x-rays. I've checked his DNA against the military lab in D.C. —no luck there either. And to top it off, no one has called in a missing persons report. You think you have something to go on, I'd love to hear it."

I felt like a minion, way out of my comfort level. "Just an idea." I coughed into my mask, trying to clear my throat. "I heard on the news you think he was killed by a Scorpion Fish?"

"He's got the poison of that genus in his system. But it doesn't make sense." He started putting the organ bags back in place. "That fish doesn't exist here in these waters, at least not the kind that could kill someone, like this." He pointed to the man on the table.

"But a Stonefish could, right? And it's in the same family as the Scorpion Fish."

He nodded, showing a bit more confidence in my ability. "Sure, a Stonefish would do the trick, but again not local to these waters."

"Can you show me the wound?"

He moved down to the end of the table and motioned to the right foot. I moved down beside him.

"Here." He pointed to the artery on top of the foot. There was discoloration and swelling around the wound.

I stood with my head cocked to one side for a second. "Just one wound?"

"Yes. I've looked over and over. There's only one wound."

"Isn't it kind of odd that he got stung on top of his foot? I mean, this fish is known for burying in the sand and minding its own business. People usually get stung when they inadvertently step on them. Don't you think this entry wound is unusual?"

"I think it's very unusual"

"And don't you think it's suspicious that the wound is directly in the artery?"

"Very suspicious."

I looked more closely. There was a deep indentation that looked like someone or something had stabbed the victim.

Hunter confirmed my thoughts. "The fish leaves a stab mark where the poison is introduced. The discoloration of the skin is a result of the poison."

I was about to look away, when my mental light bulb flashed. It doesn't flash often anymore, but I still had the sense to recognize it.

"Hunter, could the poison have been introduced in another way?"

His eyes became dark and penetrating, deep in thought. "You mean by ingestion?"

I looked at him smiling. "Or how about as simple as through a needle?"

His eyes lit up. "A hypodermic needle, yes!" He grabbed the magnifying glass from the next table and scrutinized the wound. "I think you're right, Tess. The wound could have been purposely disrupted to try to hide the entry wound of the needle." He straightened, and leaned back against the sink.

"What's the matter?" I said, worried that we'd hit another dead end.

"If we're right, we have a methodical, heartless killer on our hands. This John Doe died a very painful death, probably over a number of hours. The injection would have caused intense pain and rapid swelling of his foot and leg. If he was lucky, he lost consciousness before the irregular breathing and drop in blood pressure occurred. Within a few hours, paralysis would have set in. The killer could have saved him at any time. There was an antivenin developed in the late 50s."

My head was feeling light, and my stomach churned. "I've got to get out of here, Hunter."

He jumped up and put his long arm around me. "I'm sorry, Tess. I shouldn't have gone into the details with you."

I leaned on him. It felt good to be taken care of. "I wouldn't have missed it for the world. Just, maybe next time can we have our chat in your office?"

"You bet. You think there's going to be a next time?" We passed through the suite doors back into the world of the living. The air smelled fresh.

A cup of cold water and a Pepto Bismol seemed to bring me back to my senses.

"He was poisoned," I said rather matter-of-factly, not sure if I even believed what I was saying.

"That seems to have been the weapon of choice." Hunter leaned back in an old leather, executive chair, resting his feet on top of his desk. The stuffing was coming out of the bottom seat cushion.

I'd taken a chair in the corner of the room. I didn't feel comfortable sitting on the sofa. I knew it had served as his bed for many years until he got more office help. "So, you're telling me someone overpowered this guy, tied him up, shot him full of Stonefish poison, and dumped him in the bay to die?"

Hunter clasped his hands behind his head. "That about sums it up."

Before I could stop myself, the word tumbled out. "Why?"

"What do you mean?"

"I mean, why would someone kill somebody like that?"

"Modus of operation."

"You think we got someone here that has a habit of killing people using a similar method each time?"

"You said it, Sherlock. Not me. Now, you said this was affecting your family. You want to shed some light on that for me?"

I sank back in my chair, dropping my head over the back. It was all coming together. The body on the Pirate Ship, my Italian mugger, the stinky mushroom poison—it was like a hundred-piece puzzle in my head and I only had the outside edges figured out. I filled Hunter in on my assumption that these three events had a single common denominator—someone killing people with poisons to obtain something they think my family or I is in possession of. He thought my idea was plausible enough to put the legal arms of the law into motion.

"Do me a favor? When you talk with Sheriff Hagen, play down my involvement in all this."

He agreed and invited me to join him for a pizza out on the picnic table. I was looking for any excuse not to have to eat at the morgue, when my cell phone rang.

"Where are you?" A stern, female voice berated me from the other end of the line.

I didn't care for the tone, regardless of who it happened to be. "I'm at the morgue. Where are you?" I thought that might quiet her down. No such luck.

"I'm sitting here at a banquet for a hundred people that's ready to start in an hour. A banquet where my daughter is supposed to be sitting by my side showing her familial affections and making herself available for photo opportunities with her mother. An event that could make me look like an utter fool since it's a Mother-Daughter banquet!"

Chapter Seventeen

It was four o'clock. I had forty-five minutes to look beautiful and race to my mother's side so she wouldn't look like an idiot. Not an easy trick—the looking beautiful and arriving on time—I knew nothing could prevent my mother from looking like an idiot.

I fixed my face and hair as well as possible and slipped into an Ann Taylor sleeveless pink sheath dress. Those extra pounds made it hell to get the zipper closed. I squeezed my feet into the matching strapped shoes, and instantly remembered the pain I'd endured wearing this same outfit to a wedding a few months before. It was too late to look for something else. I grabbed the matching short jacket, threw my lipstick and driver's license into a matching bag and headed downstairs.

Before leaving, I went through a quick mental checklist: The kids are with Nell having dinner and watching a movie, check; I've got my keys, cell phone, and some money, check; I turned the curling iron off and put the meat I'd defrosted back in the fridge, check. I took one last look in the mirror and cursed myself for not having the guts to cancel out.

I raced across the county and arrived at the Water's Edge Resort with minutes to spare. The valet leaped out of the way as I came to a screeching halt and jumped out of the car. I threw him the keys. "It's got a curse on it. If you don't treat it right, I can't be responsible for what it might do to you."

He laughed and looked uncertainly at me. I gave him one of those "No really. I'm not kidding" looks and ran through the lobby doors.

I knew my way around. Every event that had any backing whatsoever was held at the Water's Edge. There were six ballrooms. I didn't remember which one the banquet was being held in, so I read the signs outside of each doorway. "Gardening Club," "Chamber of Commerce," and in front of door number three "Citizens for the Ethical Treatment of Exotic Animals (CETEA)" was Breecher pacing back and forth.

"Why, Mr. Breecher, what a coincidence to see you here."

He stopped dead in his tracks. "Mrs. Titan, a mistake I'm sure. You can't possibly be attending this meeting."

I looked closely at the sign. "Why, Wendell, I'm surprised to think that you would consider me unsuitable fodder for your little ho-down."

He squirmed, and fidgeted with his tie. "As much as I'd enjoy continuing this conversation, I must make myself available for a more professional clientele."

"Well, you might want to be careful, I don't think it's legal to solicit in such a public place."

His jaw dropped. I turned and walked towards the ladies room. I really didn't need to pee, but I did need to prepare myself mentally to be in the same room with my mother. Upon entering the powder room, I found I'd merely taken myself from the frying pan and thrown myself into the fire.

"Why, Tess Titan, I haven't seen you in ages. What in the world has become of you? How is Kevin? Katie must be growing like a weed by now. Does she still have that...what was it? Oh yes, pelican. Does she still have that pelican?"

I stood face to face with the county's star gossip. "Ferdy, so nice to see you again. I just need to grab a tissue, and I'll be out of your way."

"Oh, honey, you're not in my way at all! I'm stuck here waiting until our speaker arrives for the CETEA meeting, the acclaimed Miss Bea Wanamaker. Perhaps you've heard of her? She's been visiting our town on and off now for the last number of months, helping us to set up a CETEA Chapter in this area. While waiting for her to arrive, we've been listening ad nauseum to Bill Brannon drone on about termites and their mating habits."

I almost felt bad for her. Grabbing a few tissues, I made for the door. "Well, I certainly hope she comes soon. I know how distressing it can be to wait for someone...like my mother is for me right now. I really must go. Give my regards to your family."

I hurried out the door, and started reading the meeting room doors again. "Cheer Squad," and finally "The Walton County Women's Club." *Oh boy, I knew one thing for sure, whoever planned this event was going to be on the clean-up committee next year. Who in their right mind would put mother's event next to the Cheer Squad Awards Banquet? This was definitely a disaster in the making.*

I pinned my name badge on to my jacket and hurried through the door. Mother was busy greeting people table by table. There must have been twelve round tables with eight guests at each table. Her radar picked me up immediately. I smiled and waved. She motioned for me to join her.

"Tess. I'm so glad you could make it. I know it must have been horribly difficult finding a babysitter for the children this afternoon. You really do spoil your mother!" All of this was said just loud enough for the table of ladies to hear. She turned back towards the ladies. "Everyone, I'd like you to meet my lovely daughter, Tess. She has two children at home who keep her very busy, but she always makes time for her mother." The ladies smiled and nodded approvingly.

I pasted a smile across my face and kept nodding like a toy Chihuahua in a car window. The other daughters in the room wore the same pasted-on smile. They were probably making grocery lists in their minds and wondering if they'd turned off their curling irons.

After meeting every senior lady in the county, mother ushered me up to the head table. The other candidates and their daughters were already seated and had started in on their hearts of palm salads. I kept my head down and tried to be invisible.

The bread was too good to pass up.

"Mother, will you pass me another roll? Please."

She raised one of her parental eyebrows. "Tess, dear. Do you think there's enough room for you and one more roll in that dress? You need to leave some room for the main course, honey."

I could feel my cheeks burning with embarrassment. I turned to the other ladies at the table, "Mothers. They never know when to cut the cord." Everyone laughed a little uneasily. I reached across Mother and got a roll. I didn't feel like eating it, but now I had to. I lathered it with butter and ate it all up, licking my fingers at the end. Mother sat there trying to ignore me, but I could see the back of her neck was red...a sure sign I'd gotten to her. I'm not sure it was worth the effort. I felt like I was going to bust the zipper out of my dress.

The entrée was veal scallopini with asparagus. Mother took one bite of each and pushed the food aside. She went on campaigning around the table. I cleaned my plate. I tried to leave one asparagus tip on the plate, but it looked silly. Dessert was served while the speaker gave the history of the Women's Club and introduced the ballot of candidates for the various board positions.

"Last but not least, as I'm sure you're all aware, our very own Eudora Wellsley, of the Birmingham Wellsleys, is running unopposed for President. We all know Eudora and all the wonderful things she's done for the club over the years, so this year I'd like to do things a little differently." I could see Mother's back stiffen. She didn't like to do things differently.

"This year, I'd like to ask the daughters of the candidates to come up and say a few words about their mothers and why they think they should be elected to these positions." There was a low murmur from the audience. Next thing I knew, my name came over the loud speaker.

"Tess Titan, will you please be first to speak about your mother, Eudora?

I took my finger out of the whipped topping on my strawberry shortcake and wiped it on my napkin. Mother and I turned and stared at one another. I smiled, teeth clenched. I tried to talk without making my lips move.

"Mother, you didn't tell me I'd have to say something. I didn't prepare anything."

"I had no idea they would do this, Tess. Do you think I'd ever put myself in this position on purpose?" she replied, with the same clenched teeth hidden behind her candidate smile.

"Thanks for the confidence, Mother."

I pushed my chair back and made my way to the podium. The mike was too short. I pulled it towards me causing deafening feedback. "Sorry," I said as I backed away from the podium and leaned inward toward the mike with my hands behind my back. Just about then, the Cheer Squad started demonstrating their winning routines. Their voices boomed through the partition, each syllable clearly discernible from the next. There was some laughter in the room, while the event planner slid down as far as she could in her chair.

"It seems I'm competing with award-winning spirit revelers today, so I'll make my comments short." There was a little more laughter.

136

Mother looked like that picture of the farm woman holding a pitchfork.

"My mother, Eudora Wellsley. Well, you've certainly put me on the spot. I don't suppose anyone out there would like to trade places with me?" I heard a few chuckles from the back of the room, from other daughters I suspected. The mothers didn't look too impressed.

My mind was scrambling. What could I say? The only thing that came to mind was a favorite book I used to read, *All I Really Need To Know I Learned In Kindergarten*.

"I'm joking of course. Anyone who knows my mother is aware of the qualities and strengths she brings to this position. You won't find another candidate more capable or diligent at handling the responsibilities this job requires. She has lived in this community for more than thirty years. She's witnessed its achievements and shared in its growing pains. She offers unselfishly of herself wherever her time and talents can be utilized. One of my first memories of Mother was collecting toys for the Christmas Toys for Tots program. Her work has taught me many things over the years. It has been some of her simplest thoughts that serve me on a daily basis. Some of my favorites are: *share everything; play fair; put things back where you found them; clean up your own messes; don't take things that aren't yours; say you're sorry when you hurt somebody; live a balanced life; and most important be aware of wonder*." All I really need to know, I learned from my mother. And I'm sure you'll find her straightforward, honest way of doing things a breath of fresh of air. Thank you."

The crowd applauded. Mother looked dazed. My stomach was doing somersaults. I was sure I was going to spew asparagus tips all over the stage. I hated lying, especially for my mother. And that is just what I'd done. When I returned to the table, Mother looked at me in some sick kind of bonding fashion and patted my hands.

"That was lovely, dear. I had no idea you felt that way about me. You brought back such wonderful memories for me."

I couldn't help wonder what planet this woman was on? What memories? I'd made it all up! Leave it to my mother to turn fantasy into reality.

I patted Mother's hands back. "Believe what you need to. I'm leaving now." I leaned over and whispered into her ear, "Never ask me to something like this again, or I'll be forced to tell the simple truth next time."

She smiled, "How nice of you to say so, Tess. I know you need to get going. Say goodnight to my darling grandchildren for me."

The valet saw me coming through the lobby and took off to get my car. I waited outside the lobby doors looking at the full parking lot. *Business must be good.* All of a sudden, I saw a black Beemer parked in the lot. The valet pulled up and handed me the keys.

I made a few hand motions in front of his body. "You're now cleansed of any bad luck the car may have left on you."

"Thanks, ma'am. I know my mom will be glad you cleansed me."

I couldn't help but smile. "Say, did you happen to notice who pulled up in the black Beemer over there." I pointed toward the car.

He looked over in that direction. "Can't say for certain. There were about a dozen folks who came scrambling in all about the same time, including an older lady with a holier-than-thou attitude. Normally, I wouldn't have paid her any attention, but she said she was a speaker and was running very late."

"So, you're fairly certain it was an older woman who made those remarks?"

"Oh yeah. No doubt there. I haven't seen anyone younger than fifty today."

I held myself back from boxing his ears. I certainly didn't look fifty, and the fact he couldn't tell the difference proved to me his facts couldn't be completely trusted. But I'd still bet my last Canadian penny that the ill-natured spinster was Wanamaker. I hated to think what might have made her so late for her public appearance. What made me even more curious was if Breecher knew why she was late to the meeting? He seemed genuinely concerned that she hadn't arrived, maybe even embarrassed. It was his reputation on the line if she didn't show.

I gave him a dollar tip and pulled the VW up next to the back of the Beemer. I got out, and ran my hand along under the bumper. Aha! The gum was there. Wanamaker had been at the music show, and she was attending the CETEA function at the conference center today. I'd never seen her driving a car so I couldn't be sure the Beemer was hers. Could Wanamaker have been strong enough to knock out the sales clerk at the shooting range?

I pondered this last question while I made my way back across the county. Halfway home, my cell phone rang.

"Hello?"

"Tessa, its Nell."

"Nell? Is everything all right?" My hands tightened around the steering wheel.

"Oh, yes, dear. Everything's fine. I just thought you should know, UPS delivered the Contessa's book just a little bit ago. My neighbor called so I went right over to my house to pick it up."

"I'll be there as quick as I can. Be sure the doors are locked."

"Tessa, dear?"

"Yes, Nell?"

"There's something else."

I found myself holding my breath. "What is it, Nell?"

"The book binder found a sealed envelope behind the front cover. It hasn't been opened."

"Wait till I get there, I'm only ten minutes away." I put the phone down on the seat beside me, put the car in fifth gear, and hoped a wandering deer didn't jump in front of the car.

The outdoor light was on when I pulled up into the driveway. I could hear music playing from the kids' bedrooms. Nell was sitting in the sunroom with a cup of tea and the book in her lap.

I sat in the lounge chair next to her. "Did you find anything in the book that would give us a clue about what's going on?"

She looked up from the book. "No, dear. I've been looking through it and reading the comments the Contessa scribbled in the corners, but nothing seems out of the ordinary."

Nell handed me the envelope. It was yellowed from age. Nothing was written on the outside. I lifted the back corner. The seal broke away easily. I carefully pulled out two sheets of paper folded in half. They were hand-written in a clear, strong style. I reviewed the pages for several minutes.

Pablo Picasso – Still Life with Mandolin, 1913, Oil on Canvas, 3'10" x 2'8", hidden in Spreuerbrucke, Lucerne, Switzerland. In the center of this narrow, covered bridge is a small 16th Century chapel. The chapel has a truss system, which supports the roof. The canvas is hidden in the dark trusses. The space is difficult to access and not open to visitors.

Paul Cézanne – Still Life with Apples and Blue and White Vase,

1877, Oil on Canvas, 8.5" x 12 ¾", hidden at the Betlemska kaple (Bethlehem Chapel), Prague, in the stair risers of the 15th Century pulpit. Remove the end plank of the fourth riser from the floor, you will find the painting inside.

Rembrandt – Portrait of Saskia in a Feathered Hat, 1639, Oil on Canvas, 3'5" x 3'5", hidden at Oude Kerk (old church) in Amsterdam. This is Amsterdam's oldest church. It retains its original bell tower and some of the original windows. Rembrandt's beloved first wife, Saskia, is buried here. The painting is hidden in the circular stairway leading up to the old bell tower. Remove a series of interior wall stones on the second step from the top. The painting is hidden in a small cavity inside the wall.

Van Eyck – Madonna and Child Enthroned, 1433, Tempera and Oil on Canvas, 35.5" x 25.5", hidden in the Syon House outside of London. In the anteroom, you will find a large walk-in fireplace that was bricked up and is now faced by an elaborate iron grate. The painting is rolled up and hidden inside the original chimney.

Francois Boucher – Venus at Her Dressing Table, 1754, Oil on Canvas, 56" x 45", hidden in the Highgate Cemetery outside of London. The cemetery was abandoned in the early 20th century and is derelict. The painting is buried at the site marked by twin headstones under the name "Keller."

Hans Holbein the Younger – Portrait of a Young Nobleman, 1534, Oil on Canvas, 37" x 29", hidden below the San Clemente, Rome, basilica in the Mithraic temple (crypt) in a sarcophagus. The sarcophagus is covered with a bas-relief carving of stylized birds flanking an abstracted flowering tree. This part of the church is rarely visited and has long been neglected.

Camille Pissarro – Place du Theatre Francais, 1897, Oil on Canvas, 29" x 36", hidden on the grounds of the Villa de Castello outside Florence in the grotto near the marble statue of Hercules. The walls are encrusted with shells and rocks. The canvas is in a small niche near the floor on the north wall. It has been plastered over to resemble the rest of the wall. You will find this spot marked with an upside down scallop shell.

Cimabue, Christ on the Cross, 1290, Tempera on Wood, 12'7" x 7' 4", hidden in a mid-19th century block house (No.15) on a side street off Rue Saint-Louis-en-Ile. The altarpiece had to be disassembled to fit between the floor and stone foundation in the first floor bedchamber.

Egon Schiele – Self-Portrait, Oil on Canvas, 42" x 48", hidden in the attic of the Hotel de Ville (Town Hall) in Brussels. A tight, winding staircase provides access to the attic. The painting is nestled between the trusses and supports in the middle of the north wall.

Emile Nolde – Christ in the Temple, Oil on Canvas, 20" x 30", hidden in the 13th century ruins of the Hore Abbey at the base of the Rock of Cashel in Ireland. The painting is buried under the center stones of the nave.

The wheels were cranking. My master's in fine art was kicking in. I looked over the list a half dozen times. The pieces started making sense.

"Is it something important, Tessa? Is it a clue to why such dreadful things have been happening?"

I set the letter down in my lap.

"Tessa, you look like you've just seen a ghost. What does it say?"

I took a sip of Nell's tea and lay back in the lounger. I took a deep breath and exhaled long and hard.

"Nell, we're in more trouble than I thought."

"Start at the beginning, Tessa. We'll work things out from there."

I handed Nell the piece of paper. "This is a list of famous art objects, probably stolen from private collections or museums during World War II. If memory serves me right, these items and many others were to be incorporated into the grand new art museum in Berlin that Hitler was planning on building to house the war booty he amassed."

Nell put her glasses on and started reading the list. "That doesn't sound so bad, dear. A list is nothing more than a list. You or I could have written that with a little help from a history book."

"AND...it gives the locations of where these pieces have been hidden."

Nell read down the list. She slid the glasses off her nose. "I guess that's not good?"

"Very good for the person who's been searching for this information. Very bad for the people who have the information."

Nell put her glasses in her lap. Do you think this is why that Romeo man wants the book? Do you think he knows this list is in it?"

I let loose another deep sigh. "I have no idea, Nell."

We sat in silence for a few minutes. The kids had turned off their music. A red squirrel was up in one of the hardwoods chattering away at a cat taking a short cut through our yard.

"What are you going to do, Tess?"

"I think we should give the book to Romeo and keep the list."

"I see. You think we should keep playing this game?"

I got up and looked out the window more closely at the squirrel. He'd found a nut and was busily gnawing away at his treasure in a shell. "I know that as long as we have this list, we have bargaining power. Without it, all of us are dispensable."

Nell left the book and list with me and went home for the evening. It took me several minutes before I was ready to make the phone call to Jack. It was late. I dialed his number. When he answered on the third ring, his voice was sharp and alert.

"Hello? Who's this?"

"Jack, it's Tess."

"Tess! I'm glad you called. We need to talk."

"No, you need to listen. I've got the book. I'm ready to make the drop to Romeo."

"How did you know about Romeo?"

"Let's not backpedal, Jack. I know he wants the book. I know you're getting pictures in return, and I know it will buy the safety of my family."

There was a long, silent pause on the other end of the phone.

"Like I said, Tess, we need to talk."

Chapter Eighteen

September 19, 2001

I agreed to hold off on giving Romeo the book until after Jack and I had a chance to talk. I felt I owed him that much. Katie and I were scheduled to play in a croquet tournament in the morning. I told Jack I'd meet him at Josie's for lunch.

I rolled out of bed at 7:30 a.m. sharp, did a few stretches, and tried to regain my former croquet-winning physique. After a few minutes of stretching, I realized it was going to be an Advil week.

Katie and I started walking over to the croquet grounds at 8:30 am. The tournament was starting at nine o'clock. That gave me thirty minutes of quality time with my daughter.

Katie grabbed a stick and ran it along the outside of the white picket fences. It made a comforting thwacking sound.

"Mom, can girls marry girls?"

My mouth dropped open, but nothing came out.

Katie kept running her stick over the slats, adding a hop and jump over any cracks in the sidewalk.

"Mom?" She looked back over her shoulder at me.

I thought I knew what to say. But the words kept stopping on my lips. She'd caught me off guard. I tried to sidetrack the conversation. "Why all the interest in marriage?"

"I was just wonderin'. It just seems like moms and dads don't get along very well and that maybe moms and moms might get along better.

So much for sidetracking. I moved straight into self-preservation mode. " Hmmmm. I'd never thought of that. I don't know, though. Then there'd be two moms asking you if you'd done your chores. Two moms telling you to do your homework. Two moms asking you to wash the car. Two moms...."

"Okay, okay, I get the idea. Two moms may not be such a good idea."

We spent the rest of the walk kicking prickly sweet gum balls, like little soccer balls, down the sidewalk. It was a beautiful morning. The humidity was sleeping late, and a storm front from last night had cleared out some of the heat. The sky was crystal blue.

I could hear the chattering of voices at the grounds from down the street. The croquet competition was a popular event. It didn't matter if you were old or young, athletic or klutzy, everyone enjoyed a good game of croquet. The competition had grown each year, as new categories were added. This was the first year for doubles. Katie had me sign up months ago to be her partner. We'd spent hours knocking around croquet balls in the backyard.

Katie was our captain. She'd drawn first-ups last week at the lottery. She and I would be competing with Mr. and Mrs. Seaborne; an elderly retired couple from Alabama who vacationed here on the weekends.

The courses looked very professional. There were three 50' x 100' rectangular grass lawns marked at the corners with colored flags, corner pegs and bordered by white lines. The playing courses were set up in a standard double-diamond configuration using nine wickets. Katie and I were decked out in the prerequisite white attire, complete with rubber-soled, flat-heeled tennies.

"Titans and Seabornes, course number one," the coordinator called out into the crowd.

Course number one was at the far side of the fields, nearest the woods. A referee was waiting for us at the course. "Good morning, all. Are we ready to play some croquet?"

"Yes!" We all responded in an early morning chorus.

"Will the captains please approach?"

Katie and Mrs. Seaborne walked up to the referee.

"Youth before beauty," the referee said to Mrs. Seaborne. "That means, you get to call the coin toss, Katie. Are you ready?"

"You bet," Katie said.

The referee tossed the coin into the air.

"Heads!" Katie yelled.

The coin dropped. The referee leaned over to pick it up. "Heads, it is. Katie, which color ball would you like?"

"Blue! I want blue." Katie jumped up and down with excitement. "That means I get to go first, Mom!"

I couldn't help but laugh. "That's right, Katie. Way to go."

The rules called for me to get the black ball and the Seabornes the red and yellow ones.

Katie set her ball in front of the starting stake and struck it solidly with her wooden mallet. The ball zipped through the first two hoops.

Katie turned to me, "Mom, two more turns, right?"

I did a thumbs-up. "That's right, honey. Two more turns."

Her first hit sent the ball sailing. It stopped about six inches from the hoop, but at an angle.

"You can do it, Katie. Remember how we practiced?"

She held her mallet firmly. She looked at the hoop, then at the ball. Holding her breath, she took a swing. The ball went through the hoop.

"Mom, I did it! I did it!" She jumped up and down to the other side of the wicket.

I clapped my hands. "Good for you, Katie. Keep going."

She had one more turn. She smacked the ball hard, setting herself up for a good next shot. She took her colored clip and attached it to the crown of the wicket. "Did you see how far I got, Mom?"

"You betcha. Now let's see how Mrs. Seaborne does."

Mrs. Seaborne would have made a perfect bowling pin, not that I was in any condition to be making remarks. The white visor helped shield her fair complexion from the sun and kept her short hair pulled back away from her face. She sashayed up to the starting stake, crossed both sets of fingers up in the air, and said some incantation for luck before she took her swings. Within a half-hour of play, it was obvious Katie was beating all of us. Mrs. Seaborne had taken a more offensive approach to playing and was going after Katie.

Her ball knocked up against Katie's. "Yes! That's a roquet. I get two bonus shots." She used one of her shots to hit Katie's ball towards the woods. Then took off toward her wicket.

Katie looked a little dismayed. "Don't worry, Katie bear, you're way ahead. Besides, I need to catch up some. You can't win without me."

Katie walked over towards her ball. I was concentrating on my next shot.

"Ahhhhhhh!" Katie screamed. I turned and saw her limping towards me holding her leg. "Mom, mom! A snake bit me! A snake bit me!"

I ran over to her, sat her on the ground, and lifted her hand off the wound. Underneath was a nasty bite. "Wait right here, Katie. Don't move." I ran over to the sideline where her ball was lying. At first, I heard leaves crunching and found myself looking deep into the woods at a retreating figure.

My attention returned to my immediate surroundings. I scanned the edge of the woods until my eyes fell on the snake. I walked up carefully to take a better look. The snake was gray with black blotches along its back and about 20 inches long. It made a buzzing sound the closer I got.

"Step back, slowly, Tess," the referee said as he circled around to the other side of the snake. I was holding my breath and could feel the adrenaline rushing through my body. The next thing I knew, the referee had his foot over the snake's head and sliced its head off with his pocketknife. He carefully wrapped the snake in his handkerchief.

"We need to hurry. Hold this so I can call an ambulance for Katie." He passed me the handkerchief. It took every ounce of self-control I had not to throw the cloth back at him.

The referee grabbed his cell phone and called for an ambulance. I heard him describing the accident. My worst fears were realized. It was a pigmy rattler.

"Don't worry, Tess. They'll be here in just a few minutes. I'm sure they've got the antivenin on hand." He put his arm on my shoulder and told me the emergency first aid we needed to do for Katie while we were waiting for the ambulance.

I hurried back to console Katie with the word "antivenin" ringing in my ears.

"Don't worry, Katie, everything's going to be all right. I'll be right here with you." She held tightly on to my hand.

"Don't leave me Mom, okay?"

"I'm like glue. I'm not going anywhere." I pulled her into a sitting position in my lap, keeping the affected area below heart level to reduce the flow of venom.

Mrs. Seaborne came rushing over with a wet wipe. "Will this be of any help?"

"Yes, thank you. That will help to clean the wound." The referee laid the wipe on top of the wound and poured some cool water on top. "That should help reduce some of the swelling." He continued to take her pulse and watch her breathing.

I rubbed my hand slowly across Katie's forehead, pulling strands of hair away from her face. I kissed the top of her head.

"Mom? I don't feel so good. My stomach hurts and I feel really tired." Her eyelids began to droop, and her skin was turning pale.

"What do we do?" I looked up at the referee.

"She's going into shock. Lay her head flat." I put her head on to the ground as he raised her feet and put his jacket underneath. Someone handed me a blanket. I bundled her up and held her hand.

The ambulance arrived. Two men jumped out of the wagon and hurried over with the stretcher. They lifted her on to the pallet and raced off across the field with my baby. I ran beside her holding her hand. I knew I couldn't let go.

The short ride to the hospital was harried. The EMTs put an oxygen mask on her, checked vital signs, cleaned the wound, and radioed information to the doctor back at the hospital. Everything was a blur as I sat there holding my nine-year-old daughter's hand, listening to each breath she took through the mask.

We were met by a number of medical staff and rushed into the emergency room.

A nurse with a clipboard asked me questions as I ran alongside the gurney. "What is the child's name?"

"Katie. Katie Titan."

"How old is she?"

"Nine."

"Do you know how much she weighs?"

My mind stumbled searching for the right answer. "Eighty...no ninety pounds."

The doctor lifted the wet wipe. The wound was discolored and swollen. "Venom has been injected."

Katie started wheezing. "Blood pressure is bottoming! We've got an allergic reaction. Prepare antivenin, stat!" the doctor directed.

I held fast to Katie's hand and whispered into her ear, "Everything's okay, Katie bear. You be strong." The next thing I knew I was fibbing. "I just got a call that Fitz has been found. He's just fine.

So he's going to need you to feed him." I thought I saw her head move a little.

The doctor gave her the shot. He looked at me, knowing what I was going to ask. "We'll know in the next couple of minutes."

Time stopped. One minute, then two passed.

"Her vital signs are improving. Her color is coming back." The doctor moved around her bed checking her reflexes in her arms and legs. "Yes!" cheered the medical staff.

I squeezed Katie's hand, "Good girl, Katie bear. I knew you could do it."

The doctor settled next to me. "She'll be tired and sore for a few days. I want to keep her here under observation for two days. After that, keep the wound cleaned until it's healed."

I shook his hand. "How can I ever thank you? Nothing I could say would ever be enough."

"Her happy face eating breakfast in the morning is all the thanks I need. Do you need us to call someone? Your husband or other family?"

My heart sank. "Other," I replied.

******

I watched Katie sleep for hours, listening for each breath and watching her chest rise up and down.

Nell wrestled me out of my chair. "You need to be rested and in good spirits when she wakes up. You won't do anyone any good in the shape you're in now. Go on down to the coffee shop and get something to eat. I'll call you if she wakes up."

I hated to leave, but I knew Nell was right. My nerves were a wreck. I took the elevator down to the cafeteria. It was empty, just like my soul felt.

Sliding into a booth, I was impervious to the air conditioner vent blowing directly down on me. The coffee was very black, the grilled cheese sandwich and chips unappetizing.

"Not the best lunch to keep up your stamina." Jack slid into the seat opposite of me. He had a package of pretzels and coffee.

I stayed quiet and took a sip of the coffee. It burned my lips.

"I came over as soon as I heard. I'm glad everything turned out all right. I checked in on Katie before I came down here. She's a determined little girl. She'll come through this with flying colors. Just you wait and see."

"Thanks. Your concern means a lot to me." I couldn't hide the sarcasm.

"Tess, I know you're angry with me. I know what it must seem like. But you have to believe me, I'd never use your predicament for my own personal gain."

My hands wrapped around the coffee mug. "What about your exchange offer of pictures for the book? Who had the most to gain from that deal?"

Jack looked a little uneasy. "The pictures are an added benefit, but that's not why I made them a part of the deal. They were my only bargaining chip. I hoped they would buy us some time. I figured they wouldn't have them in the U.S. I was hoping the hits on you and your family would stop while we were waiting for the deal to go down."

My heart was relieved. I didn't have to hate Jack, but I didn't like what he was saying. "What do you mean? You think this snake thing with Katie wasn't an accident?" My blood began to boil. I turned the mug round and round in my hands.

He put his hands on mine. "I don't know, Tess. In the light of everything else going on, it seems more likely it wasn't a coincidence. What do you think? Did you see anything?"

I stopped handling the mug and stared blankly at the table. "I thought I heard something in the woods, branches crunching underfoot. I looked and caught sight of someone moving deeper into the thicket. About that time, I heard the buzzing sound from the snake."

I looked up at Jack, realizing I was refusing to accept the inevitable. "It could have been on purpose."

"Damn!" Jack hit his fist on the table. My mug jumped a couple inches.

I started crushing potato chips on the table with my spoon. "Why do you think they'd still be after my family when we already agreed to deal with them?"

"That would be the million dollar question. Either, they're keeping the pressure on to remind us they mean business, or...."

"Or? You have an or? What is it?" I stopped crushing the chips.

"It was something I said to Romeo the other day. It's been

bothering me. I told him I had another buyer for the book. Of course, I didn't. He didn't seem overly surprised, but it made him nervous. The 'or' is that there's another person out there that wants the book—real bad—and they're willing to kill for it."

I took some of Jack's pretzels, licking the salt from the sticks. "You don't think Romeo is capable of killing?"

"Oh, he's capable all right. But he wouldn't have gone after Katie. He has everything to gain by just playing it cool until the exchange." Jack took one of my chips and leaned back in his seat. "Do you have any idea why somebody would want this book so badly?"

I took my spoon and swirled it through the chip crumbs.

"Tess?" Jack leaned forward. "Is there something you're not telling me?"

I put a broken chip in the spoon, pulled back on the spoon, and torpedoed the chip at his chest.

"Do you feel better now?" He put the chip on the table.

"I guess. You just made me so mad. I wasn't going to share."

"And now?"

I looked up at him. "Now, I think I'd like you back on my side."

I took a sip of coffee and leaned back in my seat. "Nell got the book delivered by UPS last night."

I could see Jack's tongue doing circles around his teeth, pushing his lips out. "As far as I can tell, the book is a decoy. It's an old art text book with comments made by the Contessa in the borders."

Jack made a sucking sound through his teeth.

"But I know what everyone's looking for, and we have it."

He stopped sucking.

"There was a list, a very old list, hidden in the front cover of the book. The bookbinder found it and returned it with the book. The envelope looked original and hadn't been opened.

Jack took another chip.

"It's a list of Fine Art, stolen during World War II, and the locations of their hiding spots."

He let out a long, slow whistle. "Well that starts to clear up some questions. It also puts a whole new perspective on this. Tess, we need to round up your family and put them someplace safe until this is all over."

Now it was my turn to raise my eyebrows. "Well, that's a mighty fine idea, Ranger Jack, but not very practical with Katie in the hospital."

He rubbed his hand across his forehead. "You're right. We can't move her yet. We're going to need twenty-four-hour protection for her. I'll handle that while you, Nell, and Kevin high-tail it to a safe house."

I looked at him like he'd lost his mind. "I'm not leaving Katie in the hospital alone. And I'm not running away like a dog with my tail between my legs."

He gave me one of his stern looks.

I stuck my tongue out.

Jack shook his head. "I guess I don't have a response for that."

"You don't need one. I'll take care of getting Nell and Kevin into a safe place. You take care of getting some dependable protection on Katie. Tomorrow, we'll make the exchange."

"With or without the list?" Jack asked.

"Without. I want to keep an ace in the hole. It's all we've got."

Chapter Nineteen

September 20, 2001

I spent the morning with Katie at the hospital. She was doing a lot better, but was still a little pale. Nell and Kevin would have nothing to do with leaving town, so I did the next best thing and had them stay at the hospital with Katie. There was an armed guard outside her door and another guard down the hall at the nurses' station. The protection made me feel more comfortable, but not completely at ease.

"Nell, can you help me with some things in the bathroom for a minute?"

Nell got up from the armchair and joined me in the bathroom. She shut the door behind her. "Don't you think Kevin is a little too smart for this?"

I put the lid down on the commode and sat down. "I'm sure he is, Nell. But I don't want him to see this." I pulled out a stun gun.

"Here. I want you to have this—just in case. I want you to have some protection." I handed the gun over to her.

Nell hesitated, then took the weapon. "I don't like to have to do this, Tess. But I won't leave my godchildren unprotected. How do I use this thing?" She turned the weapon over in her hands.

"You turn it on here." I pointed to the switch on the side. "That makes the weapon live. Anything you touch with the end of the weapon will be shocked."

Nell tried the switch a few times. "How shocked are we talking?"

"Touch the end of this to any normal sized man and he'll be down on the ground at least ten minutes. Long enough for you to get everyone out and get some help."

Nell nodded and put the weapon in a knit bag she had strapped across her chest. She leaned against the sink. "When are you meeting Jack?"

"In just a few minutes, in the lobby. We want to get to the drop off spot early and talk along the way."

"Tessa." Nell hesitated. "This is difficult for me to say." She shifted her derriere on the sink. "I know you've known Jack a long time and that you were partners. But that was a long time ago. Do you think your trust is still warranted? There's a lot at stake."

I unraveled some toilet paper and blew my nose. "I know, Nell. I've thought everything through a hundred times. And I still come up with the same conclusion, 'Jack is our best bet.' And yes, I do still trust him."

With the lives of my family. I thought.

"Then I trust him too, Tessa." She looked at her watch. "You'd better get going. You don't want to leave the bad guy waiting."

Just as we were getting up, there was a knock at the door.

"Mom, Nell? Can you finish your conference out here? I've got to use the bathroom." Kevin raced into the john.

I went to kiss Katie goodbye. She looked up at me with worried eyes. "Mom, I was just wondering, did that man standing by the snake get bit too?"

I sat down beside her on the bed. "What man, Katie?"

"I remember when my ball got hit towards the woods, there was a man standing there."

"Near where your ball landed?" I asked.

"He was pretty close. I noticed he had a lunch bag with him. He was bent over like he'd dropped something out of the bag. By the time I got to my ball he was gone. I was just thinking that he might have gotten bitten too and had to come to the hospital."

Once again, I'd been a fool not to go with my instincts. So, the snake was planted, and meant specifically for Katie. "Katie, do you remember anything about the man? Was he tall or short? Light or dark hair? That sort of thing."

"I only saw him for a second. I wasn't paying that much attention to him. He just looked like an ordinary man, probably about dad's age and about as tall."

"Was he slim or heavy?"

"I'd say slim. And he had a real good tan."

It didn't sound like she was describing Romeo. No one would confuse him for tall and slim, but I could tell she was getting worn out from the talking. "Well, you remembered a lot, Katie Bear, for just seeing him for a second." I kissed her on her cheek. "Why don't you get some rest, and I'll check to be sure someone like that didn't check into the hospital with a snake bite, okay?"

"Okay." She was already beginning to drop off to sleep when her head popped back up off the pillow. "Mom, how's Fitz doin'? Where did you find him?"

My face went blank. I'd totally forgotten about Fitz. As usual, Nell came to my rescue.

She pulled the sheet up around Katie's neck and sat back down in the chair by her bed. "You know Katie, that silly old bird must have followed me home one day. I found him in my backyard eating food from the bird feeder."

Katie laughed. "I didn't know pelicans liked bird food."

I looked at Nell, raising my eyebrows as if to say, "what now?"

Nell wasn't even fazed. "Well, I guess they'll eat just about anything if they're hungry enough. I took him back over to your house. He seemed very happy to be back home. I don't think he'll go looking for greener pastures again anytime soon. I know he can't wait to see you."

Katie glowed from ear to ear. "Don't forget to feed him for me, okay Mom? He likes his baitfishes microwaved for a minute. He doesn't like them hard frozen."

I nodded. "Got it. Microwaved, not frozen."

Katie fell back on her pillow and started drifting off to sleep.

I pulled Nell over to the other side of the room. "I hope we're doing the right thing lying about that pelican. You think he'll show up before we get Katie home?"

Nell patted my shoulders. "Faith, Tessa. You must have some faith. And stop worrying about that bird. He'll be fine. You've got more important things to be thinking about. From what you said earlier, I guess you think someone tried to hurt Katie on purpose because of this book and that list? You think it was this Romeo character?"

I nodded. Nell handed me the book wrapped in brown paper. "You do what you have to, Tess, to keep the children safe. Don't worry about us here. I'll hold the fort down on this end."

There was a knock at the door. A nurse came in and handed me a note and a small package. "Mrs. Titan, a delivery service dropped off this package and message from your mother. I believe it's for Katie." She shut the door quietly behind her.

There was a short note scribbled on some of Mother's personal stationary.

Dear Katie, What a horrible thing to happen to such a beautiful little girl! You just lie there and get well as quick as you can. Grandmother Wellsley can't make it to the hospital right now, but she knows how much you love to read and how much you'll love this little gift. Hugs and kisses. Grandmother Wellsley

It was a mystery to me why my mother always referred to herself in the third person. My guess was that she'd spent so many years make believing she was someone else that there wasn't any "I" left anymore, only "she."

Knowing better than to count on a "normal" gift from Mother, I opened it.

"Oh my," said Nell.

"Yes, oh my, just about says it all." Lying in my lap was a book on poisonous reptiles of the world. "Are you sure she's my mother, Nell? Really, really sure?"

"I'm afraid so, Tessa. I'm certain she meant well." Nell took the book and hid it in the bottom of her suitcase. "I'll donate it to the library."

I kissed Katie gently on the forehead and hugged Nell. I held the art book tightly in my hands. The time had come.

******

"How's everyone doing?" Jack held the door to his white SUV open for me. "They're ready." I slid into the passenger's seat.

"I'm afraid to ask what that means." He got into the driver's side and buckled his belt.

"Don't ask, don't tell." I pulled the strap across and buckled it.

As we drove along, I was reminded that most cars in Florida are white. I never paid much attention to it until I visited other cities up north. In the north, people have lots of black cars, and red cars, and blue cars, but not a lot of white cars. Every time I return from a trip up north, I have a day or two of car color shock. Of course, it makes sense.

It gets so damn hot down here, you want the lightest color car you can get to reflect the sunlight. Same goes for the interior. You want a light interior. And God help you if you're a leather freak, then you'd better have the money for heavy tinted windows, or you'll burn your ass every time you sit in your car.

Jack's car had tan cloth seats and tinted windows. "So what's the plan?" I rubbed my hands over the book.

Jack looked straight ahead. "The plan is I take the book over and make the exchange while you stay in the car and out of trouble."

I drummed my fingers across the book. "Think again, Jack. It's my family, my book. I'll do the exchange. You're the back-up."

Jack threw the brakes on. "Look, Tess. This isn't some neighborhood caper. These guys load their guns with real bullets and don't hesitate to use them."

"I'm not some babe in the woods, Jack. I can handle this."

He took his foot off the brake. "I know you can handle this. You've got nothing to prove to me. But it makes more sense for me to make the exchange with Romeo. I made the deal with him. If he sees you, he may not show."

I rubbed my tongue around on the back of my teeth trying to find a reason why that didn't matter. But it did. "All right. Only because you made the deal. I don't want to scare him off."

Jack pulled across the street from the post office and parked in the lot at the ice cream shop. He backed in so I'd have a clear view of the post boxes. The post office was an open-air building with post boxes on either side. There was a small office to the right where you could mail packages and buy stamps.

Jack looked at his watch. "Almost noon." He opened his door.

I touched his arm. "Jack...."

"I know. Walk in the park. I won't be long." He climbed out and shut the door.

I watched him cross the street and make his way over to the front of the building. Romeo appeared from the coffee shop a few minutes later. Jack handed him the book. He tore the brown paper off and seemed pleased. He handed Jack an envelope. Jack checked its contents and seemed agreeable. They talked for a couple minutes. Romeo kept shaking his head "no." Jack was looking more and more perplexed. The pleasantries appeared to be over. They separated. Jack started walking back across the Village Green to the car. Romeo was walking at a ninety-degree angle toward a pathway.

I let out a long breath and sat back in my seat. It looked like a walk in the park, just like Jack had said.

Out of the corner of my eye, I saw a black BMW roadster pull alongside Romeo in the parking lot. He had nowhere to run. I heard a popping sound and saw Romeo fall to the ground. The driver slipped out of the car, grabbed the book, got back in the car and sped off through the parking lot. Jack ran back across the Green and was kneeling by Romeo by the time I got across the road and joined him.

"The bastard shot him point blank. He didn't have a chance." Jack had no feeling in his voice.

So much for a walk in the park. I thought.

Chapter Twenty

"So what was all the head-shaking and finger pointing about?" I passed the sugar bowl to Jack.

He poured a few teaspoons into his dark coffee and stirred it with a wooden stick. "I asked him about all the 'accidents' your family had been having." He slurped a small bit of coffee into his mouth.

The coffee shop was all but empty. It was after three o'clock by the time Andy finished talking with Jack. We told Andy we just happened to be driving by and were the first people on the scene. It was pretty obvious he didn't believe us, but he didn't have any witnesses to prove otherwise.

We sat in a booth in the corner, feeling more secure with our backs to the wall and eyes toward the door.

"And?"

"And he thought your family was very accident prone, but he claimed he didn't have anything to do with it."

"None of it?"

"Nada. He was supposed to keep this thing low key. That's why he was trying to handle it through me."

"Like the less people involved, the better?"

"Yeah, something like that. But by the time we finished talking, he was spooked. He must have put one and one together and figured there was another player in town. And if there was another player, he wasn't safe either."

"Did you believe him?"

"Well, I might have been wavering a bit, but since he took that shot to the chest, I'm willing to give him the benefit of the doubt now."

I had to agree. "So there's someone else, always has been?"

"Looks that way."

I told him what Katie had told me about the man on the croquet field, and her description of him.

Jack's eyes blazed. "Damn! I can't believe he's been so close to us this entire time. He believes he's untouchable."

"Well, I couldn't see anything except the big picture from the car. Did you see the driver at all?"

Jack looked frustrated. "I didn't even know anything was going down, until I heard the 'pop' from the silencer. I hit the ground and turned toward Romeo, thinking he was shooting at me. By that time, all I saw was the back of a person jumping into the car and taking off. Katie's description is probably as good, if not better, than anything I could give."

"If this other player has been in the picture from the start, why hasn't he tried to contact us like Romeo? Why doesn't he make an offer for the book? He knows we have it. Why go around killing people?"

Jack slid his coffee cup back and forth between his hands. "That's the part that makes me nervous. If we take Romeo out of the equation, we've got an unknown identity with a propensity for killing to get what he wants. Negotiating isn't high on his list of priorities."

I swept back a hair that kept stabbing me in my right eye. "Thanks for that unnerving thought. But there is a good side, right?"

Jack cocked his head to the right and raised an eyebrow. "Good side?"

"Sure. Our 'unknown identity' now has the book. He got what he came for. Now he can go home. Case closed."

"If you believe that, I've got some prime real estate in the Everglades to sell you."

"Smart ass."

"You know as well as I do that what we've got now is a cold blooded killer who's probably as pissed as a hornet caught in a screen door. He's got a book with no answers. If I were him, I'd be thinking you held out on the deal. Which of course, you did."

I started biting the inside of my cheek. "This isn't looking good."

"I'd say that's an adequate summary of this situation."

"What do we do now?"

"Oh, so now it's we."

"Don't give me a hard time, Jack. Do you see a way out of this?"

He rubbed his fingers across his forehead. "If we knew how to contact this bozo, we could set up a meet and give him the list."

"Give him the list? That's your answer to getting out of this?"

Jack looked me straight in the eyes. "He plans to kill you. He may try and kill Nell, Katie, and Kevin. Do you have a better answer?"

I thought for a moment. "No. But we need to bring him down at the meet. We can't let him walk, or I'll be looking over my shoulder for the rest of my life."

Jack nodded in agreement. "I'm with you on that one. But we need to bring in some professional help, not the local police."

"You think that's such a good idea, keeping Andy out of the loop?"

"No, I don't think it's such a good idea. But I think it's an even worse idea to have Andy staking out a meet with a professional killer."

It was my turn to nod.

"But all of this is a moot point unless we figure out a way to contact this guy." Jack noted.

We both sat stymied. Then my light bulb came on again. "I've got it."

"Well, let's hear it."

"We'll put up a sign."

"Excuse me?"

"I said, we'll put up a sign."

"A sign. And what might this sign say?"

I thought for a second. "I don't know. How about 'I'm ready to deal.'"

Jack suppressed a chuckle and wiped his hand over his face.

"Okay, okay. I know it's not some incredibly difficult, hi-tech answer, but what's to say simple won't work? He's obviously watching the house."

Jack stopped smiling. "You're right. I hate to admit it, but you're probably right. We've got nothing to lose at this point."

"How long will it take you to get the 'professional help' we need?"

"Twenty-four hours."

"All right. I'll plan to put up the sign tonight. When I get the call, I'll make the meet for the next night."

Jack pointed his coffee stick at me. "The important thing is you take control of the conversation. You tell him when and where. Don't let him steamroll you."

"Right, no steamrolling. How about Josie's? It's familiar territory. We can meet after they close. It will keep any civilian casualties to zero."

Jack thought about the location. "Yeah, I think you're right. It's out of the way, so we won't cause suspicion, and it's familiar ground for us."

"Josie's it is. I'll call her tonight and set things up."

Jack got up to leave.

I put my hand on his arm. "Hold up there, cowboy. You don't think you're gettin' off that easy, do you? Just sit your little taco right back down."

I could tell he had no idea where I was going with this. He slid back into his seat.

I took the last sip of my coffee. "We never talked about the envelope?"

"Envelope?" he said acting coy.

"Yes, the envelope supposedly containing pictures that Romeo gave to you when you gave him the book."

He rubbed his lips together a few times. "Oh, *that* envelope."

"You seemed agreeable to whatever you saw inside it."

"Yep, everything seemed fine."

I turned my Styrofoam cup upside down and crushed it on the table. It made a popping sound. "Damn it, Jack! Stop dancing around this with me."

"What? I've answered everything you asked me."

"Right. And told me nothing I want to know. Let me see if I can be more specific. How is it you came to know Romeo in the first place? Why did he come to you to try and get the book, instead of me? And what kind of pictures could his family have of you that were so damned important?"

Jack cleared his throat and looked around to make sure the shop was still empty. "You're right. You deserve an explanation."

"Damned straight, I do." A minute went by. "I'm still waiting."

Jack ran his hands through his hair and laid his head back against the booth. "My dad worked for the Rosetti family after WWII in Chicago. The family was scattered all over the world, but a small faction ended up in Chicago."

I couldn't believe what I was hearing. "I thought your dad was a cop?"

"He was. He worked for Rosetti on the side. I grew up knowing both cops and mobsters."

"Didn't anyone notice?"

"No, he was discreet. Back then, it wasn't so unusual for cops to be workin' side jobs. It was hard to make ends meet."

"So that's how you knew Romeo."

"Yeah, him and a number of guys."

"How'd he get that nickname and the scar?"

"We use to call him that because girls were always falling for him."

"And the scar?"

"One too many women. He finally slept with one who had a bigger, meaner boyfriend."

I touched the side of my face imagining the pain of a sharp knife cutting into my skin. "I guess he wasn't such a happy camper after that?"

"He found other ways to busy himself. We used to go fishing together, along with some of the other guys. I was twenty-two when my two worlds collided. I was fishing with one of the guys, Joey Carouche. We went fishing for a while, then he drops me back at the dock. He goes back out to pick up this girl he'd made a date with. Seconds later I'm lying on the dock hearing bells and Joey was lying in a million pieces in the water."

"The boat blew up?"

"It blew up, down, and everywhere else."

"That must have screwed you up pretty good."

Jack smiled. "Yeah, you could say that. Up to that point, I was walking the fine line. Everyone was waitin' to see which way I would fall. The next day I'm given a set of pictures that shows me and Joey fishing, me leaving the boat, and the boat blowing up. The pictures could have put a lot of questions in the wrong people's minds about my innocence or guilt. The pictures could have made it real tough on my dad, too."

"That's why you don't talk about your dad."

"Yeah. The Rosetti's have been holding me and my dad professionally ransom for these last twenty years, waiting for their time to collect."

"And that's what Romeo was trying to do, collect."

"That's what Romeo does best. He's a retriever for the family first, then for the highest dollar."

"Oh. So that's what you meant about him buttering his bread on both sides?"

He looked startled. "You've got a good memory for someone who can't find her car keys half the time."

We both sat quiet for a few minutes.

"So what happens now that you've got the pictures, but the Rosetti's didn't end up with the book?"

"Well, technically the meet was completed. Romeo did have the book, and I had the pictures. Unfortunately, his untimely demise, once again, doesn't shine too brightly on me."

"You think his family will blame you for his death?"

"Let's just say, if I was making a list of suspects, my name would be near the top."

I had to agree with him. "So, that just makes it even more important that we bring this guy down. The faster, the better. We both got important assets on the line, wouldn't you agree?"

"Indubitably."

I slid out of the booth. "I'm heading back over to the hospital. Do you want to join us for some exquisite hospital cuisine? I believe we're having country-fried steak with lard-laden gravy, overcooked kale with your choice of vinegar or tabasco, biscuits by Beulah the kitchen warrior, and a sumptuously sweet fruit cocktail. You can have my cherry halves."

"How could I refuse an offer like that?"

******

The hospital floor was abuzz with activity when we arrived. Dinners were being delivered to patients while visitors were sneaking in their own forms of nourishment from the local sub and donut shops.

We passed inspection by the local gendarmes and entered Katie's room to find her watching *Scooby Doo* on the television. Kevin was practicing some of his new Tae Kwon Do moves while Nell was painting her nails an interesting shade of frosted lavender. She looked up when we came through the door.

"I certainly am glad it's you. I'd hate to have messed up my nails grabbing into my bag."

Neither of the kids paid any attention to her comment.

"Everything looks normal here." I sat down on the bed next to Katie.

"Normal like a three ring circus." Jack said, picking up a magazine and scooting his chair far away from Nell. "Nothing personal. I can't stand the smell of that stuff."

Nell laughed. "I've never known a man to say anything different."

I looked over my Katie, closely, like only a mother can. The rosy color was back in her cheeks, and the blue in her eyes was as clear as the Gulf water in the beginning of October.

I slid my hand through her hair. "You look like you're feeling better."

She turned her head, smiled, and looked back at the screen. "Yeah, I feel lots better. We don't have to leave before Scooby's over, do we, Mom?"

I had to smile and shake my head. Only a child could be close to death, rebound in one day and act as if nothing had happened. I wish I had that skill.

"No problem, sweetie. I'm sure you'll be here for at least another day or two."

"Great! You know they give me all the Popsicles I want here? And the *Scooby Doo* Marathon just started."

Nell rolled her eyes. "How'd everything go at your *meeting*, dear?"

I bumped Jack out of his chair and pulled it up next to Nell. "We got the package delivered on time," I said a little loudly, then lowered my voice to tell her the rest of the story.

Nell's eyes widened when I got to the part about the new player in the scenario that appeared to be our murderer. "So, Katie did see someone, and it wasn't Romeo?"

I nodded. "We think she saw the murderer."

"Oh, my. That does put a new twist on things, doesn't it?"

"Major screw." I agreed.

Nell patted her handy chest bag. "I suppose that means you'll want me to hold on to this for a bit longer."

"I think that would be a good idea."

Jack looked over at Nell's bag. His eyes questioning what she was holding so tight to her body.

Nell smiled at Jack. "Tsk, tsk. Curiosity killed the cat."

We were saved by the dinner bell. The cafeteria sent up enough food for a small banquet. It wasn't quite as bad as I'd anticipated. Besides, who could have guessed Jack loved kale? He chose the tabasco sauce. I ate anything on the plate with carbohydrates in it and eagerly awaited a Popsicle. I could taste the sweet, sappy flavored ice melting in my mouth when there was another knock at the door.

I was expecting a bowl of Popsicles. Instead I got the UPS man. Jack stood up and put himself between the door and us. There was some heated murmuring between him and the deliveryman.

Jack turned to Nell. "It seems you have an important package from France."

"For me? From France? Are you sure? I don't know anyone over there." Nell looked confused.

The UPS man looked around Jack's shoulder. "Ma'am. I have very special instructions. I'm only allowed to deliver this package to you."

Jack put his hand on the deliverer's arm. "Who gave you these instructions?"

"I have written instructions, sir. They were given to me by my superior. He told me this was a very unusual situation. That's why I tracked Miss Nell here to the hospital." He turned to Nell and tipped his hat. "Your neighbor told me you were here, ma'am."

Jack didn't let his guard down. "Do you have the instructions with you?"

"Oh, yes, sir. They're right here." He reached for his shirt pocket and handed an old, yellowed piece of paper to Jack.

Jack took a minute to read the paper. "Are you sure the date on this is right?"

"Oh, yessir. It's the genuine article. That's what makes this delivery so special. I've heard about deliveries like this, but never had one myself."

I couldn't stand it any longer. "Would someone like to let the rest of us in on the big secret? Who's it from, Jack? And why's the date so important?"

Jack bit the side of his lip. "Nell, it's from the Contessa, and the instructions are dated September 20, 1991!"

Chapter Twenty-one

September 20, 2001

I jumped out of my seat. "That's impossible."

Nell stood. "Not impossible, dear."

I turned back to face Nell. "What do you mean, not impossible? The Contessa's been dead for years."

"You're right, Tessa. She'd been dead for years, ten years to be exact. She died on September 20, 1991."

It took me a minute to realize this was September 20, 2001. Ten years to the day she had died. I sat down on the bed. "You mean she could have sent this package to you on the day she died?"

"It would seem that way, Tessa." Nell made her way over to the UPS man. She took the box from his hands and the instructions from Jack. "Well, let's see what we have here." She started reading the instructions, then turned to Jack. "Would you be a dear and please tip this gentleman?" She shook the young man's hand. "Thank you for finding me. The Contessa always found a way to surprise me, just as you have today."

The man saluted. "Just doing my duty, ma'am." He took the ten from Jack. "You all have a nice day." The door shut quietly behind him.

We all sat in stunned silence as Nell opened the box. On top lay a sealed envelope with Nell's name scrawled across the front. She slid the envelope under her nose for a brief second. "Yes, yes. It's the Contessa's fragrance. I remember it well."

Sitting down on the end of the bed, she took a deep breath, opened the envelope, and held the letter gently in her hands.

Katie muted the television as Nell read the letter out loud.

My Dearest Nell,

This must be quite a shock. If you are surprised, then I have succeeded. I have beaten them at their own game. And with that satisfaction, know that my spirit is now free.

I must first thank you and equally ask for your forgiveness. Receiving this package now makes you a part of my lifetime struggle. Forgive me for leaving you with such a burden.

I cannot explain everything in this letter, so I have included my diary. It is an exhaustive account of my work for the past twenty years. This diary is very dangerous. Do not tell anyone of its existence.

Once you have read the diary, you will understand why I could only entrust my work to my dearest friend. I feel you with me now, just as you have been with me my entire life. Distance was a nuisance, but never a barrier to our friendship. I have missed you greatly over these years.

The spirit of your friendship was my solace when the work seemed futile and strengthened my will to continue seeking and overcome all those who wanted me to fail. The world deserves to know the truth. It deserves to see and enjoy that which has been hidden from it for so many years. It's time for the stealing, corruption, and power battles to end. You are the person I trust most in life and am depending on most in death. I know you will do the right thing.

Do not grieve my life or my disappearance. Know that I lived my life pursuing my greatest passion. My deepest regret is never having met Tessa. Her name is a good one...one to be proud of. Her bloodline comes from a strong and compassionate people; a people who strived to find balance in a world full of inequity. I know she will find her place, just as you've found yours.

I would like her to have this momento of me. It was given to me by my mother when it was time for me to leave home and make my own life. The stones represent the balance of heart, mind, and spirit.

My love and spirit will always be with you both.

The Contessa

P.S. – It would be useful to put your hands on that art textbook I gave you.

Nell dipped her hand into a red velvet bag and presented me with a gold necklace.

Katie sat forward in bed. "Look at those beautiful stones, Mom!" A ruby, emerald, and sapphire were set within a gold medallion.

Nell took the necklace from my hands and put it around my neck. "Beautiful, Tessa. It is truly beautiful."

I was overwhelmed. I couldn't ever remember having received such a wonderful gift.

"Pretty cool stuff, Aunt Nell." Kevin said.

"Like a fairytale," Katie added.

"Well, be that as it may. I think it's time for me to settle down here and read this diary to see what all this fuss is about." Nell pulled the floor lamp over to the armchair and settled in to start her reading.

"Do you want us to stay?" I asked.

"No, no, dear. Why don't you and Jack take Kevin and go to the movies or something for a few hours? I'll fill you in when you get back."

"How about it, Jack? Do you think it's safe for us to go out for some quality family time?"

"As long as I don't have to sing or dance in front of a group of people."

"I never knew you had stage fright."

"I don't. I just don't like to make a spectacle of myself."

I made the Girl Scout sign with my hand. "Okay, we promise. No spectacles."

"Very funny." He didn't seem convinced.

******

We grabbed our stuff and headed for the Mecca of entertainment in our seaside paradise, "Wally's Skateworld." It had everything a teenager could desire: bowling, skating, arcade, pool tables, large sports screens, black lights, blaring music, and food that would make any normal adult turn and run the other way. We played the video games for a while until a bowling lane opened up.

"Our lane just opened up. Come on, guys, let's get our shoes." I corralled them toward the bowling desk.

Jack looked a bit hesitant. "I don't know, Tess. This is borderline 'spectacle' kind of stuff."

"What are you talking about? Bowling is a man's game. Grunting, drinking beer, and beating the hell out of ten penguin pins. What could be manlier?" I shoved a pair of size eleven shoes at him.

"Good guess."

"Yeah, glad to know I can still get work at a carnival guessing shoe sizes."

Kevin got his shoes and the two of them went down to the lane to pick out their balls.

I was waiting for a pair of shoes my size to be returned. Just then a pair of nines came over the counter. The teenager servicing the desk handed them to me. I looked at the shoes like they had just come off the feet of the creature from the black lagoon. I held them at arms length with my index fingers carefully hooked into the heels.

I looked at the kid. "You know this town does have health codes."

He flipped his tongue ring back and forth at me. "It's not like they got a disease lady."

The only thing worse than being called "ma'am" is being called "lady." The reject obviously had no respect for paying customers. I leaned over the desk and took a close look at his nametag.

"Randy, is it?"

"That's my name, don't wear it out, Momma."

I was wrong, there was something worse than being called "lady."

"Randy, how much are they paying you an hour?"

He looked at me curiously. "Eight dollars and I'm worth every penny of it. Why? You got a better offer for me, babe?"

"Yeah, Randy, I think I do. Tell you what. You spray some disinfectant in these shoes, and I won't drag your sorry ass across this desk, rip that ring from your tongue, and use it to pierce your balls and dick together in a neat package."

"Whoa, lady. Take it easy. I was only playing."

"Then start playing the role of an outstanding employee before I call your boss and get you demoted to nacho chef."

He grimaced, shot my shoes full of disinfectant, and turned the lights on to lane seven. By the time I got there, the guys were setting up the score sheet.

"What took you so long, Mom?" Kevin asked, walking up to take a practice shot.

"Just a little difference of opinion."

I sat next to Jack in the empty chair and finished my thought. "Randy, our friendly counter clerk, was living in fantasia, and I made it clear he'd be living in the hell of my choice if he didn't put some disinfectant in my shoes."

Jack laughed.

"What? What are you laughing at? The kid was totally out of line. He had no respect whatsoever. He was violating health codes and to top it off he made a pass at me."

"Well, that does it." Jack stood up and put the scoring wand behind his ear. "Who does he think he is making a pass at a woman of your age?"

I hit him hard on the shoulder. "Oh, shut up. Am I supposed to feel flattered because some delinquent with a tongue ring wants to try his moves out on the past president of the PTA?"

Jack sat back down and added my name to the scorecard. "No. But it wouldn't hurt to chill out a bit. You're starting to sound like your mother."

I knew he was right. But that didn't mean squat. "If you want to maintain any kind of friendship with me, never, and I mean never, compare me to my mother. You understand?"

"No sweat. I won't go there."

I put my shoes on and tried a couple balls. I finally settled on a twelve-pounder. It was too heavy for me, but I liked the swirly blue color. It reminded me of those mood rings we used to wear in junior high school.

Turned out Jack was a pretty good bowler, and even offered to pay for the second game to give us a chance to win back our pride. My pride felt fine. It was the muscles in my bowling arm that were screaming to surrender. I was already breaking a sweat.

"Hey, Kev, before we start, will you go get us some sodas?"

"Sure, Mom." He took the five from my hand and went up to the "food-a-rama" to wait in line for the drinks.

I took the opportunity to talk shop with Jack.

"So, what are we giving the invisible man at the meeting?"

Jack looked at me blankly. "The invisible man?"

"Well, he needed a name. I'm tired of calling him the murderer. Besides, eavesdroppers always give us the oddest looks when we call him that."

Jack smiled. "I'm sure we'll get a better reaction using the "invisible man.""

"I'm all ears, if you got something better."

"Oh, no, no. The invisible man is fine with me." He wrote our names on the score sheet for the next game.

"So, are we giving him the real McCoy or are we slipping him a decoy?"

"I think our decoy days are over, Tess. I think we should pass him the real list."

"What's our ace?"

"'Scuse me?"

"Ace. Our ace in the hole. What's to keep this guy from taking the list and killing us and my family to keep all this quiet? We know the list is valuable. Who knows what his plans are for it? I'm fairly certain we're disposable pawns in this game."

"Disposable is right. The way this clown's been working, we have to figure he has no plans of leaving leaks."

"How about if we make copies, tell him they'll be circulated to key people if anything happens to us or my family?"

Jack hesitated. "It's not much, but it's all we've got right now. If we knew who this guy was, there might be more we could use against him."

"Maybe there'll be something in the diary, some clue, or information that we can use as a weapon against him."

Jack shook his head. "We can always hope. Let's get this game underway and get back to the hospital to see what Nell's found out."

"Agreed." I looked up to the concession stand to see what was taking Kevin so long.

"Uh oh." Three boys had surrounded Kevin and were giving him a hard time. They were shoving him around. The sodas spilled onto his shirt. I jumped up to save him. Jack pulled me back.

I looked at him fiercely. "What the hell are you doing? He obviously needs some help."

"You're right. But not from you. Let me take this one, champ."

I watched as he idled up to the boys and said a few words. It didn't seem to help. All the boys were still laughing. Jack was laughing too when he walked over to the tallest kid and went to shake his hand.

Within seconds, the kid was on his knees, a pained expression on his face. Jack was still smiling, still talking. Soon, all the boys were nodding and hesitantly shaking his hand. Looked like Jack only needed to paint one picture to show how things were going to be from now on. He put his arm on Kevin's shoulder and helped him with the sodas.

"Man, Mom. Did you see Jack put Joey Harrelson to his knees? He didn't even barely have to touch him! He was totally zoned out until Jack let go of him."

"Yeah, I saw. Nice moves, Jack. I hope his parents don't sue you."

"No bruises. His word against mine."

Kevin looked on in awe. "Way too cool, Jack. Can you show me how to do that?"

Jack looked over at me. "That would all depend on how your mom feels about that, and if you're ready for that kind of responsibility. It's one thing to use it to get people's attention. It's a whole 'nother ballpark to use it to bend people's will."

Kevin looked at me with his soulful, puppy eyes. "Please, Mom. Please. It would make me feel better, if I knew I could protect myself like that."

I knew what my answer was going to be, and I already hated myself for it. "All right. But you learn it only from Jack, and you never use it unless you absolutely have to. Got it?"

"You bet! Thanks, Mom! I'm gonna run up and wash this soda off my hands. It feels kinda sticky." He took off for the washroom.

I shouted after him, "And no practicing on your sister!"

I slumped down on one of the plastic benches. "Why do I do this to myself? Why?"

Jack sat next to me. "Because you have good instincts. You're right on this one. Give yourself a break."

I stared down at the dirty shoelaces on my red, white, and blue bowling shoes. "That's easy for you to say. You don't have kids. You don't have that nauseous feeling in your stomach every time you make a decision that could scar them for life."

Jack was real quiet. I looked over at him. His expression was grim.

"You're right. I don't have kids. And I've got no business telling other people how to raise theirs." He grabbed his street shoes. "I've gotta start checking on our back-up. Call me and let me know if there's something we can use from the diary." He turned his back on me and walked away.

I slipped further down on the plastic seat. "Great. I wonder if I was born with foot-in-mouth disease or if I just acquired it at some point?"

Chapter Twenty-two

It was almost eight o'clock by the time we got back to the hospital. Everything was quiet when Kevin and I got back to the room.

Nell looked up from her reading when we came in. "I'm almost finished, dear. Just a few more pages."

I looked over at Katie.

Nell smiled. "She finally reached her Scooby Doo capacity and zonked out."

I went over and looked at my baby. She looked fine, just out-of-place in a hospital bed surrounded by coloring books and stuffed animals. I could feel the anger rising from my gut. No one had the right to do this to my family. No one had the right to turn our lives upside down and make us worry about our very existence. Even as the anger burned in my stomach, I could feel the weariness in my head. I wasn't twenty anymore. I didn't spring back from emotional turmoil like I used to. I was tired of everything.

"Are you all right, Tessa?" Nell laid the diary on the table by Katie's bed.

"What?"

"I said, are you all right? You look a little pale."

"Oh, I'm fine. Nothing a long weekend of sleep wouldn't cure." I pulled a chair up next to Nell. "So, what revelations did the Contessa deem to bless us with?" My tone was more sarcastic then I'd intended. If Nell noticed, she didn't act it. She started right in about the diary.

"There are many private revelations in the diary about the Contessa's husband, her romances, and family issues. She lived with many burdens but shouldered them all with an ease that surely would have destroyed most of us. Her life with Robert, her husband, was a lonely one. He was more interested in business than marriage, but allowed her free reign of the homes and an adequate allowance. It was one of his business relationships that ended up shaping the rest of the Contessa's life."

I moved forward to the edge of my seat. "What happened, Nell? What changed her life?"

"In the strictness of confidence, the Count related a very important event to her. He told her it was of the utmost importance that she keep the story a secret, but never forget what he was about to tell her."

"Nell!"

"Patience, Tessa. Patience." She smiled and started the story. "One cold evening in January, 1945, the Count had a visitor at his home in Italy. The gentleman gave the Count an envelope telling him how very important this information was. He told the Count no one could ever know about the contents of the envelope, and that someone from the family would retrieve it once the war was over. The Contessa was confused when her husband mentioned 'family' coming to retrieve the information. As far as she knew, he had no living relatives. He told her she would understand when the time was right."

I nodded. "So how long did it take her to figure out he was in cahoots with 'The Family' of all families?"

"Well, it appears she didn't concern herself with the matter again until Robert's death. He had left her detailed information about how to handle his affairs. He noted that a sealed letter that could be found inside the front cover of one of his favorite books was to be kept secret and protected until a member of the "Sarducci" family came to retrieve it.

I shook my head. "Wait a minute. Didn't the Count die in the 50s?"

"Yes, I believe it was in '55."

"If I've got my history right, the war was over by, what 1947, '48? Why didn't the family return to pick up the envelope?"

"Yes, yes, that stymied me as well until I continued reading."

I looked at Nell. "Well? What did it say?"

"When the Contessa read the Count's letter and saw the name "Sarducci," she was immediately worried. She had known of the family quite well, as would almost anyone in the European community. They had reigned as the Godfathers of the Italian Mafia for as far back as could be remembered, up until the war.

The war changed the face of how business was handled, and with those changes came new leaders. The Sarducci family lost their power during the war, and moved to greener pastures. Knowing that the family was no longer prominent in the European community, the Contessa decided to open the letter and decide for herself what should be done with it."

I sat back in the chair. "Smart lady."

Nell hesitated. "Perhaps. You see, when she opened the envelope she found this list that we now have in our possession. She was excited to know that these works existed, but distraught to realize they were being used as barter to fund the proliferation of power and evil."

I sat forward resting my elbows on my knees and chin on my hands. "Wow, she had to decide between apathy or saving part of the world."

Nell agreed. "Many people would have chosen to turn their backs, act as if nothing had ever happened. But that was not the Contessa. She knew that at some point someone would come looking. She didn't know how much time she had, so she devised a plan and went about it as quickly as possible."

I stretched my legs to get some kinks out and tried to hold back a yawn. "So her plan was to hide the letter in a different book, give you the book for safekeeping, and send you her journal upon her death telling you what you had.

I wonder why she didn't just turn the list over to the authorities when she found it? Why go through all this cloak and dagger stuff? If the secret had been told, the family wouldn't have tracked her for all those years. She wouldn't have been a prisoner to her own life."

"I was thinking that myself, Tessa. She goes on to say in her diary that she didn't know whom she could trust. The police were notorious for taking kickbacks, and she was certain the family had surrounded her with spies that kept track of her movements. She decided the best thing to do was search out the missing treasures and re-hide them in new places, places only she would know about. Eventually, she felt certain she would find someone she could trust with this information. She details, in her diary, the meticulous measures she took to be sure she wasn't followed during this entire process."

My head jerked up from the back of the chair. "Re-hide? You mean she used the Count's list to find the treasures, then re-hid the pieces?"

"That's what she says in the diary, dear. She made a copy of the list to continue working from and placed the original in this book."

"So, the list we have is worthless?"

"I wouldn't say worthless. There's obviously someone very interested in obtaining this list. Someone willing to kill anyone or anything that stands in his way."

I nodded my head in a daze. "Great, the killer doesn't know the list is worthless. He thinks he's finally found the pot of gold at the end of the rainbow." I played with the back of my earring for a minute. "Nell, do you think the Contessa's death was an accident? Or do you think she was murdered because they thought they had enough information to solve the puzzle and didn't need her anymore? She had become expendable?"

Nell took a Kleenex from the table and wiped a tear from her eye. "Yes, Tessa. I believe they killed her. The Contessa's last few entries were filled with urgency. She knew she was running out of time."

Nell opened the diary to the last entry and read aloud. *"I would be lying if I didn't say I was afraid of death. I have spent a good part of my life trying to solve and control the outcome of a great mystery. It is of no comfort to have to face the biggest mystery known to mankind and have no hand in its outcome. I do not know when or how it will happen, though I hope it is quick. Know from my own lips that I am at peace with my life. I know I have done the right thing, and that one day my sacrifice will seem quite small compared to the joy this art will bring to the world.*

I have always been a good card player. My grandmother loved to play poker, and taught me well. I want you to know that I started this game with a low pair, but I'll be closing with a full house, ace high. This is the legacy I leave to those who follow."

Nell shut the diary and placed it on the table by Katie. She took the Kleenex and pushed it up inside her long sleeve.

I sat there shaking my head. "Did she give any clues about where she re-hid the pieces?

"Not that I can tell, Tessa. I wasn't looking for cryptic messages or invisible ink, mind you, but beyond those possibilities, I didn't find anything obvious."

I leaned over and kissed Nell on the cheek. "Oh well, easy come, easy go. At least now, I'll have no qualms about giving the list to the killer." I picked up my jacket and headed for the door. "I've got to run home and take care of a few things for tomorrow. I'll be back in a couple hours."

"All right, dear. Be careful. Do you need to take my buzz gun with you?"

I smiled. "Stun gun, Nell. Stun gun. No. I'm carrying a little heavier than that. I'll be fine. You all get some sleep. I'll be back as quick as I can."

******

I went home, pulled out an old yard sale sign, and wrote my message to the killer on the other side. I pounded it into the ground near the front of the driveway. I stood back to examine my work. "I'm ready to deal." That should do it. I felt the hairs rise on the back of my neck. I shook it off, and wandered around the house for a few minutes checking that the windows and doors were locked. I threw a few items in an overnight bag and was heading back out the door when Andy's police cruiser pulled up across the street in front of Breecher's house. It was almost midnight, I couldn't imagine what Andy was doing over there at this time of night.

I watched him go up to the porch and ring the bell. The outside light came on illuminating Andy, who kept one hand on his holstered weapon. The discussion got louder until I could hear angry words from Breecher. Unfortunately, my name was included with a number of other choice words. Ricochet, Breecher's terrier, started barking and growling. Andy's voice was curt. I heard him say something about "the easy way or the hard way." A few minutes later, Breecher exited his house with a leash and muzzle on Ricochet. He'd thrown on a gray sweat suit and was carrying a duffel bag. Ricochet and Breecher got into the back of the cruiser. Breecher turned towards my house before ducking into the back seat screaming some obscenity and flipping me the bird. The last words I could make out were something like, "I'll be back!"

I got a brief picture in my mind of an indestructible, mechanical Breecher tearing me and my home limb from limb. I shook my head and locked the door behind me. *What an imagination,* I thought. I'd never cared for Breecher that much, but this was the first time he'd made it into my "evil arch enemy and monster" category. "I'll be back," echoed in my ears.

I turned on the outdoor motion sensor lights, got back in my car, and returned to the hospital to spend the night with my family.

I was thankful the hospital staff had brought in another cot. It had starched white sheets and a blanket, not a wrinkle to be seen. It took me a minute to pry loose the covers so I could crawl in. I couldn't help but notice the perfect military corners at the end of the bed.

I lay there for a few minutes wondering how my life had become such a quagmire of death and mystery. I had spent years distancing myself from the likes of this situation, and yet here I was, the very centerpiece of this mess.

Who could have ever guessed that a woman I'd never met would have such an impact on me? She had woven her magic with Nell, and now even in her grave had managed to involve me in her affairs.

The Contessa had been a part of my life as far back as I could remember. In life, her closeness could be felt through the stories Nell told, and in the very warmth of Nell's voice whenever she spoke of her. In death, it was as if her life force surrounded each of us providing the strength, courage, and motivation we needed to complete her work.

I couldn't find a comfortable position to fall asleep. I rolled over on my stomach as a last ditch effort.

My last thoughts were of Breecher attacking my house, spraying it with decks of cards. He was yelling something about "full houses," which reminded me I was planning a full house for Thanksgiving and would need to find another leaf to add to the table.

September 21, 2001

I was awakened early in the morning by an odd vibration under my left side. For a moment, I thought I was at a spa having a new massage treatment. I reached down to move the masseuse's hand a little lower and realized it was my cell phone ringing.

"Hello?" I said yawning into the mouthpiece.

"Do you have what I want?" The voice sounded electronically distorted.

I thought it was a prank call. Then it dawned on me. I sat straight up in bed. "You got my message fast."

"Too bad your police friend was doing his job last night, or we could have talked at your house. Alone."

The hair on my arms stood straight up. I took a deep breath and tried to sound authoritative. "We need to deal. Not at my house and not alone." I turned my head away from the mouthpiece so the person on the other end couldn't hear me hyperventilating. I tried to take a calm, deep breath. "Josie's, tonight, midnight. Me and Mr. Daniels will be there with the list."

There was a long pause. "Agreed. But no tricks this time. You bring the list, the entire list, or that pretty little girl of yours won't be so lucky next time."

I shivered with goose bumps. The phone disconnected in my ear.

I slid my legs over the side of the cot and held my head in my hands. *What had I just done?* I asked myself. *Made a deal with the devil, no doubt*, I answered under my breath.

Nell sat down beside me. "That devil's a sly one, Tessa. Just remember, he never keeps his promises, except when your soul's at stake."

I put my head on Nell's shoulder. "Jack will be with me. He won't let anyone take my soul without a fight."

Nell patted my head. "Well, let's just hope the battle ends before it starts. I'm ready to go home."

"Me too." Katie echoed jumping onto the cot.

"Me three." Kevin joined in.

The cot had taken all it could take. "Crash!" The next thing we knew we were all lying on the floor laughing hysterically.

The guard opened the door, and looked frantically at us with his hand over his holstered weapon. "Is everything all right?"

I looked up at the guard while wiping my nose on my sleeve. "Yes, sir, we're all just fine."

Nell looked over at me. "Well, you may be fine. But I think I just peed in my pants!"

We all started howling over again. The guard shook his head and retreated back to the safety of the other side of the door.

Chapter Twenty-three

I called Jack and let him in on the secret of the list. Like me, he hoped the murderer knew as little about the authenticity of the list as we had. "I'll be busy until tonight getting everything ready. I'll be at your house by 11:00 p.m."

"I'll be ready."

I went back home to worry over what I should wear to a dangerous night meet where I could be potentially maimed or killed. Geena and I sat together in the wicker loveseat with a half-eaten pan of brownies between the two of us facing the king size bed covered with clothes.

Geena snapped a tissue from the table next to her and wiped some crumbs from her fingers. "I still think the tight black stirrup pants, black sweater, and ankle boots. Oh! And don't forget the neck scarf. It really makes the outfit."

"Whose outfit are we talking about? Some over-the-hill-talk show host?"

"Some of the sexiest, best dressed female detectives wore this very outfit! Look at Mrs. Peel in *The Avengers*, Barbara Feldon in *Get Smart*, or even Cat Woman in *Batman*. They were all very stylish upholders of all that was good and important!" Geena danced around the room holding a scarf over the bottom of her face, looking very Mata Harish.

I ate another brownie and pondered my options. "Geena, I need something more sensible. The black stirrup pants can stay. The ankle boots have to go."

Geena pouted. "But they give you height, make you look slimmer."

"I'm fairly certain the murderer can shoot me whether I'm 5'6 or 5'8. I'm more concerned about making less noise and being able to scurry faster than a black racer snake getting out of the way of a lawn mower."

Her face scrunched up. "You know I hate snakes."

"Well, I don't relish being shot. So let's go with the Air Nike's."

"At least let me spray them black and put black laces in them." Geena picked them up and put them beside the loveseat.

"Is there some good reason you're going to ruin my 100 dollar pair of sneakers with black shoe spray?"

"Well, duh! Everybody knows you wear as much black as possible so you don't stand out so much. Otherwise, you'd be like a white rabbit in the middle of a dark forest."

If it was dark in the forest, I couldn't imagine seeing a rabbit, regardless of its color. I raised my eyebrows, adding a questionable smirk.

"Don't you look like that at me, Tess Titan. You want to go get your feet blown off because it's the only thing the killer can see?"

Ouch. Now that was a painful thought.

"Or what if you need to hide behind some curtains or under a table. What do you think is going to be standing out brighter than a red sock in a load of white laundry?"

"Okay, okay. I give in. Spray the shoes."

The sweater was too damned hot, so I opted for a black tee shirt and a dark canvas jacket that would hide my shoulder holster. I laid out my jewelry on the bedside table.

"What are you doing?" Geena asked.

"Laying out my jewelry, so I don't forget it."

Geena shook her head back and forth. "You don't wear jewelry on a night job."

"You don't?"

"Not if you want to stay alive. You never know if a glint from your earrings or a necklace will give away your position. And what a perfect target, your head or chest."

I opened the drawer and pushed the baubles back inside. "What about my watch?"

"Yes, of course you have to have a watch. How else will you know when it's time to make your move? Just keep it under the sleeve of your jacket. You don't want to lose a hand."

I looked down at my hand and wondered how I'd ever made it through ten years in the Patrol without all this vital accouterment information.

While I contemplated wearing my hair in a ponytail or straight down, the phone rang. Geena and I both jumped, and just stared at it. It rang again.

"Are you going to answer it?" Geena asked.

"I guess I should, since I'm closer."

Geena nodded. "Makes sense."

We both tensed as I picked up the receiver. "Hello?" The fear dropped from my face. "Are you certain? That's hard to believe. Well, I'm sure you've got the details and I don't. Of course, I'll be over within the hour." I laid the receiver back in its cradle.

"You're never going to believe this."

Geena stopped hanging clothes. "What, what is it?"

"Remember how I told you Andy picked up Breecher last night in his patrol car and took him and the dog with him?"

"Yeah. Did they finally catch him at some devious deed like transplanting mole crickets or red ants into other people's yards?"

I sat down on the bed. "No, nothing so middle class."

Geena sat on the footboard. "Well, what then? What'd they finally get the beady eyed nuisance neighbor for?"

"Grand theft and accessory to murder."

Geena almost fell off the footboard. "What?"

"Accessory to manslaughter to be exact."

"You've got to be kidding."

"I wish I was."

"No way. Old long-nose helping snuff someone out. I don't believe it."

"Well, I guess you'd better start. That was Andy on the phone. He wants me to come down to the station and make a statement."

"A statement? What are you going to say? 'Yes, I must admit that I've lived next to a bony-assed, complaining sonnafabitch for the past twelve years. Yes, he lets his dog poop on my lawn regularly and he has the manners of a poodle in heat—Breecher AND his dog.'"

I couldn't help but smile. "That would be too easy. Andy's not interested in my character assassination of Breecher. He wants details about Wanamaker's visits, and information about their on-going relationship."

"Did Andy say who Breecher allegedly accessorized?"

"Geena, he didn't fit someone with a bad hat. He helped murder someone!"

"I know, I know. Did Andy say who Breecher was working with and who they took out?"

"No, you know Andy. No details on the phone. But I'd bet the house that Wanamaker's at the bottom of this." I started to grab my purse and head out the door to the station.

"I hate to be a fashion fart, but don't you think your caped crusader attire might be a little inappropriate for an afternoon at the police station?"

"Shit. I totally forgot." I ripped my clothes off. "Find me something quick, Geena. Something that says, 'This is a smart, intelligent woman. I should believe everything she says.'"

"How about something that says, 'I love myself, I love my clothes, and you should love me too?'"

I looked up at Geena with my pants caught down around my ankles. "What the hell are you talking about? Didn't you hear me? I need something that looks official, something that looks like I mean business, something..."

"...that fits." Geena looked around at the collection of clothes. "Most of your tailored clothes don't fit you anymore, remember your Honor? Let me see. Pull your black pants back on. Kick off the tennis shoes." She threw me some black knee-highs. "Put these on with the black pumps." She grabbed a yellow short-sleeved two-piece knit sweater set and helped slip it over my head. I straightened my hair and face as she spritzed me with some gardenia perfume and handed me some pearl studs.

I took a look in the mirror. "Not bad."

Geena looked from behind. "Not a problem. We had a lot to work with."

We high-fived each other and I took off for the station.

******

The station looked unusually busy as I pulled into the parking lot. There were two rental cars I didn't recognize, a black Taurus and a blue Crown Victoria. As I approached the porch, I could hear a loud discussion taking place. Something about jurisdictions, collars, and quarters.

I wasn't worried about the collar. I was wearing a respectable jewel neckline and had a number of quarters in my purse if that became an issue. I smiled at my own personal joke and made my way into the station.

I pushed open the door. "Good morning, everyone." I could see two men bent over Andy's desk looking like tigers ready to pounce on their morning meal.

"I'm sorry. Did I come at a bad time? I can come back later." I started to back out the door.

Andy jumped up from behind the desk. "No, no. This is a perfect time. As a matter of fact, it would probably be beneficial if Mr. Feester and Mr. Trumball were both here to listen to your statement."

"Well, if you think so. I'm not exactly sure what information you think I might have, but I'll help if I can." After taking one look at Feester and Trumball, I decided that playing a thoroughly southern woman would be to my advantage, at least for the time being.

Andy motioned me over to the chair by his desk. The two men stood behind me.

The hair on the back of my neck started to rise. I raised my voice an octave or so and added a slow southern drawl, "Andy, do you mind if I turn my chair around? I feel so rude talking with my back against your guests." He looked at me a bit oddly, but helped me turn the chair around so that Andy and I were now both facing the two men. At least that evened the odds.

Andy took out a tape recorder and placed it on the desk between the two of us. "You understand that we're going to record your statement, so there won't be any misunderstandings or forgotten details?"

I straightened my sweater and fussed with my hair. "If that's procedure. Then you do whatever it is you need to do. I'm just here to help."

Andy looked at me like he'd just seen a Sasquatch. He knew something was up, but started dealing with initial procedure on the recording.

I looked over at the two men who had now taken a seat on the leather sofa. They looked like two warts on a frog's ass.

I turned to Andy. "I'm sorry. Can you put that on hold for a minute?"

Andy fumbled over the buttons for a second until he found stop.

"I apologize, gentlemen. I've just realized I'm at a terrible disadvantage. It just occurred to me that we haven't been properly introduced. Now, that just doesn't seem right."

The two squirmed uncomfortably in their seats for a second. The first mumbled something unrecognizable from behind his hand.

"I'm sorry, Mr. Feester, isn't it? I didn't quite get that?"

He took his hand away from his mouth, and stated quite clearly, "Detective John Feester, State Animal Control Division."

The second man straightened up noticeably and pulled his tie a little tighter. "Special Prosecutor, Adam Trumball, Gulf County, Florida."

I smiled at the two gentlemen. "Thank you for that introduction. And I think you know that I am Tessa Titan, writer and mother." I tossed their titles over in my minds realizing Breecher had gotten in way over his head. I didn't like the man, but I wasn't about to lead a lamb to slaughter. And that's what this was beginning to look like.

I looked back at Andy. "Oh, are you waitin' on little ol' me?"

He rolled his eyes, and hit the play button. "Please state your name for the record."

"Tessa Elizabeth Titan."

"Your address?"

"Two-forty-five Azalea Lane, Paradise Pointe, Florida.

"Do you have a neighbor who resides across the street from you at 246 Azalea Lane?"

"Yes, I do."

"Please state his name, the length of time you've known him, and your relationship."

I had to bite my lip from smirking at that last part. "Why, I believe that would be Mr. Wendell Breecher. He's lived in that house almost as long as we've been in ours. That would be about fourteen years." There was a pause.

Andy looked up at me. "And your relationship with Mr. Breecher?"

I clasped my hands together in my lap, and straightened my shoulders. "Mr. Breecher and I did not have a relationship. As I stated, he lived across the street from me."

Mr. Feester got up from the sofa. "Now, Mrs. Titan, you're telling me you lived fourteen years across from Mr. Breecher and have nothing to say about him"

I looked at Mr. Feester and batted my eyelashes. "I didn't say I didn't have anything to say about Mr. Breecher. I said we didn't have a relationship. Mother always said, 'if you didn't have anything nice to say, don't say anything at all.' I think that's very wise, don't you, Mr. Feester?"

Feester nodded his head. "Yes. No. I mean, why don't you continue?"

"Well, I don't know that there's much more to say. Mr. Breecher and I didn't see eye to eye on most things. We kept our distance as much as possible and conversed only on a necessary basis."

Feester jumped up again. "What about the afternoon—"

Andy cut him off. "I believe I can handle this, gentlemen."

Feester nodded and sat back down looking like a heavyweight fighter being held back by an invisible piece of string.

Andy started back up. "Now, Tess. Do you recall where you were on Friday afternoon at lunchtime?"

I paused for several minutes, then remembered mother's luncheon. "Oh yes, now I remember. I was attending a luncheon at the Water's Edge. The Women's Club was meeting and mother had been nominated as president for next year." I smiled at Feester and Trumball.

"Do you remember when you arrived?"

"I was running late. I should have been there at 11:30 a.m., but I didn't get there until noon."

"Do you know when you left?"

"Oh yes, it was right after I gave my speech, 1:00 p.m."

Andy nudged the recorder closer to me. "Now, Tess. Do you remember seeing anyone at the hotel that you recognized?"

I looked at Andy like he was nuts. "Why Andy Hagen, you know you couldn't pee in a cup around here without everybody knowin' about it." I giggled and tried to blush.

Trumball laughed from the other side of the room.

Feester wasn't as pleased. "Mrs. Titan, please try to keep your comments pertinent to the questions at hand."

I nodded my head in Feester's direction, "I apologize, I know bodily functions make some people very uncomfortable."

Andy wiped his hand across his mouth to hide his smile, coughed, and started back up. "Now about seeing anyone else you knew at the hotel?"

"Well, I remember the place was packed that day. I recognized the names of a number of the groups. Most of the meetings were already in session. There weren't a lot of people milling about. But there must have been hundreds of folks there that day."

"Do you remember one of the groups meeting that day to be the Citizens for the Ethical Treatment of Exotic Animals?"

"Oh yes, they were there. Sort of stood out being wedged between the Chamber of Commerce and the Cheer Squad.

"And did you see anyone you knew attending the CETEA meeting?"

It was pretty clear where this line of questioning was going, but I couldn't very well claim amnesia at this point. "Yes, Mr. Breecher was waiting outside the doors to the CETEA meeting room."

"Did he appear calm?"

"I don't think the word 'calm' and Wendell Breecher can be used in the same sentence."

"So, he was nervous?"

I shifted in my seat. "He was obviously bothered about something."

"Do you know what was disturbing him?"

"How do I know? Maybe his hemmies were acting-up."

Andy shook his head, ready to call it quits.

I snapped my fingers. "Sorry about that, I did it again, didn't I, Mr. Feester?" I focused my attention back on Andy. "I would say he was waiting for someone, and he looked a bit out of sorts. But then that's somewhat of his normal state, wouldn't you say?"

Feester jumped up again. "Mrs. Titan, just answer the questions as they are given to you. Acting familiar with the recording officer can contaminate your statement."

I looked at Andy. "Oh, mustn't do that now, should I?" Andy continued. "Did you have the opportunity to find out who Mr. Breecher was waiting for?"

I thought about lying for an instant, but remembered my conversation with Ferdy the Foghorn in the restroom. They already knew the answer to this one. I would only be verifying.

"It just so happens I did. I went in the ladies room to powder my nose and saw Ferdy Callahan. We had a brief conversation. She mentioned the speaker, Miss Wanamaker, was running quite late and couldn't be found. It seems she was to be the speaker for the meeting, and the group was getting a little edgy after having to listen to Bill Brannon talk about the mating habits of termites."

Andy held back a laugh. Feester glared at Andy and rolled his hand to get on with it.

"Thank you, Tess. Now moving on to another occasion. Did you visit Mr. Breecher at his home on the evening of September 18?"

"Well, visit infers somewhat being invited, so I'd have to say 'no' to that one. I did knock on his door asking him what he'd done with our pelican, Fitzgerald."

"You had some reason to believe that Mr. Breecher would have something to do with the disappearance of your pelican?"

There were a hundred nasty words zooming through my brain. I was having trouble finding the most appropriate southern reply for the stuffy figureheads sitting opposite me. "My experience with Mr. Breecher was that he did not share in my daughter's interest for taking care of injured animals. He particularly did not like Fitzgerald. He felt that F. Scott scared away the other birds from feeding in his yard."

"And how did he react to your accusation that evening?"

"He denied having anything to do with it. Our conversation was cut short by the appearance of Mrs. Wanamakit."

"Wanamaker," Andy corrected.

I turned to Andy as if I hadn't heard him. "I'm sorry, I didn't catch what you said."

Andy took a deep breath. I'm sure he was counting to ten. "Her name is 'Wanamaker,' not 'Wanamakit.'"

I tittered into my hand. "You could have fooled me."

Andy forced the issue. "Was she coming for a visit?"

"Oh, I think visit is more the right word for her. She had definitely been invited, if you know what I mean?" I winked at Mr. Feester.

Andy pressed on. "So, she was already in the house when you arrived?"

"Oh yes, she'd been there long enough to be in her Victoria's Secret nightgown. She seemed like a take-charge kind of woman. I doubt poor ol' Wendell even realized he had a tiger by the tail."

Feester and Trumball turned red as a pair of roosters caught in a hen house. Andy smiled at me and pushed stop on the recorder.

I looked a bit surprised. "That's it? I'm all finished?"

Andy helped me out of the chair. "Yes, you're definitely finished. I can't imagine we'll need you for anything else. You've been a great help." He pushed me towards the door. I waved over my shoulder. "So nice to meet you, Mr. Feester, Mr. Trumball. Do come back and visit our little town under better circumstances."

Before Andy could shut the door on me, I asked, "Is Betty here? I need to drop some donations off for the school auction."

Andy looked at me suspiciously. "No, she's up in the city running errands for me today."

"Ah." I nodded. "I'll catch up with her later." *Damn, I won't know what's going on for days.*"

I couldn't tell if my feeble attempt at southern ambiguity had earned any points in favor or against Breecher. I just hoped I hadn't been the one to put the nail in his coffin. As much as I disliked the man, I knew he wasn't a murderer. At most he was an ignorant bystander that had been lured into playing a dangerous game.

I leaned back against my car, and raised my face toward the sun, taking in a few rays. The warmth felt good. The heat was relaxing the muscles in my otherwise tense body. I opened my eyes slowly, only to have them fly open in amazement. Across the street in front of the bookstore was the black Beemer.

Chapter Twenty-four

I trotted as fast as I could across the parking lot. Not seeing anyone approaching the car, I wandered up behind it, and ran my hand under the bumper. It only took a second for my hand to feel the sticky gum.

This was the same car that had been at the Water's Edge Conference Center, and now it was parked outside the bookstore. I wondered if it was the same Beemer that had been at the gun shop? This was a chance for me to get a first-hand look at the driver.

Would it be Wanamaker? I'd still never seen her driving a car; she was always being chauffeured around by Breecher. Could she be the culprit responsible for everything that had been happening? Could she be the murderer? If it was her, I'd recognize her as soon as she stepped out of the bookstore.

I took a seat on a bench nearby and waited, and waited, and waited. Almost a half-hour passed and no one appeared. I felt conspicuous on the bench by myself doing nothing and decided a woman eating an ice cream cone on a bench outside a bookstore on a nice sunny day would seem more normal.

By the time I'd decided on an ice cream flavor, cone type, and sprinkles or nuts, the car was gone. I stood there in disbelief holding a Mount Olympus ice cream cone in my hand.

Geena appeared from around the corner. "I thought you were trying to lose weight?"

I shoved the cone at her. "Here, hold this a minute. I've gotta talk to the clerk in the bookstore."

The "dingle" of the doorbells was annoyingly quaint as I raced around the browsing customers. I made my way to the checkout counter, perturbed at the current customer who couldn't decide if she wanted two or three bookmarks.

I finally had to intercede. "I couldn't help but notice your dilemma. I've often been in this same predicament. And you know whenever I don't buy the extra one, I always find that I should have. Someone drops by unexpectedly with a gift or I need a small something to give someone at the church or school."

The woman nodded in agreement. "I'll take all three."

The sales girl smiled at me as the lady shuffled off to the café section to drive someone else crazy.

"Pardon me," I said to the young girl across the counter. "I need a little help. It seems I've just missed the person I was waiting for. They drive the black Beemer that was parked out front."

The girl smacked her gum a few times. Her eyes brightened. "Oh, you must mean Mr. Sarducci! Tall, slim, very suave, and very Italian?"

That took Wanamaker off the list. It looked like our "invisible man" was taking center stage. I watched the girl's eyes go in and out of a very clear fantasy state. "Yes, yes, that's him. Mr. Sarducci. Say, he didn't happen to mention where he was going, did he?"

"No, I don't remember him saying anything. He was just following his usual routine."

My eyebrows rose. "Routine?"

"Oh yes, he has come in several times over the last week. He comes in just about this time of day, finds a book, has a cup of coffee while he looks it over, and always says 'Arrividerci, my bella donna'." Her eyes were getting glassy again.

I tried to give an honest laugh. "Oh yes, that's Mr. Sarducci, all right. You wouldn't happen to remember the books he's been buying or what section he buys from, would you?"

She looked at me a little suspiciously.

"It's no big deal. I was just hoping you might have noticed. You see, he and I are in a book club together and I got his name for the Secret Santa party. I thought it might be nice to get him something that he enjoys reading."

She popped her gum again. "Christmas in September?"

I was ready to knock my head on the counter. But I kept the ruse going. "Yes. That's exactly what we call it. 'Christmas in September.' Clever, isn't it?"

She didn't look like she was buying it. I had to go to new levels of deception.

"I'm sure *you* of all people would understand—knowing Mr. Sarducci so well. You're certainly aware how much he misses his own little village in Italy, his family, and many friends. He liked the idea of the 'Christmas in September' party, because he said it reminded him so much of a similar festival they have in his town this time of year."

Her eyes were getting all soppy. "It sounds like your group is just what he needs." She leaned over the counter and whispered in a low voice. "He likes books about nature."

"Nature? Like trees, and birds, and chipmunks?"

"Well, sort of. He likes the more exotic things. I guess it's just in his nature." She started with the mooneyes again.

"That's interesting. Exotic, you say. You know, I wouldn't even know where to begin looking for something like that. Could you show me?"

"Oh sure, that would be in this direction." She led me over to the nature aisle.

"Oh, one more thing. You know, I'd hate to accidentally buy him something he's just recently bought over the last few weeks. Would you happen to remember some of his selections?"

"Yes, I think I can help you there. His chooses some pretty unusual stuff. " She made her way down the aisle, first stopping in front of Flora & Fauna. "Let's see, he got this book on mushroom identification." She handed it to me and walked around the aisle to the other side. She stopped in front of Florida's Animals. "Then, he got this book on poisonous fish. I told him he didn't need to worry too much about that sort of thing here in the northern Gulf. But he said, 'You could never be too careful.'" She stood up and blew a good-sized bubble, then popped it. "Last week, he got a book on snakes. I specifically remember because he said he was planning on attending the Garden Club meeting and the topic was "Gardening with Poisonous Animals." He said he wanted to bone up some, particularly on rattlers before the meeting. I told him we have a lot of pigmy rattlers around here."

I couldn't believe what she was telling me. This had to be the man. The murderer and scourge of my life had been at the Water's Edge attending the Garden Club meeting while I was promoting mother for president, and moments before, he had been standing right where I am now. I could feel his filth surrounding me. I moved a little way down the aisle.

"And today?" I asked. "Anything special today?"

"Funny, you should ask. He did buy something a little different today." She walked back over to the Flora and Fauna section and pulled out a rather thick book. "This is it."

I read the title out loud. "Indigenous Flora and Fauna of Northern Florida."

"Hmm. Did he say why he was interested in this?" I could hear the customers getting restless at the front counter.

The cashier waved her hand. "Be right there." She quickly turned to me before heading back to the register. "He didn't say anything specific. But you know, he seemed to have a preoccupation with things that were deadly or poisonous. I felt sorry for him. He was far from home. He must have been paranoid about all the bugs and stuff around here. If I were you, I'd buy him a large can of mosquito spray and some citronella candles. Maybe it would lighten up his mood a little."

I nodded in an appreciative way. *I don't think Deet and citronella will get rid of this vermin.*

Chapter Twenty-five

I got Jack on the cell phone and updated him on my discovery about the identity of our killer.

He sounded worried. "Did you say, Sarducci?"

"Yeah. Isn't Sarducci the name the crime family the Contessa mentioned in her letter to Nell?" It was very quiet on the other end of the line. "Hello? Am I reaching out and touching myself here?"

"It's nothing to joke about, Tess. I think I've got this puzzle figured out, and we're about to get glued to the puzzle board."

"As romantic as that sounds—being stuck next to you for eternity on a puzzle blanket—you want to let me in on what the hell is happening here?"

I pulled my car off the side of the road. The water looked perfect. There was a young family walking down the beach, probably collecting shells. I should say, the parents were walking. The kids were dashing in and out of the waves, laughing and throwing sand at one another.

The bite in Jack's voice brought me back to realty. "Hello? Tess? Did you hear me?"

"What? No, sorry. There was some static on the line. Can you repeat it?"

There was an anxious sigh on the other end. "I said, Sarducci is a member of the *other* crime family."

The wheels were cranking very slowly. "Other family? What do you mean?"

"You remember when the Contessa wrote 'she knew they were coming,' but she didn't know how much time she had?"

"Yes, but what's that got to do with this?"

"Did you ever wonder why she ended up having so much time?

Probably more than she'd ever anticipated?"

"Sure, I wondered. But I just figured, anybody who was somebody had died during the war, and it took a long time for someone to get interested in what appeared to be a rumor."

"Somethin' like that. You see, during the war, the Sarducci Family got hit really hard."

"Right, that's why they hid the antiquities. They suspected that might happen."

"Will you let me finish? They got hit harder than they'd expected. They were all but obliterated. The few that lived through the massacre took off to the four corners of the world. There was an up-and-coming family that used the opportunity to take over."

The picture got clearer for me. "Right. The Rosetti Family, the family your father was involved with, took over, found out the rumor was true, and sent their friendly, village eraser, Romeo, to eliminate any competition. But before he finished the job, he was taken out by Sarducci."

"Well, you're partially right. It was the Sarducci Family that was in power during the war. They were taken over by the Rosetti family, which continues to be in power today. Though their presence is pretty shaky if you ask the locals."

I started searching around the car for a piece of gum. "Well, that answers my question about why Sarducci never tried to contact us to make a deal. His family is out of power, desperate to re-establish themselves. He's not interested in deals."

Jack's voice was sounding loud and clear. "You got that right. But Romeo was working with a fair amount of 'good will' I guess you'd call it, to acquire the document and any other information you had. Since his family, the Rosetti's, are still in power, he had every reason to continue working under a reasonable code of ethics and to keep things low key. It wasn't to his benefit to have bodies popping up everywhere and drawing attention to his purpose for being here."

Jack added, "According to Romeo, he hadn't been involved in the murders and dirty deeds affecting your family, and that made him nervous."

I found a half piece of gum in the coin holder that didn't look too grody. "Nervous because he thought he was playing solitaire and it turned out to be poker. He didn't know Sarducci was in the game, until it was too late."

Jack sounded a bit nostalgic. "Too bad he didn't figure it out a little earlier. He might still be here today, fighting with us instead of having his ashes scattered over the Mediterranean Sea."

"You think he'd have fought *with* us?"

"No doubt. Who the enemy is or isn't can change on a dime. Right now, we wouldn't be the enemy, Sarducci would be, and Romeo would be using all his resources to erase the real thorn in his side."

My light started blinking on my cell phone. "My battery is running low. Let's plan to meet at my house an hour before we head to Josie's. You can let me in on our 'secret forces' and we can talk strategy."

"Strategy would be good, Titan. You have to remember, Sarducci has probably been sent to find the answer to restoring financial power to their family, or given the order not to return. He *has* to succeed. Nothing can stand in his way." The phone started losing power. The connection was getting worse. Jacks words were going in and out. "He...has...nothing...to...lose."

The line died.

Chapter Twenty-six

As I pulled into my driveway, I couldn't help but notice the real estate agent putting up a rental sign in Breecher's yard.

I meandered up to the corner of his property. "So, Mr. Breecher is taking a holiday?"

The young toots jumped around. "Oh! You scared me. I wasn't expecting anyone home around this time."

"Oh yes, I'm in and out all the time." I extended my hand. "I'm Tess Titan. I live across the street." I tried not to stare at the size 40 Ds falling out of her scooped tee shirt.

She gave me one of those glamour girl smiles and daintily shook my hand.

"It's so nice to meet you, Mrs. Titan. I'm sure you're concerned about who might move in, but I want you to know I'll do my very best to make sure we get someone quiet, dependable, and friendly."

"Sane would be a step up," I said.

She cocked her head to the left a bit, like the light bulb had slipped, and gave me a vague smile. "I'll do what I can."

"Great, that would be great. Well, I've got to get going. Nice to have met you...uh?"

"Oh! I'm Suzanne. Suzanne Dimple."

"Of course, you are. I should have known. Well, see you around, Suzanne."

Suzanne went back to tapping in her 25 x 25 rental sign with a tack hammer. At that rate she'd be pounding for the rest of the afternoon. A nice person would have gone in her garage and gotten her a bigger hammer. But I figured she was going to need all the muscle building she could stand to keep those puppies perked up.

I had a good six hours before I had to dress and be ready to meet with Jack and his recruits. I should have used the time to clean, fold laundry, or update my address book. Instead, I decided to shave and pluck unwanted hair from my body. That accomplished, I took a nap.

Donning my skulking attire, I double-checked my gun and put on some fresh lipstick. Jack appeared at the doorstep at 11:00 p.m on the nose. I held the door open and looked behind him as he settled himself in the living room.

"Where's everyone else?" I shut the door and sat down opposite him on the sofa.

"Where they're supposed to be."

"And I hope that's somewhere near where we're putting our lives in danger in an hour?"

He smiled and nodded. "Would I let you down?"

"This is not a good time to be asking me rhetorical questions. This is my life we're talking about here."

"I know. I don't mean to make light of the situation. Are you carrying?"

"Yep." I patted my pockets. "Gum, Glock, and a quarter in case I need to make an emergency phone call."

"Very funny. With our luck, we'll get one of those pay phones that charges thirty-five cents."

I went over to the drawer, pulled out an extra dime, and added it to my pocket. "Can't be too prepared. So, what's the plan, great leader?"

"The plan is we go to Josie's. I'll walk in first, you follow. I'll keep the list. We make contact, we give him the list, and we get the hell out of there."

I nodded my head. "How long did it take you to figure out that master plan?"

"Don't start with me, Titan. There's no need to go ballistic on this meet. It's neat. It's simple. It's a..."

"...walk in the park. Yeah, I'm already brutally familiar with your park walking scenarios."

Jack fidgeted in his seat. "There's no way we could have known that was going to happen."

"And we know what's gonna happen tonight?"

"Yeah, we do. And we're covered. This guy works alone. We don't. The odds are with us, big time."

"Well, it eases my mind to know that if we do bite the dust that it will have been a mere fluke, an 'odds buster,' I believe Nell would call it."

Jack stood up and tossed his keys back and forth from one hand to the other. "Don't go getting all bent out of shape about this. We're ready. He's not. Tonight will be the end of all this. Tomorrow morning, you'll be a worry-free woman again."

Does such a being exist? I wondered. A picture of Suzanne Dimple shot into my head. Even she had to worry about straining her back or getting bra burn.

I made a call to the hospital and spoke to the kids and Nell. Everything was quiet. They were planning on watching some *Tarzan* classics and eating as many Popsicles as the nurse would bring them.

"I'll call you as soon as this is over. Okay, Nell?"

"I'll be waiting. You just do what you need to do. I don't mean to complain, Tessa dear, but after tonight, I never want to eat another Popsicle for the rest of my life."

I had to laugh. "You've paid your debt to the frozen sugar god. I promise, no more Popsicles."

I put the phone back on the receiver and couldn't help the sinking feeling in my chest. This wasn't a walk in the park. This was real. I could be hurt or killed. I knew Nell would take care of the kids, but that didn't soften the sting in my heart. Then I realized custody would go to their father, Michael. "Not in this lifetime," I said out loud.

"What did you say?" Jack asked.

"Nothing. Nothing important. Come on, let's get out of here. We've got a rat to exterminate at Josie's."

"By the way, I hope you didn't tell Josie too much about tonight. We don't want to put her in any danger."

I turned on the front porch light and locked the door behind us. "She doesn't know anything. I told her I needed some private time with you, out of the way of spying eyes."

Jack got a surprised look on his face. "You told her what? You know what that sounds like?"

I hit him in the shoulder. "Hey stud, what do you care? It only enhances your reputation."

He mumbled something about "married women" and "bats in the attic." I didn't quite catch it all before we got in his car. We hadn't gone far before I felt obliged to inform him his tank was almost on empty.

He patted his pockets, then turned towards me. "I hope you've got some money, sweetheart, because I believe in sharing expenses on a first date!"

Chapter Twenty-seven

It was 11:30 p.m. when we pulled the SUV into some brush about a half-mile from Josie's.

"Is there some reason we can't just park up front? It's not like he's not expecting us." I tried not to sound like I was whining.

"Yes, there's a reason. Besides the fact that I'm sure you can use the exercise."

I flicked my fingers under my chin in a rude gesture.

"I'll act like I didn't see that. Secondly, because I don't want anyone messing with my car. There'll be enough going on without the boys having to keep track of someone boobytrapping the car."

I popped a piece of Double Bubble in my mouth. The sugar coated my throat so strong I had to gasp out my words. "Right. Boobytrapping. Just testin' you."

Jack shook his head. "I don't know how you chew that stuff."

"You have to build up to it. It's not for lightweights."

We could see Josie's in the clearing. She had left the back porch light on for us.

"How are we supposed to get in?" Jack asked.

"She said she'd leave the key under the crab pot by the door."

We found the key easily enough and entered the restaurant through the kitchen entrance. It was eerie, even though Josie had left "mood lighting" on for us. It felt like I was sneaking around someone's house uninvited.

Jack pushed the swinging door open from the kitchen to the dining room very slowly. I hung on his shoulder. "Do you see anything?" I whispered into his ear.

"No. Everything looks clear."

"Where should we wait for him?"

"I'd suggest the dining room, too many weapons here in the kitchen."

I looked around and saw all the knives and pans hanging from the rafters. "Good idea." What I really wanted to do was take a few minutes and hide all the knives, but I didn't think Jack would go for it.

We went into the main dining room. I followed in Jack's shadow. It was so quiet you could hear Bugsy, their pet macaw cracking sunflower seeds in his cage. Jack took a quick look around. "I don't see anybody. But we're early." He walked over to the bar. "Josie left us a note. 'Know how much you all like marguaritas, left you a batch in the bar fridge. Enjoy.'" Sitting by the note were two marguarita glasses, rims salted.

"I hate to pass up a free drink on the house. You want one? Seems appropriate since it's our first date and all." Jack got the pitcher from the fridge.

"You think that's a good idea?" I hopped up onto one of the bar stools and made sure I could see everything going on behind me in the bar mirrors.

"In this situation, I'd say a few sips would be good for calming the nerves." He filled our glasses and slid mine down the bar. It stopped right in front of me.

"I'm impressed. You may have a second life as a bartender, if you ever need it."

"Been there, done that, wore out all the bad tee shirts." He ran his tongue around the rim of the glass and took a long drink. We both drank in silence.

Jack put the pitcher back in the fridge behind him. "It was nice of Josie to keep the bar stocked for us."

"Nothing's free. She'll want all the sordid details."

"Let's just leave her a tip instead."

Out of the back north corner, the shadows spoke. "I'll remember to do that for you."

I jerked around on the barstool. Jack reached for his piece. We both looked into the corner trying to discern human flesh from the darkness that encircled it.

The figure walked slowly from the shadows. "So sorry to disturb your little get-together, but I have other things to do tonight. I'm sure you understand."

A few more steps and we were finally face to face with our assailant. I was surprised. After all the gruesome atrocities this man had inflicted, I was expecting a cross between Frankenstein and Dr. Jekyl. Instead, I sat staring at an attractive man, about 5'11", 175 pounds. His skin was olive tone, the hair dark and full. Katie had described him to a tee. He didn't have any facial hair, but I could make out a gold chain around his neck. I could see why the young girl at the bookstore was so attracted to him.

"Did you bring the list, Mrs. Titan?" The man stood deathly still as he spoke to me.

"I have it." Jack came out from behind the bar.

The man's eyes jumped back and forth from me to Jack. "Slowly, Mr. Daniels, very slowly."

Jack walked up casually to the table that divided the two men, taking the list from his pocket, he tossed it on the middle of the table.

"The man reached for it and held it delicately by its corners. His eyes brightened. His smile turning into a lecherous laugh. "Yes! After all these years. Success!"

Jack sat down in one of the chairs at the table. "As much fun as it is to see you gloat, Mr. ..."

"Cobra" is all you need to know."

Jack kept his hands close to his weapon. "Well, as much fun as it is to sit here and watch you gloat, Mr. Cobra, perhaps you could find the time to fill us in on what this mystery is all about? And why it's brought you and your family from across the sea to wreak havoc on our sleepy little township?"

He rolled the list up and placed it gently inside his jacket pocket. "I believe I have a few moments, Mr. Daniels. Then I really must be on my way." He took a seat opposite Jack. He showed no fear. He must have known we were carrying, but seemed completely unconcerned. I decided to stay perched like an owl on my barstool.

Cobra leaned back in his chair and rested his arms across his chest. "Ah, where to start such an unlikely tale?"

"How about with the guy they fished from the lines of the Pirate Ship?"

Cobra nodded. "An unfortunate miscalculation on my part. I didn't expect the competition to be so close on my heels. He had to be dealt with swiftly, and a statement made of him for any others that were considering following."

I shuddered at his complete composure, as if he merely had stepped on an ant. "But why the Stonefish poison? Why not just shoot him and be done with it like Romeo?"

"I'm impressed, Mrs. Titan, that you knew where the poison came from. As I said before, he was a statement. Competitors would think twice before coming up against me."

I rested my feet on the barstool. "So let me see if I've got this straight. You were sent by the Sarducci family to find this list of hidden antiquities that, unbeknownst to my godmother, was given to her years ago by the Contessa. This list will supposedly fund the resurgence of your family's place in the Italian Mafia hierarchy."

Cobra placed his palms together, crossed his fingers, and ran his index fingers from his lips to his chin. "You know quite a lot for a sleepy township resident, Mrs. Titan. You have come to be as frustrating a foe as the Contessa."

He smoothed out the front of his jacket. "After the war, we were spread all over the world. It took decades to bring continuity to the Sarducci family once again. It wasn't until then that the tale about this list came to light. At first, it was looked upon as nothing more than the rantings of old men. But times became desperate. Anyone still living who had first-hand knowledge about the list was brought together. Soon, we were able to piece together the truth behind the tale and realized that this was our salvation."

"But why involve the Contessa?" I rubbed my fingers over the amulet hanging around my neck.

Cobra threw his fists to the table. "Stupid wench! She caused us years of waiting, years of humiliation kissing the feet of the Rosetti Family. Our fathers never considered she might become involved when they left the list with the Count for safekeeping. No one suspected it would take so long to return and retrieve the information. No one could have guessed the untimely demise of the Count.

We watched the Contessa for years for any proof that she knew about the list. We suspected her from the start, but were never able to put our hands on the information. Upon her death, we searched the home. Our only lead was pictures she'd kept of she and your godmother. We never could find that damned book your godmother was holding in one of the pictures! That is what brought me here to your little hideaway in Paradise," he said waving his arms around the room and laughing.

He stopped in mid laugh. His eyes had turned into lifeless black holes. "The book had to be found, and any proof of the pictures destroyed."

My stomach was beginning to turn. "But you weren't the man who mugged me and stole my satchel. How did you know about the timing at the photo shop?"

"Ah, yes, Frederico. He was a free-lancer."

My mouth was stone dry. "Was?"

"He had to be disposed of...more quietly." The sickly smile returned to his face. "Luckily, I was watching nearby when the idiot stole your purse. I was the end recipient of the contents. Those damned pictures kept popping up everywhere!" He slammed his fist on the table. "They all had to be destroyed."

A frightening calm came over him. "In some ways, we were lucky the Contessa found the list and didn't accidentally dispose of it. Then where would we have been?"

I bit my tongue. "Making cheap leather shoes in America?" My head was feeling fuzzy, and my tongue was numb. I didn't dare say anything to Jack.

"Ah, a sense of humor. You are going to need it, Mrs. Titan." He rose and pushed in his chair. "I understand the Contessa was much like you: a strong woman, a stubborn woman, and a brave woman. My father told me how she stared right into his eyes, never flinching, even as he helped throw her overboard on that blustery day." He patted his jacket pocket where he had secured the list. "I don't think you're holding any more cards, Mrs. Titan. I think it is your turn and Mr. Daniels' turn as well to fold."

I looked over at Jack and could tell he was out-of-it. "What have you done to us, you bastard?" His words were slurred, his eyes unfocused.

"I took the advantage of stacking the deck before you got here. Quite unfair of me, I admit. But it was two to one, you know. I felt I had some justification. It wasn't difficult this time. Nothing like taking poison from that atrocious fish or digging for those nasty smelling mushrooms or managing that unsociable rattler, much simpler. I merely edged your marguerita glasses with a powder made from the leaves and roots of a Belladonna Lily. Very poisonous, I'm afraid."

My vision was beginning to blur, and my skin was feeling hot. I could feel my heart banging against my ribs.

"You look uncomfortable on that stool, Mrs. Titan. Please allow me to sit you next to Mr. Daniels." He moved me into the chair next to Jack. I was stumbling as he helped me to the chair. I could barely keep my head up. The next thing I knew, he was setting two large salads in front of us. He washed out the marguerita glasses and dumped the pitcher from the fridge. He stood back as if surveying the outcome of his work.

"Yes, I do believe that's everything. You see, you'll both be found quite dead tomorrow morning."

I could see Jack try to move his hand for his gun, but the paralysis was too far along. I could feel sweat start to roll down my brow. "Why? Why kill us, when you have what you want?" My speech was slow and labored.

He walked over and held my chin in his hand, raising my eyes to meet his. "You know 'belladonna' comes from the Italian, meaning beautiful woman. During the Renaissance, women applied an extract of the plant to their eyes to dilate their pupils and give a wide and beautiful appearance. Bella, Mrs. Titan. Bella." He dropped my chin. "There will be no loose ends. The tale ends here, tonight."

"I'm sure your godmother and children will be as beautiful in death as you are proving to be." He walked back into the shadows. "Ciao."

I could feel the darkness closing in on me. *I failed,* I thought. *I failed myself, I failed my family, and I failed Jack.* Inside my head came the little girl's voice, "I promise. I won't touch it again. I promise. I promise. I promise."

Chapter Twenty-eight

Within minutes, I felt someone forcing me to drink some foul liquid, then shove my head in a bucket to vomit. After a few reruns, someone sat me up, cleaned my face, and gave me a shot in my left shoulder.

"Ouch! Hey buster, that hurt."

He smiled at me and looked at his partner. "She'll be just fine. How's J.D.?"

"He's coming around. He must have gotten a stronger dose of the poison. I don't think he's gonna be drinking margaritas for awhile." Our two saviors laughed.

I rose slowly out of my chair.

"Take it easy, Mrs. Titan. Wherever you think you're going will have to wait."

"No, no! You don't understand." I choked on my words, spitting the unsavory leftover taste of poison and bile from my mouth. "Cobra is on his way to the hospital to kill my godmother and children! We've got to go now. Got to call someone to alert them."

"Calm down, Mrs. Titan. We heard it all. Jack was wearing a wire. We don't know how Cobra got in and out of here. We had the place covered. But we heard his plan and alerted our other crew. He'll have a welcoming committee waiting for him at the hospital."

I should have felt better. I didn't. Now Jack was trying to get out of his chair.

"What is it with you two? You have a death wish? Sit down, take it easy, the other crew will pick this guy off." Just then his cell phone went off. He looked grim when he closed the lid.

"No!" Jack grunted furiously. "It's too important. We have to be sure. Get us to my car as fast as you can. You'll have to drive us to the hospital."

The guy didn't give Jack any more lip. "I think you're right. All the phone lines have been cut to the hospital. Seems the power line has been cut as well. They're working off an emergency generator." He spoke into a radio and within a few minutes, Jack's car was outside the door. Jack sat in front with his cohort. I sat in the back seat with his buddy.

Jack opened the glove compartment and pulled out what looked like another radio. The driver cocked his head. "Remote?"

Jack nodded. "To the hospital room."

"One way or two?"

"One. I didn't think we'd need two-way, since the hospital has phone lines."

I sat forward on the seat and put my head between the two front bucket seats. "What are you talking about? You have a remote to the kid's hospital room? Can we talk to them? Can we see if they're all right?" My words started running together as too many thoughts filled my head at one time.

Jack shook his head. "No. It's one way. I hooked it up through the nurse's intercom in the hospital room. We can hear what's going on, but we can't talk on the line."

Jack turned the remote on and turned the volume on high. There was some static and interference as we shot out of the woods back onto the main road to the hospital.

I strained to hear the faintest noise, a word, a hiccup, anything to keep my hopes alive. Then I heard it, clear as a bell, Nell giving orders to the children.

"All right, now. It's probably nothing, but we need to be prepared. The guard is still right outside the door. Katie and Kevin, I want you both to get into the bathroom, lock the door, and stand in the shower. Kevin, here is some mace. Use it if you have to."

"Where are you going to be, Nell? Shouldn't you be with us?" I could hear the fear in Katie's voice.

"Now, don't you worry about your old Nell. Why, I once took down a charging bull with nothing but my bare hands and intellect!"

Katie laughed.

"Go on take her in, Kevin. If this person gets through the guard, I'll have a trap set out here. Whatever you do, do not open that door unless you hear someone's voice you trust, do you understand?"

"Yes, ma'am. Be careful, Nell."

"Pish posh. This is like a walk in the park."

I could hear the door to the bathroom closing. Nell was walking around the room. It sounded like she was moving the furniture. Then I heard the sound of metal on metal as the curtain was being pulled around the bed. I felt like I was going to explode from tension.

"This is worse than an Alfred Hitchcock movie. Isn't there anything else we can do?" My hands clenched the sides of the front seats.

Jack looked over his shoulder at me. "We're doing it. Our two other men have reported the guard is still at his post. They'll move in at the first sign of anyone trying to enter the room. We'll be there ourselves in another five minutes."

I could do nothing but sit, listen, wait, and pray. Once I'd done that, I still had four minutes forty-five seconds to live through.

The driver's cell phone rang. He hung up quickly. "Your mother's on her way up to the room."

"My mother?"

"That's what he said."

I fell back into my seat and rubbed my hands deep into my forehead. Everything was falling apart. The next thing I know, we hear mother entering the room.

"Nell? Tess? Why are the lights all out?" I could hear her trying the switch.

Nell's voice broke the silence. "Oh for heaven's sake, Eudora. What are you doing here? You're going to get yourself and all the rest of us killed!"

I could hear a little squirmish. "Don't push me, Nellie Sharp. What are you doing? Where is everybody? What in the world are you talking about?"

"Eudora, I don't have time to explain. You'll just have to get in the shower stall with the children."

"The what?"

"The shower stall. Now hurry up."

"I certainly will not go stand in a shower stall. Really, Nellie. I can take a hint when I'm not wanted. A simple, 'this isn't a good time to visit' would suffice. Stop pullin' on me. You're as persistent as that darn pelican."

There was complete silence.

I'd never heard Nell's voice sound so intense. "Eudora Wellsley, what do you know about the disappearance of Katie's pelican?"

Mother hemmed and hawed. "It's really very simple. I didn't think everyone would make such a fuss over the disappearance of that old, scraggly fishmonger."

Nell was losing her temper. "Eudora..."

"All right. All right. I called Water World and had them come over and get him. I told them he was a menace around the children and that Tess just couldn't keep him anymore."

I could hear war drums beating. It was probably my own blood pressure rising forty points.

Nell spoke. I could tell she was madder than hell. "Dora Jane Pittman, I don't know who the hell you think you are. But how dare you! How dare you butt your nose into something that's absolutely none of your business! How dare you take something that was never yours to begin with. And how dare you be so selfish and self-centered not even to consider the feelings of Katie and Tessa."

"Well, I never!" Mother spouted back.

"That's right. You never, Dora Jane. And you'd better start soon, or I'll, I'll..."

Mother's reply sounded snotty. She'd obviously regained her composure. "Or you'll what, Nellie Sharp? You made your promise to me forty years ago, I know you'll never go back on it. So don't start getting all high and mighty with me. You'll be who you are, just the way you are for the rest of your life. I would have thought you were used to it by now. And my name is Eudora Wellsley of the Birmingham Wellsleys. Don't you ever forget it."

I couldn't believe what I was hearing. Of course, I didn't understand what I was hearing either. But it wasn't like Nell to take flack from mother. Why wasn't she fighting back?"

Jack looked back at me. "Who's Dora Jane Pittman?"

I shook my head in confusion. "I have no idea what the hell they're talking about."

Nell's voice sounded restrained. "I apologize, EUDORA. I made a promise and I'll keep it to the death. But I won't stand by and watch you railroad my goddaughter and her children. You will go get that pelican and put him back before Katie gets out of the hospital."

"Apology accepted, Nell. And I will take your suggestion under consideration regarding that beast, as long as you promise me you won't let them know where the bird's been or how he got there. Agreed?"

"Another deal with the devil, Eudora? I suppose one more won't make a difference. But I must insist you get in the shower stall now."

I could hear Nell knocking on the door and shoving mother into the bathroom with instructions for Kevin to lie on top of her if she wouldn't stay put.

The cell phone rang. The driver turned to Jack. "Fire alarm just went off. They're evacuating the hospital. Eagle one reports the guard is holding his position at the door."

My adrenaline started rushing. "Something's up, Jack."

Jack nodded. "Step on it, and tell Eagle one to take the room now," he said to the driver.

"Ssshhhh! Listen. Jack, turn up the volume all the way."

Jack rolled the button to high.

"Can you hear it?"

Jack nodded. "Footsteps. Someone's in the room."

Then came the voice. The one that didn't belong. The one with no conscience.

"Hellooo? Knock, knock."

I could hear a light switch being clicked on back and forth.

"Very clever, Miss Nell. But come now, you know this is an exercise in futility. You're only making it harder on yourself and the children."

"Sonnofabitch!" He'd obviously run into something.

"Really now, let's bring this charade to an end, now." The voice sounded anxious and angry.

"You get him, Nell. You get the bastard. I know you can do this. I know you can!" My words echoed throughout the car.

We were swerving around the last few corners to the hospital. But I knew whatever was going to happen would happen in the next few seconds, long before we reached the door to the room.

"Where's Eagle one? Where are they?" I screamed into the front seat.

The driver shook his head. "No response from Eagle one, Jack."

"Shit. She's on her own in there. Hold on, Nell. Hold on just a few more minutes." Jack had his hand on the door ready to leap as soon as we got there. The driver pulled up behind a black Beemer.

Then I heard it. The sheet surrounding the bed was ripped away. There was a scream. First it sounded high pitched, almost surprised, then there was a low, gut-wrenching moan.

Only one voice followed, only two words, "I win."

******

People were still coming out the doors when we pulled up in front of the hospital. We pushed our way through the crowd and took the stairs two at a time to the third floor. Eagle one was on the floor behind the nurse's station. The guard was lying on the floor by the door. They'd both been sedated. The door to Katie's room stood ajar.

I kicked the door with my foot and rolled to the left. The room was dark. I tried the switch. It didn't work. A light was coming from the bathroom. Jack opened the door and went in low.

"Nothing in here."

"They're not here. I leaned against the wall and took a long breath. "Where could they be?"

Jack found a light bulb on the table and screwed it into one of the lamps. He looked around the bed. "No blood. He's either taking them somewhere else to kill them, or they got away and he's hunting them."

"I'll kill him," I said. "Whatever it takes, I'm killing this son of a bitch."

"Anger is good. So is control. Stay with me here on this one, okay Tess?"

I nodded and wiped the sweat from my hands.

Jack looked around the room. "First we have to find them. We'll have to start on this floor, and work our way down." Jack moved toward the door. I'll meet you by the entrance on the first floor. Will you be okay on your own?"

"I have to be. Go. Hurry up. I'm going to take a last look around here."

"Okay." He took off down the hallway.

I looked around the room for anything out of the ordinary. I was ready to give up when I saw something on the bed. Sitting on top of the sheets was a wadded up piece of paper. I opened it and flattened it out on the bed. It was a picture of a rattlesnake. "It's Nell," I said to myself.

"They're pictures from that horrible reptile book."

I hurried into the hallway looking down the corridor, left and right. I found another one to the right, and another farther down the hall.

The wadded balls led me to the stairwell. I ran up and down the couple flights looking for another clue. Fear was creeping into my body. *I've got to find them now! I'm running out of time.*

I opened the last wadded ball and spread it out on the wall. The paper felt sticky. I sniffed it, then licked it. *Jell-O. Strawberry Jell-O. They're in the cafeteria.*

Chapter Twenty-nine

I took the stairs to the first floor and quietly made my way towards the cafeteria. There were voices coming from inside. Positioning myself outside the open doors, I could hear Cobra.

"All of you. Against the wall, now!" He yelled.

"Please don't hurt us. Don't hurt us." Mother was crying.

I looked around the corner. He had them off to the left against the wall. The doors were in his blind spot.

"Mr. Sarducci, I believe that's your name, isn't it?" Nell had her arms wrapped around the children. "There's no reason for the children to be involved in this. Why not let them go? You can keep Eudora and me."

"Spoken like a true diplomat, Miss Sharp. I can see why the Contessa chose you." Cobra moved chairs out of his way.

Eudora unfolded her hands from around her face. "The Contessa? Is she the one to blame for all this? She turned towards Nell. "You and that woman have been nothing but trouble my entire life, and now your shenanigans are going to get us all killed. Damn you, Nellie. Damn you and that friend of yours!" The tears were pouring out.

"My, my. Not much of a family reunion, is it?" Cobra laughed. He leveled his gun at Nell. "Don't worry, I've planned for the entertainment."

"No!" I screamed planting myself directly behind Cobra.

He turned. The gun was now pointed at me. "I guess we have a stand off, don't we Mrs. Titan?"

Sweat trickled down my forehead. My eyes started to blur. I could feel the slap on my face, and hear the words from my own mouth, "I promise. I promise."

He laughed again. "Why Mrs. Titan, you don't look very good. Do guns make you nervous?" He waved his around in the air.

"Don't move!" I yelled.

He stood still. "Or what, Mrs. Titan? You'll shoot me? I don't think so." He pointed the gun at me. I could see his finger pulling on the trigger.

"No!" Eudora yelled. "Tess, you have to listen to me."

"It's not a real good time right now mother, do you think this could wait?"

Cobra stayed ready, but I could see his finger loosen.

"No. It can't wait. It's rather important. I've been meaning to tell you this for a long time. But the moment never seemed to be right. Right now doesn't seem particularly good either, but sometimes you just have to hope for the best, don't you? Or not. Maybe now isn't such a good time."

"Mother! What is it?"

Eudora stood up straight and tried to gain some composure. "You know how I always disapproved of you being in the Patrol?"

"You're right, Mother. This is not a good time."

"I disapproved because I made you promise me when you were a little girl that you would never play with a gun again."

"My eyes started to clear. What are you talking about?"

She held her hand to her head. "Well, you see one day I came home from doing the shopping. It seemed like I was always shopping, or cleaning, or doing laundry. Anyway, there you were in the living room holding your father's gun. You pointed it at me and pretended to shoot me. The gun went off. I was screaming thinking you had shot me. But you had missed. I was so angry. The gun was supposed to be locked away whenever your father was off-duty. I hated that gun. I hated his job. I was frightened to death for me—and you, of course."

"You slapped me."

"Well, I really don't remember if I did or not. I was very angry."

"You made me promise never to shoot at a person again."

Eudora looked surprised. "Yes. I did make you promise."

Cobra smiled and started to pull the trigger.

I leapt to the right and heard thunder.

******

Cobra was dead. I nailed him.

I should have been dead, too. My saving grace? The Contessa's pendant. The bullet shattered the stones, and gave me a bruise to nurse, but I was alive. With the Contessa's gift and my mother's confession, I'd managed to cheat death.

Jack was by my side in minutes. "You did it, Titan. And it looks like you're going to live to tell about it."

"A walk in the park," I said. "It was a walk in the park."

Chapter Thirty

September 22, 2001

We all sat around Nell's big kitchen table chowing down on a wonderful seafood lunch, compliments of Josie.

Geena scarfed down a piece of pecan pie, shaking her head in disbelief during the entire story. "But how did you get him, Nell? How did you get him cornered so you had the chance to escape?"

Nell pushed her own pie plate to the side. "Well, you see, Geena, I remembered that story about the blind girl who knew someone was coming to kill her. She did everything she could to improve her odds. That's just what I did. I took out all the light bulbs, and moved the furniture. I knew he would eventually make his way to the bed and have to throw the curtain back. With his attention diverted, and the noise from the curtain on the metal rod, I knew he wouldn't hear me coming up behind him. I zapped him with that stun gun and got everyone out of there as fast as I could. I knew Tessa would be looking for us so I grabbed that reptile book and ripped out the pages. I knew she'd figure out where we were headed."

We all applauded. Nell blushed.

Jack pushed back from the table, fat and happy. "You know, I'm still stymied by how Cobra got in and out of Josie's without my men noticing him."

I picked up my plate and put it in the sink. "I'd been thinking about that, too. On a hunch, I went back over to Josie's and talked to Rick about it. He showed me the secret door that's back in that north corner. Smugglers used it to get in and out of the restaurant unseen."

I rinsed my plate off and put it in the dishwasher. "It's just too bad we couldn't figure out what the Contessa did with her list of the real hiding places for the art pieces. I guess the mystery died with her."

Nell rose from the table. "You know, Tessa. I've been giving that some thought. You remember in her letter, her closing words? 'I started with a low pair, but will be closing with a full house, ace high. This is the legacy I leave to those who follow.'"

"I remember. Does it mean something to you, Nell?"

"Well, after a few restless nights at the hospital. I thought about something so simple, I didn't think it was possible. I haven't checked yet. I thought you might all like to be here to see if I'm right."

I was dyin'. "Nell, you're killin' us here. What is it?"

She laughed and disappeared into the living room, reappearing with a frame in her hands. "This frame was included with the jewelry when the Contessa's estate was settled years ago. It included a short note from her saying, 'life should always be a full house, aces high'. She said this was the very hand that she'd played against a ruthless opponent. She wanted me to have it as a reminder that the impossible is always possible."

Nell turned the frame around. Inside were five cards, three aces and a pair of deuces.

We all held our breath as she carefully cut away the paper from the back of the frame.

She smiled and tears appeared in her eyes as she pulled out an old envelope. On the front it said, 'Thank you for finishing my work.' Inside, on an old folded piece of stationary, was a list of the antiquities and their new hiding places.

******

September 23, 2001

I sat at my kitchen table with Geena sipping a cup of hot English tea. She even let me use the artificial sweetener.

Geena used the real stuff. "Did you ever find out what happened to Breecher and Wanamaker? I noticed the rental sign is gone."

"I don't know anything about the rental sign, but I did get some of the details from Sue when she got back from running errands in Panama City for Andy. You know, I think he sent her there on purpose."

Geena's eyes got wide. "No. You think so?"

"Very funny. Do you want to hear the details or not?"

"Does a woodpecker love termites?"

"Yuck. Thanks for that picture. I'll be seeing that for days. It turns out Wanamaker was using the CETEA organization as a front for stealing exotic animals."

"You mean she was a modern-day poacher?"

"Yeah, something like that. She'd use her affiliation with the group to explore locations where exotic animals were known to be housed. She'd find the male leader of the 'animal community' and use him to help introduce her to the owners of these special animals. She'd talk a good story about starting a chapter in the area and how each owner had a responsibility to maintain the safety and health of their animals. She got to know their daily routines and, more importantly, their security systems."

Geena sneaked a cookie from a covered plate on the table. "So it was a piece of cake for her to steal the animals."

"People made it easy for her. She'd steal a few animals from one town and move on to the next hit. She used the guise of the 'outraged exotic animal activist' when the animals were taken during the conference times. She would tell the police it was a conspiracy against the organization."

"What about the manslaughter charge? Did Mrs. Lubbock die?"

"She's still hanging on. She was so distraught from the loss of her pet chinchillas that she went into cardiac arrest. If she dies, Wanamaker is liable, and Breecher's case will get stickier."

"What about Breecher? Is he taking the fall with her? He doesn't seem like the felonious type to me."

"I know what you mean. Once the police figured out the scam and verified her mode of operation in each town, they could see that men like Breecher were being used as saps. Unfortunately, being a sap doesn't stop you from being responsible for your actions. And his actions made him look real bad."

"You mean, they think Breecher is an accessory to her crimes?"

"Not only think. All the owners verified that he was with Wanamaker whenever she visited their homes, and he had suggested the type of security system that all the victims had installed."

"That's an interesting twist."

"That's what I thought, so I called the security company. Turns out he was getting a kick-back from each of the installations he referred to them."

"Well, that's not a crime."

"Nope, that's just Breecher. It also didn't help that his fingerprints were all over the victim's houses and the cages where they found the animals. Plus, there were all those late night personal meetings with Wanamaker at his house. That didn't look too good for him either."

"You don't think he really did it, do you?" Geena asked.

"No. I'm sure there's a logical explanation for all of it. I just hope he's got a good lawyer."

"So, where's he in the meantime?"

"In some white collar detention center over in Pensacola. He probably never had it so good."

"What about Ricochet?" Geena sounded genuinely concerned.

"Ricochet?" I couldn't help but tease her. "I think they sent him to the pound. Nobody wanted to adopt him so they put him to sleep. I think they sent his remains over to the butcher to be ground into dog food to feed the strays."

Geena stared at me horrified.

"I'm kidding. I'm kidding. You know they don't do that sort of thing. The dog food thing, I mean. They put him at some terrier puppy farm up in Alabama. Turns out, old Ricochet's got what it takes to produce some fine show heirs."

Geena let out a sigh of relief and poured herself another cup of tea. "What about Nell? Did you get around to asking her about her promise to your mother, and why she called her Dora Jane Pittman?"

"Oh, she was real sly when I brought up that subject. First she gave me what-for for listening in on other people's conversations uninvited. Then she told me I'd heard it all wrong and that she wasn't going to repeat it because she wasn't proud of the language she'd used."

"Do you believe her?"

"Absolutely not. She's lying through her teeth."

"Do you think you'll ever know the truth?"

"Only when she wants me to, not a second before. She's a tough ol' broad when she wants to be."

We both laughed.

"You know, Geena, I thought nothing could ever make me feel like the last few weeks have. I was consumed with fear, anger, helplessness, frustration, and joy. Life dealt me a monster, but through the help of my family and friends, we brought the beast to its knees."

Geena raised her mug for a toast. "To monsters with no knees."

Our mugs clanked together.

"Geena?"

"Yeah, Tess?"

"How many monsters do you think any one person deserves in a lifetime?"

Geena smiled. "No one *deserves* more than one."

I took a sip of tea. "Right, that's what I thought."

A moment later the phone rang. I was going to let the machine pick up. But what if I'd won something? I was feeling lucky.

"Hello?"

"Hello? Is that you, Tess?" There was some static on the line. I covered my other ear to try and hear more clearly.

"Yes, this is Tess. Who is this? We have a bad connection."

"Yes, we've had a bad connection for years, sweetheart."

"Michael? Michael, is that you? Where are you?"

"Yes, it's me. I'm still in Europe, England to be exact."

My eyes brimmed with tears. I wanted to ask him all about his trip, as if he'd just been away on business. Some fools never learn. "Why are you calling, Michael? Is everything all right?"

"Oh yes. Everything is more than all right. Tess, I've decided I'd like to return home and be a family again."

My mouth stood open wider than a full moon. My words were slow and I heard myself stuttering in incomplete sentences. "Come home? Here? Now? You've decided?"

"Yes, I know how stunned you probably are, and how inconvenient it may be, but I'm sure we can work things out."

Stunned didn't begin to describe what I was feeling. "You want to work things out?"

"Yes, I'm sure we can think of something."

Geena was in the background shaking her head "no" furiously.

"I just don't know, Michael. You, me and the kids all under the same roof again. We've just gotten used to you being gone. Now you want to come galloping back into our lives?"

The line was quiet. "I'm sorry, Tess. I thought you understood. I don't want to come back to live with you and the children. I want to come back and bring my male lover with me. We would live somewhere nearby so we could be close to the children. I miss them more than life itself. I want to be there with them as they grow up. I want to be an active part of their lives. I want to file for divorce."

I laid the receiver back in its cradle, sat back in my chair, and took another sip of tea.

Geena stared at me for a full minute. "Well? What did he say? What does he want to do? You're not going to let him come live here again, are you?"

I took another package of sweetener and emptied it into my mug. I stirred it gently, barely raising the level of tea in the cup. I finally answered.

"Geena, do you think monsters come in pairs?"

The End

Printed in the United States
21912LVS00004B/170